'Updating Philip K. Dick via William Gibson and Lewis Carroll, Noon sets his cyberfiction in a fantastically imagined futuristic Manchester, where humanity and technology have evolved and mutated. His latest release, *Pixel Juice*, is a collection of fifty short stories that showcases the best aspects of his talents. Noon blends Orwellian satire with pure surrealism to create darkly humorous parables in which technology has developed at an exponential rate and fused with human desires . . . the short story is the perfect form to accommodate Noon's hyperactive imagination. There are literally hundreds of ideas in *Pixel Juice* and by keeping them separate, he demonstrates his versatility and gives each the space to shine. Furthermore, his confidence and competence with the form have allowed him to find room for some much needed humour . . . *Pixel Juice* is a fantastic kaleidoscope of a book, demonstrating the wide range of Noon's vision and talents, encompassing a variety of styles, genres and voices. It is an excellent introduction to the surreal, confusing world of Jeff Noon, and paradoxically his best work yet' Laurence Phelan, *Independent on Sunday*

www.booksattransworld.co.uk/jeffnoon

By the same author

VURT
POLLEN
AUTOMATED ALICE
NYMPHOMATION
NEEDLE IN THE GROOVE

PIXEL JUICE

STORIES FROM THE AVANT PULP

JEFF NOON

BLACK SWAN

PIXEL JUICE
A BLACK SWAN BOOK : 0 552 99937 7

Originally published in Great Britain by Doubleday,
a division of Transworld Publishers

PRINTING HISTORY
Doubleday edition published 1998
Anchor edition published 2000
Black Swan edition published 2000

3 5 7 9 10 8 6 4 2

Copyright © Jeff Noon 1998

The right of Jeff Noon to be identified as the author of this
work has been asserted in accordance with sections 77 and 78
of the Copyright Designs and Patents Act 1988.

All the characters in this book are fictitious,
and any resemblance to actual persons, living or dead,
is purely coincidental.

Condition of Sale
This book is sold subject to the condition that it shall not,
by way of trade or otherwise, be lent, re-sold, hired out or
otherwise circulated in any form of binding or cover other
than that in which it is published and without a similar
condition including this condition being imposed on the
subsequent purchaser.

Set in 11/13pt Granjon by
Phoenix Typesetting, Ilkley, West Yorkshire.

Black Swan Books are published by Transworld Publishers,
61–63 Uxbridge Road, London W5 5SA,
a division of The Random House Group Ltd,
in Australia by Random House Australia (Pty) Ltd,
20 Alfred Street, Milsons Point, Sydney, NSW 2061, Australia,
in New Zealand by Random House New Zealand Ltd,
18 Poland Road, Glenfield, Auckland 10, New Zealand
and in South Africa by Random House (Pty) Ltd,
Endulini, 5a Jubilee Road, Parktown 2193, South Africa.

Printed and bound in Great Britain by
Clays Ltd, St Ives plc.

DEDICATION

some stories for MICHELLE and BILL;
and some for STEVE and BARBARA;
Super-Easy-No-Tag-Special for GORDON;
Xtrovurt and *The Perfumed Machine* for

THE BULLETS OF AUTUMN ~
www.bulletsofautumn.co.uk;
Shed Weapons for JIMMY;
Orgmentations for MATTHEW;
Bug Compass for POLLY and VANA;
Hands of the DJ for DOUG;
Homo Karaoke for MICHAEL;
and the rest for PAT and JACK

the whole, and everything
for JULIE

ACKNOWLEDGEMENTS

to the following publications
for the original mixes

THE BIG ISSUE for *Call of the Weird* and *Solace*;
CITY LIFE for *Homo Karaoke*;
the GUARDIAN for *Tweedles*;
RAISE for *Before it Disappears*;
RANDOM FACTOR for *Blurbs*;
WATERSTONE'S DIARY 1997 for *The Shoppers*

with thanks

CONTENTS

PROLOGUE

WATCH

When I was a young kid in junior school, perhaps seven or eight years old, one day this lad called Colin Bradshaw comes up to me in the playground.

'What time is it, Noony?' he asks.

'I don't know,' I reply.

'You mean you haven't got a wristwatch?'

'No.'

'I've got one. It's a special watch, like spies use. It's invisible.'

Now this Colin Bradshaw was the toughest kid in the class, and he was always hanging around with his gang, and playing tricks on the other kids.

'Wow! Invisible!' says I. 'Can I see it?'

'It's invisible, stupid! Anyway, I haven't got it on me today. It's at home. You can have it if you want. We can do swaps.'

So we made this deal, that Colin would bring the invisible

watch in the next day, and I would bring my model of the James Bond Aston Martin DB5 (complete with ejector seat and guns that came out of the front and everything). This was back in the Sixties, and the James Bond car was easily the best toy of the time, everybody wanted one. Especially Colin Bradshaw.

'OK,' he says the next day. 'Give us the car then.'

So I gave him the car.

'Right. Hold your hand out. Palm up, stupid.'

I hold my hand out, and he puts his hand into his pocket and pulls it back out, holding the invisible watch. And he places the watch, gently, in my trembling palm.

And I believed . . .

PART ONE

ILLUSION'S PERFUME

THE SHOPPERS

In the first shop they bought a packet of dogseed, because Doreen had always wanted to grow her own dog. In the second, a pair of bird shoes, which fluttered slightly as Matthew put them on. In the third shop, Little Tommy bought half a dozen singing biscuits, five of which he swallowed straight away, because shopping made him hungry.

There were only nine shops in the entire city. In fact, the shops *were* the city, so vast they were and all encompassing. It was difficult to know where one shop ended and the next began. No wonder the children were tired already.

In the fourth shop Doreen chose a box of shadows, some of which she used to mask the pain in the head that Tommy's constant singing gave her. In the fifth shop, Matthew floated over the umbrella-pig cage in his bird shoes, claiming that if Doreen had bought the shadows, then he should have at least a *single* pig to keep the rain off. Doreen reminded him it never rained inside the shops, and that he should instead buy an egg of words. Matthew was becoming angry at the way this shopping trip was going.

The three young shoppers were determined to buy a single product from each of the nine stores. These precious items were to be the children's gift to their mother, for her birthday. Their mother, you see, had never once ventured outside the first shop.

In shop six, Tommy bought a penny ghost. In shop seven, Doreen purchased a Girl-of-Eternal-Flame Doll. In shop number eight, Matthew wanted to buy a genuine piece of cow, but Doreen told him they could no longer afford it. Instead, he was forced to buy a mansion house in London. In the ninth and final shop, Little Tommy bought a smoke-map of Manchester, which they used to retrace their steps through the aisles of the city.

On the way home, however, the dogseeds slipped from Doreen's fingers, caught on a slight breeze. The bird shoes tried to catch the seeds, only to crash into a display stand, tumbling poor Matthew to the ground. He landed on Tommy, who swallowed his last song biscuit accidentally. Doreen used many more of her shadows to wipe away Tommy's wailing. Matthew's egg hatched prematurely in his pocket. The resulting cloud of words gathered over the Flame Doll, forming the word 'locust' in the air. The doll ran screaming into the mansion house, shooting electric sparks from her hair. The house burned so fiercely that not even the fire brigade could put it out. They'd forgotten to bring their hosepipes.

Tommy smoked his map completely to get them home to Mother's little kiosk. All that remained was the penny ghost and a single shadow. The children were in tears by then, but their mother accepted gratefully the gift of the shadow and told

Little Tommy he could keep the ghost for his trouble and kindness. That night he played with the spirit, as his mother wiped her sad eyes with the birthday shadow and told them the story of the mythical tenth shop, the one that lay beyond all the others.

SOLACE

Remember Spook?

—No.

Sure you do, came out when you, me and the rest of the world were just a bunch of kids. It was a bit of a craze for a few years, a new soft drink product. Ninety-nine per cent sugar; one of those things that tastes disgusting first off, but you can't help getting hooked if you persist with it. It was called Spook, I guess, because it was like clear liquid to start with, no flavour, with this neat gimmick in the cap. You could twist the cap six different ways to get six different flavours. Nothing special looking back, just some cheap chemicals released according to which flavour you chose, but the sort of thing that kids go mad for.

—Oh, right. Orange, strawberry . . . apple . . .

That's it. Lemon, cola or elderberry. Anyway, remember Nesbit?

—Who?

Come on, that scrawny little brainbox with the rich parents? He was the one who first introduced us to drinking Spook, because it wasn't advertised or anything, you just had to know it was there somehow. Whenever we went to the shop, it was always, 'I'll have a Spook'. That's all he ever asked for, especially after he'd discovered that turning the cap in a certain clever way, you could get to mix the flavours. I'm not sure if the manufacturers even knew you could do that, and we had to pay Nessie to do the combinations for us, because only he knew the secret.

—Nessie?

Nesbit. Now you've got him. He got us all hooked on the stuff for a while, trying out different combinations. It was neat, the way the two colours merged to form the new flavour. He was good at maths, I remember, and he'd worked out with six starting flavours you could have more than sixty different flavour combos, if you could only discover the correct ways of turning the bottle top. I can't remember the exact figure.

—He made up names for them?

That's right. Orange and cola he called orancola. Strawberry and elderberry he called elstrawb, and so on. He'd found out all the ways to combine two of the flavours. Then he started on mixing three of them. It was tricky stuff, getting the cap to twist just so to release three at the same time. He'd spend hours with the bottles – playtime, after school, whenever. I went round to his house one time, he was sat on his bed with dozens of bottles all around him, twisting at one like he was in a daze, like it was the best puzzle ever.

The first trio flavour he discovered was apple, cola and lemon. He called it appolamon. Tasted horrible, but he was so excited, the taste didn't bother him. It wasn't the taste anyway, that drove him, it was just finding out the new flavours. He had this thing that he would find all the trios and then move on to four different flavours, then five and so on.

—He started to put on weight?

Yeah. Real skinny to start with, but the body just can't take that much sugar. He was visiting the dentist's nearly every week, and he was the first one of us to have spots I remember, really bad ones. He used to be good at school, but now his grades were dropping daily. His parents were worried; they tried to ban him from buying any more Spook, stopped his pocket money. Which was a mistake because then he started stealing the stuff, drinking it in secret. It was strange, because the new combinations he was coming up with, they must have been vile. You'd think he'd be happy to just mess with the bottles, but no, he had to drink every single one, even the ones that were failed experiments.

By this time the rest of us were growing up, you know. Moving on to more sophisticated pleasures. Like beer, for instance. And girls and ciggies. But Nessie was still in there, still searching.

He gave me a taste of his first ever four-flavour combination. Elorcolem, he called it. Elderberry, orange, cola, lemon. I tell you, one sip was enough; I was nearly throwing up! He drank the concoction in one, no trouble, but from the look on his face, I could tell he was hating it. He couldn't stop himself.

I called him a spookaholic. He didn't laugh.

Instead, in this really clear voice, he told me that he was searching for the solace.

—Solace?

The ultimate combination. All six flavours: strawberry, orange, lemon, apple, cola, elderberry; all mixed together. He took the initial letter of each fruit: S, O, L, A, C, E. That's how he came up with the name. Solace. He said it might take him years to find the right way to twist the bottle cap, but he was determined to get there, even if he died doing it.

—He said that?

Even if it kills me. That's what he said. Exact words.

—Did he ever find this . . . what was it?

Solace? Well, we moved apart then, because it was time to go on to high school. I did all right, got a good place, but Nessie, who everyone thought would make university one day, he ended up at the worst school. He'd given up on being brilliant, I guess. That's addiction for you. Cheers!

—Bottoms up. That's a hell of a story.

It's not over yet. I bumped into him the other day. Christ, it must be fifteen years since I last saw him.

—Did you? Whereabouts?

You know that pub, the Cut Above? In there, last Friday. It was late afternoon, the place was quiet. Just me and this other guy, a great fat bloke wedged behind one of the tables. Looked like he needed two chairs to sit on. I avoided him of course, propped up the bar. He called my name out. I looked around, he was waving me over like he knew me. It took me a second or two to recognize him.

—Nessie?

I went over. God, he looked bad. Fat, like I said, and still spotty even at his age. When he smiled at me, his teeth were black, what was left of them anyway. Looked like he was on his last legs. I asked him if he wanted a drink, you can guess what he said.

—I'll have a Spook?

You got it. The table was filled with empties, must have been a dozen of them. I didn't know they were still selling the stuff, should have been banned years ago, I reckon. Anyway, I bought him another, just for old times' sake. The barman didn't open it, like he was following orders. I placed the unopened bottle on the table in front of Nesbit, who just stared at it for a while. I was trying to make conversation, asking him what he'd been up to, if he was working, married, kids of his own. He said he was out of work, divorced, a kid he never saw.

I fear for that kid, I really do.

—What do you mean?

He told me the story. Remember the Introvert scandal, from way back?

—Vaguely. He wasn't one of them, was he?

That's the explanation. He'd only found out when he was twenty-one; his parents finally got round to telling him, the bastards. That's why they were so rich, you see. Spook, the company that is, they paid them a small fortune, them and about two hundred other young couples. It was meant to be the next wave of advertising; get them hooked in the womb. I don't pretend to know the details, something to do with feeding the DNA with subliminal messages. They targeted poor people, of course, and promised no side effects. Of course, now we know better, but those two hundred kids have to live with it for the rest of their lives.

Introverts; interior adverts, I think it stood for. The original idea was that they would just promote the product, you know – word of mouth being the best advert of them all. Remember how Nesbit almost got us hooked. Then it went wrong; the hook was too deep, too sharp. The product took over.

—They were paid compensation, weren't they?

Sure. Very generous. That's why Nesbit didn't have to work. Little good it did him, the poor bastard, because you can guess what he spent the money on. And I'm scared for his kid, because if it's genetic, you know, it might be passed on.

—Jesus. Want another?

I'll stick with this, thanks. Anyway, Nesbit finishes his story, then he finally picks up the bottle of Spook I've bought him. I was all set to grab it out of his hands by this point, because I didn't want to be blamed for anything. But he was too quick for me, his left hand was gripping the bottle tight, the right twisting the cap this way and that, lightning fast. It was like watching an expert at play, like a magician or something. I tell you, I was frozen in space, as these six streams of colour – red, orange, yellow, green, brown, purple – all started to appear in the clear liquid. For a few seconds a rainbow was there in the bottle, a small tornado of colour. Then they finally merged, and the whole bottle turned black. Midnight black! Nesbit gave the bottle a final shake and then removed the cap. He poured the drink into an empty glass and placed it in front of me.

Solace, he said.

I picked it up, real slow. Looking deep into it, I swear I could see sparkles of light, like stars in the night sky.

I put the glass to my lips, and took a sip.

—And?

What?

—What did it taste of, man?

Tasted like heaven, I tell you. Like heaven was washing over my tongue.

THE CABINET OF
NIGHT UNLOCKED

Now that the existence of the Olmstaff Method is public knowledge, it may well be time to offer a brief history of the procedure. The fact that the Method itself is currently an illegal act, and that even a description of the actual ritual is a punishable offence, should only persuade us more strongly to consider the moral problems it has brought to light.

Of Brother August Olmstaff himself little need be said, beyond the standard biography proposed by Professor T. P. Lechner in his now famous but hardly seen *The Sacred Wound* (Cargo Press, 1967). The facts are quickly sketched: Olmstaff was born to a poor farming family in Lancashire, England, in 1455; he was the last and weakest child of nine siblings; he was born mute; his father ordered him to join the local Silent Order of Nazarenes, at the tender age of seven. Like many who joined the monasteries of that time, Olmstaff's subsequent history has vanished into the secret chambers of dust and slow tolling

bells. Lechner places his death in the year 1487, in disagree-
ment with more recent writings, which find evidence of
Olmstaff's life as late as 1524. (Interested parties are directed
to my own 'The Blinded Sundial' in *Items of Moral Philosophy*,
April 1995, for a detailed overview of the 'biography problem'.)
It should only be noted here that it was to Lechner's advantage
to give Olmstaff an early death, and to point out the (allegedly)
curious state of the corpse.

Of the three extant manuscripts attributed to Brother
Olmstaff's hand, the first two may be dismissed in passing,
being only a fair copy of Plato's *Republic*, and a rather beautiful
illumination of Egberg's *On the Chronologie of Certain Insectes*.
That Plato's philosophies evidently concerned the monk less
than the life cycle of the horsefly, has been of interest to some
observers.

It was only with the uncovering of the third manuscript in
1959 that the world paid any real attention to the obscure
'tongueless monk of Barnstrop'. How this Latin text found its
way from a tiny Lancastrian village to the abandoned library of
a household in Düsseldorf has yet to be fully mapped. It
was found there by the antiquarian Sir John Bosley, who
published his English translation in 1962, the year of his
death. This coincidence, of translation and death, has not been
overlooked.

Bosley called his translation *The Cabinet of Night Unlocked*,
a rather poetical rendering of Olmstaff's original Latin.
Despite this, his work, being of an overly academic nature,
attracted interest only from his fellow scholars. The public
imagination was stirred only when Lechner later brought the
manuscript to their attention.

For all our academic distaste at Professor's Lechner's
shallow popularization, and our suspicion of his decadent

lifestyle (a known drug-user, associate of Timothy Leary, and a champion of the Acid Tests) we have to admit that but for his death, the Olmstaff Method (as it became known) would still linger in obscurity.

Many have claimed to have seen the public appearance Lechner made in 1974, at which he performed the Olmstaff ritual; only a few can have actually been there. None of them would be unchanged by what they saw.

To say it was my *fortune* to have been in that audience is to stretch the meaning of the word too far. I was on a short university tour of America at the time, promoting my second book, *Morality and Death in the Age of Mass Destruction*, and found myself sharing a platform with the charismatic professor. I had no knowledge of his work, but we quickly found ourselves on the same side against the rest of the panel. Our shared position was to make suicide a legitimate undertaking, given the discovery and proliferation of the nuclear bomb. One of our opponents was a bishop of the Roman Catholic faith, so you may picture the ferocity of the arguments. This bishop (I shall refrain from mentioning his name) had read Lechner's *Sacred Wound*, and was making a mockery of the book's heretical claims. That Lechner was calling the book a religious text 'produced by a brother of your very church!' and a work of God's bounteous goodwill, obviously hit a bare nerve, because the bishop (no doubt to his eternal shame) called for him to offer proof of 'the Devil's sacrament!'

Lechner paused for a moment then, as though drawing strength. He told the bishop that the ritual took approximately fifteen minutes to perform, and that he had no intention of boring the audience for that length of time. The bishop insisted, however, and took a straw poll of the audience. It was a close count, and it may well be that my own raised hand tipped the balance. Who can tell?

'Very well, then,' Lechner said, quite calmly.

He closed his eyes and began to mumble some Latin phrases to himself. I was seated two places along from him, and could only catch a word here and there, and my Latin was nothing like it is now. Every so often he would raise his arms to make some complicated patterns in the air. At one point, perhaps after five minutes, he touched his left hand to his heart. A little later he stamped his right foot. During these movements he was continuously whispering the Latin text. The audience had laughed to begin with, but quickly became bored. Only the bishop could be heard making a spluttering sound.

I had glanced at my pocket watch as Lechner began the ritual, and after thirteen minutes passed, I was becoming quite tense. Even the bishop lapsed into silence as the final minute ticked away. Somebody in the audience dropped a notebook, and the sound of it echoed around the hall, causing me to jump in my seat. But fifteen minutes came and went, and Lechner was still intoning to himself, and so I started to breathe again, and even to smile a little, especially when Lechner opened his eyes finally and smiled right back at me.

The bishop guffawed a final time, and made some derogatory remark.

Lechner closed his eyes, let his head fall gently to one shoulder and then down to his chest. He appeared quite relaxed, and the audience was talking loudly amongst themselves. Some of the rowdier students were even booing, and demanding their money back.

The bishop had risen from his seat, and was now slapping Lechner on the back, calling him a liar and even a false prophet. The professor leaned forward under the force of the slap, until his head was resting on the podium. A glass of water, touched by his forehead, tumbled to the floor, where it smashed.

A silence, deeper than before, once again fell over the auditorium.

Somebody laughed, but then stopped, as the bishop pulled Lechner's head away from the desk. His eyes were closed, his lips still fixed in that beatific smile. Of course, like the bishop, I suspected an aimless joke was being pulled, or that a drug-induced torpor had been achieved. I went over to admonish Lechner for bringing our argument into disrepute, but no words from me would rouse him. I started to shake him vigorously, all to no avail.

I demanded an ambulance be called immediately, which announcement caused a small commotion in the audience. A few students were making their way to the platform, some more were hurrying out; the vast majority of them were fixed to their seats, as though in reflection of Lechner's fate.

By this time the bishop had moved away slightly, and was crossing himself, as though fearful of the consequences.

Perhaps he was already thinking of his own guilt.

The media were slow to pick up on the story, which hiatus allowed me to find a copy of Lechner's book, *The Sacred Wound*, in an alternative bookshop on Haight-Ashbury. I was still badly shaken by the professor's strange death, especially when, three days later, the story finally made the local press. I spent a few tense minutes in Customs coming home; it felt as though I was *smuggling* the work into Britain.

The book had never been published in this country, and never would be. Of course, an enterprising party quickly produced a pirate edition, which was said to fetch a handsome price on the black market. Mine was one of the few legitimate editions.

I was determined to keep an open mind about its contents, but for some reason I hid the thin volume within my prized first edition of Vesalius' *De Humanis Corporis Fabrica*. There it rested for another two weeks, unread, as the strange story of the American professor who had 'killed himself with words' briefly made headline news. The few details released told only of a doctor's puzzlement at the exact cause of Lechner's death.

Only when the story had faded, did I dare peruse *The Sacred Wound* for myself.

It was a short book of ninety-nine pages, barely more than a self-produced pamphlet. It was arranged in four sections, the longest being Lechner's introduction. This introduction consisted of the already mentioned biography of Brother Olmstaff, a brief history of the Method, a pseudo-scientific explanation of the Method's effectiveness followed by a plea for its acceptance, and finally a set of guidelines for the correct performance of the ritual.

Lechner had traced the Method back to certain obscure, forbidden texts said to have been lost in the fire that destroyed the Library at Alexandria. He has no explanation as to how Olmstaff came upon these original manuscripts.

The second two sections of the book detailed the Olmstaff Method itself: first the text to be spoken, secondly the movements to be made. Lechner wisely divided the two elements to prevent the casual reader from accidentally performing the ritual in its entirety. The professor made it clear in his guidelines that the two elements, the words and the movements, were completely safe if performed separately; only when combined would they activate the body's natural processes.

Still, as you can imagine, I read these two sections with no little trepidation.

The final section of the book was Lechner's improvisation

upon the Method's spiritual meaning, which owed a rather heavy debt to Leary's LSD-fuelled take on *The Tibetan Book of the Dead*. This section is, perhaps, the least interesting.

Indeed, finishing the book still 'alive', as it were, led to a feeling of anticlimax.

And, although I decided I had witnessed nothing more than one of life's sadder coincidences, that night in San Francisco, nothing would make me perform the ritual as per the instructions.

Nothing more was heard of the Olmstaff Method for a few years, until Dr Elizabeth Cunningham published her paper, 'On the Body's Self-Destruction', in the *Journal of Alternatives*, September 1985. This offered for the first time a medically approved explanation of the Method.

The fact that Cunningham was later arrested for murder should not prevent us from admiring her pioneering and courageous work. In the simplest terms the doctor had discovered a small gland (which now bears her name) in the lower abdomen. The gland had been noted previously, but no use had been found for it. Cunningham connected it to the Method in a very precise way: the combined performance of the spoken text and the ritual exercises activated the gland, which then, and only then, secreted a small amount of poison into the bloodstream. This poison (Lechner's Fluid) very quickly, and quite painlessly, overcomes the body's defences. Death follows within twenty seconds of completing the Olmstaff Method.

Cunningham's work, of course, was highly controversial, not least the fact that she had experimented on human guinea pigs, two of whom had died during the process. Both of them had terminal cancer. They were willing victims, and the doctor had signed-disclaimers proving such. This did not prevent her arrest and subsequent trial for assisted murder, of

PIXEL JUICE

which she was found guilty. She received a sentence of not less than twenty years.

Cunningham's cause was championed by the euthanasia lobby, who campaigned vigorously on her behalf, alas with little effect. The doctor was found dead in her cell on 1 August 1989. No explanation could be given for her demise. Her trial and death brought the Olmstaff Method to the forefront of public consciousness.

One should not be surprised at this. Suicide has been a constant companion to the human struggle for progress. Before the Method came to light, it was thought that the human psyche contained a fail-safe against self-destruction; witness people's pathetic attempts to hold their breath for long enough to suffocate, or the violent convulsions that pull even the most desperate back to the surface of the darkest lake.

The Olmstaff Method broke this hold over the body's defence, with the added quality of guaranteeing an entirely painless death. Of course, this last fact cannot be empirically verified, but all witnesses of the ritual (myself included) can point to the beatific smile and relaxed posture that accompany the final moments. To quote Lechner's most famous sentence: 'God has provided an off-switch.'

Despite the fact that nineteen separate studies have shown the Method to be a legitimate process of the human physiology, none of the world's governments could be persuaded to make it a legal act, or to allow publication of any books offering instruction. The incident in Denmark sealed the Method's fate, and was the strongest proof yet of its universal effectiveness.

Prior to the incident the world had hardly noticed the so-called Offspring of God's Illumination, beyond a few rumours of the cult's supposed 'sexual worship'. Even the good people of Copenhagen were taken by surprise at the extent of the group's beliefs, when all 207 members were found dead one icy cold morning in October 1992.

The bodies were tested by the Danish authorities for drugs or any other means of self-destruction. It was no surprise to me that they found none, and that the group's final statement gloried in the 'next life that awaited all true believers, through the portals of the Sacred Wound'.

The fact that the Method was undertaken in the Danish tongue is of interest, and can be briefly examined here. It should be remembered that Lechner himself had performed the sacrament in Latin, even though his own book gave the text in plain English. In the introduction to *The Sacred Wound* he notes that the ritual can be spoken in Latin or English, although he believed the Latin expression to be more pure, 'closer to the wound itself', as he puts it.

Around this time I happened upon an edition of Sir John Bosley's *The Cabinet of Night Unlocked*. Curiously, although the book is long out of print, it has never been banned in this or any country. Certainly, Bosley's is an academic study, and his translation from the Latin is dense with secondary and tertiary meanings. It is of little use to any but the most convoluted or desperate mind.

It is interesting to compare Bosley's version with Lechner's, mainly because Lechner had simplified the more complicated passages, and even eliminated entire sentences in his quest for the purest form. Both versions are effective, which leads one to believe that the exact nature of the text is of less importance than the overall 'truth' of the sacrament. The same leeway is allowed with the accompanying movements, with different cultures producing their own, slight variations.

Hundreds of illegal translations have been made over the

PIXEL JUICE

years, and all of them activate Cunningham's Gland successfully. One curious exception is the pictograph language of the K'dhall Islands in New Guinea. Here the Method does not work. Research continues into why this should be so.

Is it any wonder that the Method became so popular? The suicide rate increased noticeably as the ritual became known, not least in death cells around the world. For the victims of painful incurable diseases, it is quite easy to find a doctor who, for a price or for his conscience, will tutor the sufferer in the correct words and the movements. Other stranger rumours abound. For instance, Lechner had stated that the Vatican held similar manuscripts in their vaults, and that the facts had been suppressed for centuries in order to maintain the Christian way of death. Certain warrior sects had known of the Method as long ago as the tenth century, using it to ensure that captured soldiers could kill themselves without succumbing to torture. The US Army is said to have employed the Method in the Vietnam War. It is, perhaps, not entirely untrue that the Method was used to effect a kind of escape from the Nazi concentration camps. One famous, perhaps non-existent heretical text is said to contain certain proof that Jesus the Son of God used the Method in his dying moments on the Cross.

My own obsession with the Olmstaff Method is fuelled by my professional interest in the morality of suicide, and by my personal involvement in the first reported case. With these two not unworthy weapons at my disposal, I was, after a lengthy bureaucratic battle, allowed a brief perusal of the original *Cabinet of Night Unlocked*.

Sir John Bosley, in his last will and testament, had bequeathed Olmstaff's manuscript to the British Museum, where it was expressly to be kept under lock and key in the rare volumes chamber. I was escorted there, one dismal afternoon in December of last year. I was allowed only one hour with the volume, and the guard was to be with me the whole time, whether for protection of the manuscript, or for protection of the reader, I cannot say.

How strange it was, that one hour. The manuscript was kept under glass, and was open at the page that began the sacramental text. The calligraphy and the illuminations were of the highest standard, far higher than Olmstaff's other known works. So rich were the colourings, I almost felt they were rising out of the parchment towards me. It was, quite literally, a pleasure to gaze upon it.

I had learned a little more Latin since my first (and last) meeting with Professor Lechner, and I tried as best I could to decipher the work's meaning. I mean not the textual message discovered by Bosley, nor the wild extrapolations given flight by Lechner; rather I was seeking the *hidden* message of the work. The mechanism – the magic, if you will – that allowed a few words, marks on paper, to affect the human body so drastically. And always, as I read, how could I not be aware that Bosley, Lechner, Cunningham, and perhaps Olmstaff as well, had all taken advantage of the Method. They had all died by the book.

I came out of the museum early, twelve minutes before my allotted time was up, and never before had the dirty London rain felt so glorious on my face!

I will finish this short history with an account of my own experiments with the Method. My main preoccupation is to establish the exact limits of the ritual's effectiveness. For instance, I have already agreed with Lechner that the words and the movements are quite harmless when performed separately, by the simple expedient of performing them myself. I have followed his instructions precisely during these experiments.

During the last few months I have taken to performing the words and the movements together in various combinations; for example, speaking the words in reverse order, or making the movements in mirror-image. None of these variations has had any effect upon my body.

I am currently in the process of performing the Method in its correct order, but stopping off at various points to ascertain the cumulative effects. From these experiments I can conclude that the first ten minutes of the sacrament have no obvious effect at all. Only at the eleventh minute does a certain light-headedness descend upon the body. It is not unpleasant. At the thirteenth minute this is replaced by a momentary fear, which may be a physical symptom of the Method, or else a legitimate emotion brought about by the approach of death. The four-teenth minute passes almost unnoticed.

As the final passages of the Olmstaff Method are under-taken, a feeling of intense expectation and desire takes over the whole body, as though it were eager to complete the ritual forthwith, and to leap joyously into the realms of darkness!

It is only with immense self-will that I have managed to hold off from making that final execution. To descend from such heights so crudely brings with it a despair I would never have thought possible.

I have only a single word left to say, and a single movement to make.

The word is 'circumference'. The movement, a gentle touching of the right thumb and middle finger, to form a small circle of flesh.

Thus.

SUPER-EASY-
NO-TAG-SPECIAL

So they threw me out of Strangeways with a packet of stale fags and the clothes I went in with. And a letter from the governor praising my good-boy behaviour and my spirited reform, and claiming I was perfectly capable of holding down an honest job, given the chance. Right, so that's why the last thing inside, they stick this tagging device around my left ankle. Radio bleeper, satellite mapping, locking encryption, nifty little sonic ball-and-chain. I had to wear the thing for two years, two years of being followed, of having my every movement logged on some giant cop computer. Don't ask me how the thing works, I'm just the guy that has to sport the accessory. Two years of never leaving Manchester.

Betsy was waiting for me outside the prison, the sweet-hearted old girl. We gave each other a kiss, and said hello and she told me that nobody was wearing trousers like that any more, and I said you should try being off the scene for four years, see what you come out like. Then she said we need to get you out of those trousers, and I said we most certainly do.

First she was a touch put off by the contraption strapped tight around my ankle, then she got kinda excited like it was some weird bondage device, then when it was the third time over, she said it was sad that I'd never be naked, not really naked, not for two whole years anyway. Me, I was just thinking that some greasy cop was watching this little bleep on a computerized map going jigger-jigger. It was like having a voyeur in the boudoir. Gave me the shivers. Then we talked about the job, and the money and where the fuck was Danny Boy with the takings. Then she went quiet, and turned away.

So, Danny Boy. Good old faithful Danny the Boy, trusty assistant of yesteryear, now gone AWOL with the loot. London, said Betsy. Last month, said Betsy. And she said, I wanted to tell you, visiting times, but I thought it'd only make your time go slow. And I said, no, the anger would've sped it along no end. And she said, so when are you going after him, Dex? And I said, now that's the problem, I can't.

I can't wait two years, because Danny will have spent it all by then, if not already. So I did some enquiries, and the friend of a friend said there just might be a way out of it, but it would cost. I said name it, cause it's gotta be less than I stand to make if I catch up with the bastard. And it was, a whole load of cash, but a lot less than the big takings. I had to pull in some bad debts, and make some bad debts myself just to raise the unlocking money.

The guy said his name was the YoYo, which is pretty damn stupid, but he did have a way of bouncing up and down when he got excited, which is when I showed him the fee. Of course he had to come visit me to do the operation, because no way could I let my bleep-bleep show up on the bad part of the map.

He had all the equipment with him, which fitted inside a case you might keep a pair of spectacles in, posh ones. Things have gotten smaller since I was put away. Soon the whole world will vanish, I swear. So this guy, this YoYo guy, he gets this gadget out of the case, presses some keys on it, holds it against the tagging device on my ankle. The gadget goes whirrrrr, and the tag goes wheeeep! And I said, that's it, is it? And he said, that's it. Super-easy-no-tag-special. Just like that. Super, easy, no tag, special. Proud of it he was. But I was nervous, and I said, you're sure this is safe? I mean, I can really leave Manchester now, no problems? And he said, leave right now, your bleep still shows up on the cop map. It moves around the streets just like you're still living here. It's a phantom bleep, isn't it? Because I've hijacked their fucking system, haven't I? Any trouble, call this number. Twenty-four-hour care line. And he went off on another bouncing spree, a little heavier this time on account of the fee I'd paid him.

So I went down to London, and I found Danny, and it took five days all told, and we had a nice little tête-à-tête, and he handed over the money. Just my rightful share mind, because that shows the difference between us, I'm fair, me, even when I've been cheated. So it was good, everything was back on plan. Get back to Manchester, sit tight on the loot, wait out the two years, get to know Betsy all over and all over again. Easy. Like the man says, super easy!

I got back to Manchester on the Saturday, the afternoon it was, and I thought maybe I should go see that YoYo right off, get him to turn me back onto the real map. But then I thought maybe not, maybe I'm needing to leave town again some time soon. He didn't say anything about a time limit, did he? So I thought instead I'd go round and see if Betsy was up for a night out, but who should I see on the way but Nasty Dave, who was an old acquaintance and not at all nasty, not if you ignored the business with the Kumar Brothers anyway. And he says to me, hi Dex, you're out then? And I say, yeah. And he says, I thought it was you. And I say, well it is me. And he says, no, last Wednesday I mean, I saw you on the street, thought it was you but I was on the bus, so I couldn't stop. And I says, nah, you're wrong there, cause I was away last Wednesday. Oh, he says, must have been someone else then. And I says, yeah, it must've been. Strange, he says, it sure looked like you.

I give Betsy a call, but she's not in. Now, I could go round there if I want, cause I've got a key. I'm more or less living there until I get settled. Instead, I'm thinking, well it's a Saturday night isn't it? Let's do the town, just like the old days, me and my shadow working the clubs and playing the chances. I have a pretty good time, meet up with some of the old guys, get drunk. Someone says, can't remember who, that he sees I'm back with Betsy. And I say, well kind of, just messing around you know. And he says, well it looked serious to me. What did? I ask. Holding hands and everything, he says. Of course this gets a laugh from the boys, the thought of me holding hands with anything, never mind a woman. When was this? I ask. And he says, Thursday I think. Yeah, Thursday. In the park. I was walking the dog. Yeah, holding hands and everything.

I left after that, laughing with the rest of them. I took a cab over to Betsy's flat. More than anything, it was an insane surge of jealousy that drove me there. Strange this, considering our relationship, which was always loose and easy. Maybe it was the fact that she was taking up with someone else, so soon after I'd got out of Strangeways. And the fact that the guy looked like me, that was the killer. OK, maybe it showed her love; I'd been away for four years, and so enamoured was she, the only person who could keep her company was a lookalike. These thoughts didn't help me any. And when I got to the flat, and I rang the bell to no answer, and when I tried the key, and it didn't work . . .

So I bust the door down. Straight away, I could see that the nasties had been done recently, and with some vigour, because the bed was in a mess, and the smell, and the stains . . . Jesus! Who was this guy? And the cheek of Betsy – right under my nose. I didn't know what to do for the best, except just to wait there, perched on the bed, slowly getting angrier. My only problem was who to hit first, the man or the woman. I must have dozed off at some point, because the next thing I know it's gone one o'clock and all the lights are off. I wake up wondering where I am, and then who I am. I shake myself out of the feeling. Then I hear noises down below at the door. Well, here it comes. Betsy will see the door is smashed, she'll know. Maybe they won't come up. No, here they come, two sets of footsteps. I can hear them moving through the living room. I sit up, get myself in a relaxed position. The bedroom door opens. Two men come in.

It was the cops. Inspector This, Deputy Inspector That. The bastards only arrest me, don't they. I'm screaming at them, what have I done wrong now? They inform, kindly, that a robbery took place Friday night, and that, according to my location on their tagging equipment, I was in the exact vicinity, the exact time. I protest at this, but what can I say, no, I was in London, I'm innocent? Eventually, when we get to the cop station, I'm more or less pleading with them to believe me, I was in London! London! Does no good, and I get my one call. I think about a lawyer, then about Betsy, then about the only person who can really get me out of this mess. I call the number that YoYo gave me.

It was a dead line.

ALPHABOX

The bookshop on Deansgate Boulevard in Manchester is filled with many words, most of them for sale, only a few of which manage to find their way into customers' bags. Most of the staff take their lunch at the Bluefinch Café, on John Dalton Street. Donna Clarke, who worked in the shop, was walking towards this place of refreshment one lunchtime, her head filled as usual with strange ideas of becoming a writer herself one day, when she happened to notice a man walking towards her carrying a wooden box.

The box was not too large, but the man seemed to be struggling with it. Perhaps it contained something heavy. Strangely enough, the next day he was there again, same time, same place, still struggling with the weight of the thing. And the rest of that week, whenever she went to lunch, the man was always there, walking towards Donna and then past her, a pained expression on his face.

Donna was curious. Why did he keep carrying the box around with him? If it was the same box every time, that is. Maybe the man had a number of these boxes to deliver, but then why not send them all at once and by delivery van? And if it was the same box, where was he taking it and, more importantly, what was inside it?

One day, Donna had to take an early lunch due to a staff mix-up. When she got to the café, the man was there. He was eating his meal, with the box on the table beside him. Donna slid into the empty seat opposite to him, ordered her usual, and then tried to start a conversation. The man answered her statement about the weather with a simple, 'Yes, isn't it?' and then carried on eating. The box, Donna could now see, was rather ornate and antique looking, decorated with flowers and songbirds. It appeared to have been carved from a single piece of wood, with no lid to it, no obvious way to open it up.

The man was silent until he had finished his simple meal (eggs, chips, beans) and then ordered his cup of tea. Only when this arrived, did he look directly into Donna's eyes. 'I suppose you're wondering what's inside?' he said.

Donna stopped eating, her fork poised halfway to her lips.

'It's a letter,' the man said.

'A letter?' asked Donna.

'Yes. Today's letter.'

'It's a large box to carry a single letter in, isn't it?'

'I have to use this box. It's in the contract.'

'I see,' said Donna, not seeing at all. 'To whom is it addressed?'

'Addressed?'

'Yes. The envelope. Are you a postman?'

The man laughed, gently, and then pressed upon the box in certain places. Until, with a whirring sound, the flowers and the songbirds parted company, making a small aperture. 'I shouldn't be doing this, really,' the man whispered. 'Just a tiny peek now.' Feeling somewhat foolish, but curious nonetheless, Donna put her eye to the opening and peered inside.

It was a world of febrile darkness, in which something barely breathed, gleaming in silver. Almost liquid it seemed, like mercury is almost liquid.

'Do you see it?' the man asked.

'Yes,' answered Donna. 'It's the letter W.'

'What!?' The man was suddenly agitated. 'Let me see that!' He pulled the box away from her, and quickly placed his own eye against the opening. 'Oh, I see what has happened.' He breathed a sigh of relief. 'The little bugger was upside-down. There, take another look.'

Donna did so, and saw now quite clearly that a small letter M was moving around inside the box, moving as if alive.

The man gently performed the secret operation, and the box closed shut. 'It's my job to deliver the letters,' he announced proudly; 'one for each day, according to the contract.'

'The contract?' Donna asked.

'The signed contract between myself and the writer.'

'Which writer?'

'Oh, he's very famous, miss, and does not like to be named.'

'He only writes a single letter a day? He must be a very slow writer.'

'Each morning he sends word of which letter he next needs. I pick it up from the suppliers, and then carry it across town to the writer's house. For one moment there I thought I'd picked up a W by mistake. That would have been disastrous.'

'Can he not have it delivered, by van for instance, or through the postal service?'

'It is in the contract that I must carry the letter personally, and contained within this box.' The man stood up. 'But now I must be going. I am already late, and the writer must have urgent need of the letter M. He gets very angry, miss, if I do not deliver on time.'

The man picked up the box.

'Wait!' cried Donna. 'You haven't told me what he writes about.'

But the man had gone already.

METAPHORAZINE

Johnny takes Metaphorazine. Every clockwork day. Says it burns his house down, with a haircut made of wings. You could say he eats a problem. You could say he stokes his thrill. Every clingfilm evening, climb inside a little pill. Intoxicate the feelings. Play those skull-piano blues. Johnny takes Metaphorazine.

He's a dog.

Lucy takes Simileum. That's not half as bad. She's only like a moon gone slithering, upside-down the sky. Like a tidal wave of perfume, like a spillage in the heart. With eyes stuck tight like envelopes, and posted like a teardrop. Like a syringe, of teardrops. Like a dripfeed aphrodisiac, swallowed like a Cadillac, Lucy takes Simileum.

She's like a dog.

Graham takes Litotezol. Brain the size of particles, that cloud inside of parasites, that live inside the paradise of a pair of lice. He's a surge of melted ice cream, when he makes love like a ghost. Sparkles like a graveyard, but never gets the urge, and then sings Hallelujah! Hallelujah! Hallelujah! like a turgid flatfoot dirge. Graham takes Litotezol.

He's a small dog.

Josie takes Hyperbolehyde. Ten thousand every second. See her face go touch the sky, when she climbs that rollercoaster high. That mouth! Such bliss! All the planets and the satellites make their home inside her lips. It's a four-minute warning! Atomic tongue! Nitrokisserene! Josie takes Hyperbolehyde.

She's a big dog.

Alanis takes Alliterene. It drags a deeper ditch. And all her dirty dealings display a debonair disdain. Her dynamo is dangerous, ditto her dusky dreams. Dummies devise diverse deluxe débâcles down dingy darkened detox driveways. Alanis takes Alliterene.

She's a dead dog, ya dig?

Desmond takes Onomatopiates.

He's a woof woof.

Sylvia takes oxymorox. She's got the teenage menopause. Gets her winter-sugar somersaults from sniffing non-stick glue. She wears the V-necked trousers, in the blind-eye looking-glass. Does the amputated tango, and then finds herself quite lost, in the new old English style! Sylvia takes oxymorox.

She's a cat dog.

But Johnny takes Metaphorazine. Look at those busted street lamp eyes, that midnight clockface of a smile. That corrugated tinflesh roof of a brow. The knife, fork and spoon of his fingers, the sheer umbrella of the man's hairdo! The coldwater bedsit of his brain. He's a fanfare of atoms, I tell you! And you know that last, exquisite mathematical formula rubbed off the blackboard before the long summer holidays begin? Well, that's him. Speeding language through the veins, Johnny takes Metaphorazine.

He's a real dog.

ALPHABOX

'**W**hat does he write about?'

This was the one question that Donna kept asking the man with the alphabet box, whenever they bumped into each other. During the last few weeks they had become quite friendly, sometimes even taking their lunch together in a small park behind a department store.

He told her stories, stories of his own. Stories of the factory he visited every morning, the way the letters were bred and tamed, and of the writer and his cruelties. He often let Donna see inside the box; the silvery, slippery letters that flowed to the corners as though afraid of the light.

'What does he write about?' the carrier finally replied to Donna one day. 'Ah, that's the trouble, you see. The writer doesn't get out much any more. Not at all, actually. He's very old. That's why he pays me to deliver the letters. Now when he was a younger man, why he was famous for his cruelty and cunning in hunting down the letters. And not these tame little factory-produced letters, oh no; back then, he would track down wild, fierce letters, and drag them screaming back to his rooms. And his books were wild and fierce, in turn. Now, unfortunately, his stories are quite tame, and always about the same subject.'

'Which is?'

'He writes about writing, of course. What else does he know?'

And then, one wonderful lunchtime, in the autumn of the year, with the sun moulded from brass, the carrier showed Donna how to open the box for herself. The secret manoeuvres; the slightest pressure to the wing of a songbird, to a flower's petal, to a thorn. The box opened up for Donna, and she put her eye to the gifted darkness.

It was the letter Q.

A flash of quicksilver, curling to meet inside itself, to flick out a tail.

QWERTYPHOBIA

The trouble began at the christening. The joyous announcement, 'I name this child Quentin Thomas King', was disturbed by the baby boy's sudden retching cough. The holy water in the font swirled red with blood.

During the first years of his life, Quentin suffered daily from this attack. His mother would call out his name, to stop him from doing that naughty thing, whatever it was, this very instant. The boy would start to cough. His father would read him a bedtime story: '"Off with her head!" cried the Queen of Hearts.' The child's skin would inflame. His mother would say to him, 'Oh, you're such a queer boy!' A trickle of blood would flow from his lips.

Experiments were made on his body, checking for all the common allergic reactions. Neither milk nor pollen nor even the household cat made any impression. All the tests failed to find the cause of Quentin's discomfort. Some small relief was taken from the fact that the abreaction was becoming less pronounced as he grew older, with the shock of blood slowly giving way to a severe, burning rash.

For all the tests done by various doctors and experts, it was Quentin's own mother who first discovered the cause of the problem. This came about when she was trying to teach the young boy the alphabet. When asked to repeat the letters after her, the poor child managed all the way to the letter P, quite successfully, only then to go quiet.

'Come on now,' said his mother, 'the next letter is called Q, isn't that right?'

The usual reaction set in. The pupil's skin was livid with his pain. Mrs King immediately made an appointment for her son to see a psychiatrist.

This psychiatrist, a certain Dr Crombie, confirmed the mother's suspicions. 'Mr and Mrs King,' he said to the parents, 'your son, I'm afraid, is allergic to the letter Q.'

Quentin was in the room at the time, and of course the very sound of the pronouncement was enough to set him off.

'Your child is not alone,' continued the psychiatrist, once Quentin was safely in bed. 'I have found a number of cases in the literature. Most of these have occurred in the last five years, which may prove worrying. There was the case of a young girl in 1999, who was scared of the letter E; a rather more serious case, I think you'll agree.'

'But what have I done wrong?' cried Mrs King, 'to cause this . . . this *disease* to happen?'

'Oh, it's not a disease, madam; think of it more as a negative reaction, a mental dismissal. Your dear child has a deep, deep hatred for the seventeenth letter of the alphabet, whether written down or spoken aloud. This hatred causes a psychosomatic response in his bodily functions.'

'Can nothing be done?' asked the father.

'The root cause of the condition is unknown,' replied Dr Crombie, 'although research has shown it to occur mainly in the more well-off, dare I say it, upper-middle-class families, such as your own. Until the cause is found, we can do nothing except treat your son with the utmost tenderness.'

'Oh my poor, poor child!' Mrs King was in tears.

'I would advise', added the psychiatrist, 'that your son lead a more isolated life.'

So Quentin's parents started calling their son by his middle name, Thomas. His bedroom was stripped of all offending posters and all the books, of course, for how could they check every one? Only the simplest picture books were allowed, and even these had to have certain pages torn out. Thomas was not allowed out to play, and none of his friends could visit, except under the strictest instructions, and then only for a few minutes at a time.

At first, the Kings found it hard not to say the dreaded letter in their son's presence. Quixotic, query, quincunx, quoits, quotidian; these words, and others – quaff and quiff, quiver and quagmire and quantum mechanics – all had to be forsaken. Eventually, however, they became expert at their task. They would read to Thomas, see the dreaded letter coming up, and with a deft turn of phrase, substitute the offending word with a more suitable one. By this technique, Thomas received an education of sorts, and even started to write his own stories; magical tales they were, and not entirely because of the restricted vocabulary.

Even in their own private, intimate conversations, and without thinking about it, Mr and Mrs King found themselves avoiding the letter Q. In this avoidance, strangely, they found a renewal of their love for each other.

When Thomas was seven years old, the good Dr Crombie brought news of a new treatment. 'I must warn you,' he said to the parents, 'the drug is still in its experimental phase. Basically, if you agree to his being treated, your son will be a guinea pig. It will not cure him, please take note of this. It will only hold the reaction at bay. If he should desist from the treatment . . .'

The Kings signed the required paperwork.

The medication turned out to be a cloudy liquor, pale green in colour. Thomas took two portions a day, every morning and evening. Without cease, this washing of the tongue. Until, on one fair spring day, a trembling nine-year-old boy wrote these words in his diary: 'My name is Quentin Thomas King.'

There was a slight quickening of the pulse, a flush of heat to his forehead, a nervous twitch in his arm.

And then a smile, a play of sounds in his mind, on his lips.

At the age of eighteen, Quentin King joined a self-help group called Word Up Positive. They met every Thursday evening, in a room above a public house in the centre of Manchester. At any time there could be between twelve and thirty-nine members present. They led a more or less normal life, thanks to the continuous intake of certain drugs, but at these weekly meetings, all use of the medication was banned. Instead, they talked in their own tongue, feeling more natural doing so, and not wanting to lose the gift it gave them.

The language they used was entirely dependent on which particular members were present. Sometimes, when the gathering was sparse, it was almost English they spoke. Other times, when the room was crowded, they could hardly speak at all, with so many letters dangerous. Even then, they managed to hold real conversations, expressing more in those two hours together than they had all week in more liberal company.

Thirteen of them were writers of fiction. Quentin King, led by their example, became the most successful of them all, with three best-selling novels to his name. The critics praised the 'majestic restraint' of his prose.

At the age of twenty-four Quentin married another member of the group, Molly Unwin, who could not stand the letter U. One year later their first child was born, a boy, a completely normal, healthy boy.

They called him Charles Gordon Alexander King.

PIXEL JUICE

ALPHABOX
(in the mix)

After learning the secret of opening the box, Donna didn't see the carrier for a few weeks. Perhaps he had chosen a new route; perhaps he had lost the job because of being late, or for bringing the wrong letter; perhaps the writer had finished the book. No matter how Donna varied her lunchtimes, no matter where she searched, still the alphabet box eluded her. She started to feel lonely, depressed even, and could not explain why, especially to the manager of the bookshop, who kept on at her for not working to her usual high standards.

Eventually, about two months after she had last seen him, the carrier turned up again at the café. He was looking very tired. He clattered the box down on the table, with none of his former loving care. And when Donna asked him what was wrong, he said:

'It's the writer. He's driving me mad. He's desperate to

finish his book, you see. His last great masterpiece, he calls it. He's dying. He's got me carrying two, sometimes even three letters over in one day. I just can't manage it.'

'Put two letters in at once,' suggested Donna.

'Two letters in the box! At once! Are you crazy? They would mate. Have you ever seen the offspring of a G and a P? It's a horrible sight, let me tell you. No, if I'm to keep this job, I must work harder, that is all. Look, I only came in to say, well, I won't be around much any more. I have enjoyed our conversations, but . . .'

'Don't worry, I understand.'

'Perhaps when this story is over . . . ?'

'Yes. Let's.'

The man picked up the box, and left the café. Donna finished her meal, hardly knowing what to think. Suddenly, the idea of returning to the shop didn't appeal. But she had to make a living. On the way back, there was a crowd gathered on the corner of Deansgate Boulevard, and the traffic had come to a standstill. As Donna got closer, she realized there had been an accident. Pushing through the crowd, she saw the man's body on the ground, somebody kneeling over him. A car had mounted the pavement.

The box lay some way off, unnoticed. Donna heard a voice, from somewhere.

(Hardly anything is true about me.)

She bent down to the box, touched it in secret. (I want everybody to know that.) The carvings slid apart, making darkness. (Read the true confessions.) She put her hand through the aperture. (Reveal all, reveal all.) Clutched at something wet and slippery, like catching a fish with bare hands.

(Let someone write it for me.)

Donna didn't know where the writer lived, didn't know

where the letters were made. (It wouldn't be truthful.) She was already late for the afternoon shift, but suddenly nothing mattered any more, nothing at all. (You have to be special.) This was hers now, this warm, squirming thing inside her palm.

(You have to be very special.)

She didn't dare open her hands until she was five streets away.

(It wouldn't be truthful otherwise.)

It was the letter J. Without knowing why, the young bookseller knew it stood for Junior.

(Reveal all, reveal all.)

Donna started to run.

JUNIOR PIMP

First of all I want everyone to know that hardly anything that was said in the other papers is true about me. The other papers know nothing, and only in this paper will you read the true confessions of the world-famous Junior Pimp. I intend to reveal all, no holds barred, pimples and all, and if the police and the church people and all the other stuck-up people don't like it, well they know what they can do. I reckon they're only jealous anyway, because I bet they had boring old childhoods, and it's not everybody that gets to be a famous Junior Pimp, you have to be special.

My name is William Wheeler, and I wish my mum and dad hadn't given me those two Ws, but there's nothing much I can do about it except call myself Liam. Which I tried for a few years, but the other kids just kept on calling me Willy Wheels, and that's just one example of the things I've had to put up with. And people wring their hands in shame, and dare to ask why it was that I became a Junior Pimp.

Well, keep reading, because I'm going to tell you exactly how it happened, and I'm going to tell it in my own way. The paper offered to let someone write it for me, but I refused, saying it wouldn't be truthful otherwise.

I'm eleven years old, nearly twelve. I became the famous Junior Pimp when I was only ten, which I think must be a record, certainly for this country. I've given up being the famous Junior Pimp now, and I'll give the reason for that as well, but to learn why you'll have to keep buying this newspaper, won't you?

DEPRIVED

I lived with my mum and dad and my little dog, Tango, in a nice little house in Ashton-under-Lyne, which is a town near Manchester. There's some rough areas in Ashton, but we don't live in them, oh no, we live in one of the posher bits. We're not very rich or anything like that, just not rough, that's all. I'm telling you this so you won't get the idea that maybe I was forced into being a Junior Pimp because of a deprived childhood.

Nothing could be further from the truth. I've always done pretty good at school, especially at art, which is my favourite. I like to draw, and my hobbies include watching television, listening to music, and reading. I've never been very good at things like football or tennis or cricket, and my dad was always telling me off about this, saying when was I going to be a proper man like the other kids? But apart from that, I've had a very happy childhood, compared to some, the kids from the Shakespeare Estate that backs on to our street for instance. My mum was very angry when the council built the estate, apparently, so my dad kept telling me, and she wanted to move straight away. They were saving up for a better house, in a better part of town.

My mum says it's a joke that the council called it the Shakespeare Estate, and that all the streets are named after characters from his plays. She's a bit of a snob really, and I hope she doesn't mind me saying that, because I know I've caused her problems lately, ever since it came out that I was a Junior Pimp. But I've promised to be truthful, so she'll just have to put up with it, anyway she's not complaining about the money I'm getting for writing these world-exclusive confessions.

I always liked to play with the kids from the estate, because they were more fun than the ones in our street, far less boring. There was one kid in particular that everybody wanted to hang out with, his real name is Paul Holland, but everybody called him Dutch. He lived on MacDuff Park, which is really grotty and not a park at all, but who's to blame for that, the council I reckon. Dutch was the same age as me, but older if you know what I mean, and the leader of a gang that called themselves the Parkas, because they lived on the Park, and also because they wore these long parka coats, even in the summer. You had to have one to be in the gang. I asked my mum to buy me one, but she wouldn't, they weren't posh enough. But I really, really wanted to join Dutch's gang, and would do anything to hang out with them, even if they were always making fun of me and calling me Willy Wheels.

GIRLIE MAGS

It was the summer holidays, very hot and nothing much to do, except think about how close it was to going back to school. We were going on to the secondary school after the holidays, and I think that got Dutch going a little, because he seemed to get madder, braver, more outrageous in his schemes the closer it got. I guess he was worried, or something, and really wanted to make the most of his time.

I'll tell you how I got to be a member of the Parka Gang, without even needing one of them snazzy coats. Dutch and his mates were hanging out at the busted playground one day, when I came to find them. I think they liked to have me around just to make fun of, but I was beyond caring by then. Anyway, they had these magazines that Dutch had got from somewhere. Girlie mags they were. I'd never seen one before, not close up enough to study. I was amazed! Open legs and everything. They weren't hardcore or anything, but I'd never seen a woman before, naked I mean, even if they were only photographs. I wasn't excited by them, not in my body I mean, and it's important to remember that fact for later on. No, it was just the idea of them that got me going. I was excited in my head. I wasn't thinking about sex, like Dutch and his mates were. They were going crazy over them, and telling dirty jokes about the women, and explaining how big their thingies were getting, and moaning about the fact that the pictures weren't explicit enough. Me, I was just fascinated by the shapes, the hidden details, the secrets. I tried to pretend that my thingy was getting big as well, but I didn't know what they were talking about. I guess I've always been young for my age.

I asked Dutch if I could borrow one of these mags, and he said OK, only don't bring it back with the pages stuck together. I asked him what he meant, but all he did was laugh at me. I don't care that he laughs at me, at least it's something.

I had to smuggle it into our house under my coat, so my mum wouldn't see it. It was bad enough me hanging around with the estate kids, never mind bringing home pornography. But I had a plan, see. I waited till bedtime, and then got the magazine out and studied it for a while. Then I got my drawing kit out. Like I said earlier, I've always been pretty good at drawing, ever since I was little.

Anyway the next day I turn up at the busted playground again, carrying the mag with me in a carrier bag. I hand it back to Dutch, and then I tell him I've done some of my own. He says, what? I say I've done some pornography of my own. And I pull these four sheets of paper out of the bag, hand them round, one for each member of the gang. And their faces, you should've seen them! Because I'd remembered all the things they said about what they really wanted the pictures to show, and I'd painted just that, as realistic as I could manage. Which wasn't very realistic at all, because I got a lot of the details mixed up.

But Dutch was amazed, I just know he was, because he couldn't stop smiling and drooling over my drawings. So that's how I became a true member of the gang, and that's why Dutch stole me my very own parka, because I'd turned myself into a Junior Pornographer! Pretty neat, eh?

TARTY

I just assumed that Dutch had nicked the girlie mags, from the newsagent, or even from behind his dad's workbench, but when he told me where he'd really got them from, well it was my turn to be amazed. Because he'd been given them by his sister!

Now I'd seen this sister a few times, just hanging around, you know. Her name was Fiona, and she was seventeen years old. She was pretty good looking, I think, a bit tarty with it, but most of the girls on the estate looked that way, I think it was the fashion. But you always got the impression with Fiona that it wasn't just fashion, it was more a way of life, if you know what I mean. Sometimes she'd turn up with a bruised cheek, or even a black eye. She could be hard-faced when she wanted to be, but she always had a little smile for me. The other kids in the gang were always trying it on with her, even though they were only ten and wouldn't know what to do with it anyway. She'd just tell them to shut up and come back when they were men, but with me it was different, I never bothered her. I think she saw me as just a little kid really, innocent, you know. So she'd smile at me, and I'd smile right back.

I had this famous smile. I know I had it, because my aunts and uncles were always calling me 'Smiler'. I just couldn't be tough like the other kids, even if I tried. When I did try, it came out all funny, so in the end I gave up on ever being tough.

Fiona even called me Liam, which was the best thing of all. She never made fun of me. Still, I was shocked when Dutch told me that it was her that had given him the porno mags. I didn't think girls could get hold of that kind of thing. I mean, I knew she was easy because all the lads said she was, but porno mags! So I asked Dutch where she'd got them from, and he said that it came with the job.

Job, I thought. What job could possibly let a girl get hold of porno mags, and she didn't even have a job as far as I knew, because she was often hanging out at the busted playground during the weekdays. That's when Dutch told me that Fiona was a prostitute!

I was shocked of course, who wouldn't be. I didn't believe him at first, I thought he was just joking with me. But he wasn't, and I found out for sure a few days later.

FIFTY POUNDS

You have to understand that we didn't do much with our days, just hang around the busted playground mostly, and talk about pop music or football, or maybe we'd go down the high street and try and nick things from the corner shop. We were never very successful at this, and that's one of the reasons I liked to hang out with the Parkas, they weren't really, really bad like some of the other gangs I could mention.

One time we were messing about outside the shop, steeling up courage, and it was pretty late, I know because I kept looking at my watch. I had to be in by a certain time or else my dad would go mad at me. My dad could be pretty mad at times, and even violent, although he mostly took that out on our dog, Tango. I don't care who knows this, because it's true. It was strange, because I had this parka on, that I wasn't supposed to wear. I had to hide it in the shed, go out in my normal coat, swap it for the parka, and then swap back before I went back in. I kept thinking it must be nice to be able to do just what you want, like Dutch, like Fiona. Their parents didn't seem to mind what they did.

Anyway, so we were hanging out at the shop, and it was getting late, just starting to get dark, when Fiona comes running out of the pub opposite. She's got a man with her, some older guy, real fat and ugly and I wonder what's she's doing with him. Dutch says to me, There, I told you. That's her latest punter. No way, I said. Watch, he says. The man and Fiona are talking, and I actually see the man give her some money, then they walk off together!

Where's she going? I ask. Oh, they usually go to her flat, Dutch replies, or else just to a dark street if it's just a blow job the bloke's after. She gets twenty quid for a blow job. Twenty quid! I say. Sure, he says, and fifty for the whole thing. Fifty quid! I shout. Bloody hell, that's a fortune! And then they laugh at me some more.

Uh huh! whispers Dutch. He's looking over to the pub where this young bloke's come out, a real hard-looking type, all tight trousers and bare arms with muscles and everything. Who's that? I ask. That's Melv, says Dutch. Melvin Flowers, he's Fiona's pimp. I ask what a pimp is, and then they really start making fun of me. Willy Wheels! Willy Wheels, doesn't even know what a pimp is! Stuff like that.

Of course I'd heard the word before, but it was one of those words that I never got round to really finding out about, mainly because until then I'd never had the need to. So Dutch tells me how it all works, how this Melv character gets 70 per cent of everything that Fiona earns, and in return he's supposed to look after her, protect her from violent clients. And that this Melv has got about fifteen girls working for him, and that instead of looking after her, usually it's him that's the cause of all the bruises on Fiona's face.

This Melvin looks over at us then, and Dutch gives him a wave, but all he gets in return is a dirty look.

It just didn't seem fair somehow, but just think of all the money he must be earning for doing hardly anything at all, and that night, when I was lying awake in bed, it was all I could think about, how lucky he was.

BRUISED

Nothing much happened for a week or two, and then we had to go back to school. I kind of lost touch with Dutch then, because when we got to the secondary school, he started to change, become more serious. And when we did meet up, it wasn't the same. He suddenly seemed a lot older, I think he must have been reaching puberty or something, after all the pretending. He even stopped wearing the famous parka coat. Sometimes I'd go to the busted playground, expecting the gang to be there, but they hardly ever were.

I still went anyway, with the parka on just in case. I think I just liked to get out of the house, because Mum and Dad were arguing a lot by then, lots of shouting and one time my dad actually hit my mum. It wasn't a bad hit, more of a slap really. But I was an only child, and I felt pretty helpless, because how could I help my mum, I wasn't much use to anyone.

So I'd just sit on the busted roundabout, feeling pretty sorry for myself, and thinking that maybe there wasn't much use in love or whatever you wanted to call it. And who should come up, but this Fiona.

She was looking real bad herself, with a black eye again, but worse than usual, and plenty of bruises. She sits down on the roundabout and we don't say much to each other for a while, just lost in our own little worlds I guess. It was nice, being like that, as though we didn't even need to talk. Eventually she says, That's it, I've left him. And I knew who she meant, without even asking. I've got to get me a new pimp, she says.

Do you have to have a new pimp? I ask.

Of course I do. Who would look after me otherwise? I'd get beaten up.

You're getting beaten up anyway, I say.

I know, she says. It sucks, doesn't it?

And then she asks what's up with me, and I tell her about my mum and dad and all that trouble. She comes close then, round to my side of the roundabout, and sits back down beside me. We're a couple of right losers, aren't we? she whispers, and it's only then that I realize that she's crying.

And there's nothing I can do but put my arm around her. We must've looked a right sight.

RUNAWAY

It was a week after this that I left home. I'd come home late one time, and I was expecting to get told off for it, but what should

I find but Mum and Dad arguing again. I was growing used to this by now, but this time was different, worse than ever. Tango was howling as well, like he wanted to get in on the act, and my mum was crying, and my dad shouting his head off and waving his fists around. I just knew he was working up to hitting someone, either me or Tango, or even worse, my mum. I'd just about had enough, so I shouted back at him which felt good because it was the first time I'd managed it. That stopped him for a moment, just a moment, then he started in again, even louder this time. I don't know, something must have broken inside me then. I went up quietly to my room, collected a few things into a rucksack, came back downstairs and out the back door. Nobody noticed me leaving, not even Tango, which was sad. But I just had to do it, although I suppose I was only making a scene of it, not really running away.

I didn't have a clue where to go, except the busted playground. It was late by the time I got there, and dark. I was hoping Fiona would be there. We'd met up nearly every night since the first night, just to talk and share a laugh or two, and I couldn't think of anywhere else to go. But she wasn't there. Of course Fiona hadn't left Melvin, her pimp, because she couldn't, could she? Every pro had to have a pimp. She'd taught me all about how the system worked, and how there was no escape from it, once you got started. I think that's why we felt good together, both of us were trapped, in our own ways, I suppose. Although I've never quite managed to work out what was holding me back. Maybe just boredom.

But she wasn't there. I hung around for a bit, but then I got scared. I didn't want to go home, not yet, it was too soon. I wanted Mum and Dad to be really sorry for having argued. But where could I go? I didn't know where Fiona's flat was, she'd never told me, I think she kept it secret on purpose, part of the pimping system. I walked over to the high street. It was about eleven o'clock by then, and the pubs were chucking out. It was a Saturday as well, so the streets were pretty violent, that special tensed-up feeling like a fight was just about to break out. I kept my eyes to myself, because that's the best way to avoid getting beaten up. It was strange, because the tough guys would go quiet when I passed them, as though they were embarrassed by me being there, a young kid on the street like that. I always did look innocent, my mum was so proud of it, the way I looked, I mean. Mummy's little angel, she called me, if you can imagine that! No wonder I ran away.

Anyway, I was hoping to see Fiona, and I got lucky. Well, not that lucky, because this was her big night for working. I was using my brain, wasn't I? I saw her coming out of the pub with some over-eager bloke. I didn't know what else to do, so I followed them. First of all I waited to see if Melvin turned up. Sure enough he did, but only to talk to the bloke like he was warning him or something, then he turned to see to one of his other girls, who was making a right noise because some drunk had slapped her.

So, I followed them, Fiona and the punter. It was pretty easy, with the dark, and with me being so small. I kept to the shadows. Fiona's flat was only around the corner anyway, above a newsagent's. There was a side door that they went through, and when I got there of course it was locked. There was a little panel with her name in it, just her first name that is, Fiona, and a little bell and a grille beside it you could speak through.

I didn't know what to do next, so I just hung around, maybe to wait until the guy had finished. There was a window above the shop, and that's where Fiona lived, because the light was turned on almost straight away. I saw her close the curtains, but she didn't see me. I couldn't help thinking about what was happening up there. All I had to go on was the naked pictures I'd seen, and the jokes of Dutch and the gang. Somehow, I couldn't imagine Fiona doing anything dirty like that, which just shows how innocent I was in those days!

INNOCENT

I must have waited down there for about ten minutes when suddenly I heard a scream. It was Fiona! I looked up at the window, and there were shapes moving there, and then the light went out, and the scream was almost lost, you know, something you can only just hear. Straight away, not even thinking about it, I ran to the door and pushed the bell. I kept my finger on it. I could hear it from upstairs, making this piercing sound. I just kept pushing it, till my finger went numb. And suddenly Fiona's voice came screaming through the little grille, Help! and the door buzzed and swung open. Fiona must have got to the switch somehow. I ran up the stairs. No, that's not true. I walked up the stairs. I was suddenly scared, you see, really scared, thinking about what I might find. Where was this famous Melvin the Pimp, wasn't this his job, protecting his girls? And what could I do, just a kid.

Anyway, I got to the top of the stairs, where another door led to her flat. This one wasn't locked, so I pushed it slowly open. I couldn't see anything, not at first, because the light still wasn't on. There was a noise coming from somewhere, another room I think, so I headed towards it. I was shaking something rotten, but what else could I do? Fiona screamed again, and called out Melvin's name, she must've thought it was him coming to rescue her, not me.

I walked into the room, Fiona's bedroom it was. Pitch black, but my eyes had started to get used to the darkness. There was a shape on the bed, and a shape standing over it. I called out Fiona's name.

Fi . . . on . . . a . . .

Just like that, very quietly

Everything seemed to stop then. The standing shape made a noise, turned towards me. Fiona must've got to her bedside light, because it came on then, and I saw this man, big man he was, half naked and carrying his belt in his hands like a whip. He turned on me like he was going to hit me with it this time.

But then he stopped.

Fiona called my name out loud.

What's going on? said the man, only he swore, which can't be repeated in a family newspaper. Leave her alone, I said. Don't be a bully. The man laughed, just once, and then he stopped laughing. He looked confused, more than anything, like I was the last thing he expected to see, which is the truth I suppose. He almost looked scared himself. Then he picked up his shirt and his jacket, and he walked out of there, just like that!

Weird, eh?

Fiona stood up, and hugged me. She was nearly naked. But it was nice, you know, just nice. I wasn't excited by it, just glad she was all right, that's all. Just glad I'd managed to protect her. She let me sleep there, for the night. I slept in the living room, on the couch. Just so you don't get the wrong idea or anything.

CAREER

I guess that's when my career as the famous Junior Pimp started, although I didn't know that then. The bad man had already paid for his stupid pleasure, and Fiona gave me some of the money for helping her out. Not a lot, but I was happy to take it, who wouldn't be? I went back home the following morning, which was the Sunday. Of course there was some explaining to do, but mainly my mum was just glad to have me back, safe and sound. My dad promised to never argue ever again. I didn't tell them where I'd slept, just saying I'd stayed at a friend's house, which wasn't a lie.

My dad kept his promise, for a while anyway. They wanted to keep me in at night from then on, but I told them they couldn't, I was eleven years old now. It was my birthday that week, you see. But I put up with their wishes, till the next Saturday that is. They went out for the night, which was something they hadn't done in ages, so my dad really was making an effort. Of course, as soon as they were out the door, so was I!

I went straight round to Fiona's. It was early yet, and she was in. She was alone and glad to see me. She said she hadn't been out since last Saturday, said she was sick of the game. That's what she called it, the game. I suppose it did have rules, but who was the winner? The pimp, I think. Melvin. He'd been round, she said, to ask her what was going on, where was his money? She'd told him she was ill, a bad disease that meant she couldn't have sex. Of course she didn't have this disease, she was just kidding him. He'd said she was no use to him in that state, and she'd said, good, because she wanted out.

It was me that persuaded her that she didn't want out, that she was just feeling scared. I told her that she should go out, find a punter, because didn't she need the money? And if there was trouble, wasn't I going to be there to protect her, just like I'd done that week?

If this sounds like I was being very grown-up, well I suppose I was. What I'd seen last week had changed me, made me realize things about adults, how bad they could be, how stupid.

If I had to grow up, I was determined to be different, I was going to be in control of my life, like they said on the American chat shows on the tele. I wasn't going to be stupid like other men, that's what I promised myself anyway.

Fiona was reluctant at first, but she gave in eventually. She had to eat, didn't she? So we made a plan, and out she went to find a punter. My job was to hide in the living room until they'd finished whatever it was they had to do. Only if there was trouble would she call for me. Then I'd come in and sort it out.

The first punter didn't make any bother, and neither did the second. But the third was a nasty piece of work. Sure enough, Fiona called for me, and in I went. I put on my most innocent face, and the famous smile. I just smiled at this big tough guy, like butter wouldn't melt. And sure enough he couldn't take it, he left sharpish. What it was, I think, is that the punters just couldn't think about sex or violence, not whilst there was a kid in the bedroom. Does that make sense?

Anyway, it worked. I made a load of money that night, more than I'd ever seen before. It was part of the deal, you see.

NINE GIRLS

So that's how I became the Junior Pimp. I more or less moved in with Fiona. I know mum and dad called the police about me, but I stayed in the flat as much as possible. Fiona did the shopping. It was the Easter holidays at school, so that was all right, and when the holidays were over I just didn't bother with school at all. Fiona was angry with me about this, but what could she do, she'd hardly been a perfect pupil herself. She got used to having me round. It was like I was her younger brother, the younger brother that Dutch should've been, if only he hadn't been so stupid.

She introduced me to some of the other girls, and I would do specials for them, if they had to see punters that had caused trouble in the past. I tell you, nobody caused trouble when the young boy turned up. Eventually I was looking after nine different girls, which was neat but involved a lot of juggling. We decided that all the difficult punters had to come to Fiona's flat, so Fiona became what she called a madame, which is French, isn't it? Me, I just stayed in the flat, going out at night sometimes, for air. I wasn't needed all that often, because most of the punters behaved themselves. But I was always there for them, the girls that is, if they ever needed any help.

Fiona and the other girls were so used to me, they more or less walked around naked when I was there, as though I wasn't there. I'd do drawings of them sometimes, in various states of undress. They made nice shapes. The only rule we had was that I would never get to see them actually doing it, the sex I mean. Anyway, I didn't want to.

Of course it all had to go wrong, and that's what I'll tell in the final part of my confessions, which you can read in tomorrow's paper.

EXCITEMENT

I was a Junior Pimp for three weeks altogether, which doesn't seem very long, but how long have you ever been a Junior Pimp? tell me that. And anyway, I sure packed a lot of living into those three weeks, and made a whole lot of money. But everything has to end sooner or later, even the good things. This is how my career finished.

I had the police looking for me still. I'd see my face on television, and read about how I'd gone missing in the newspaper. But it wasn't the police that finished my career. And Dutch, he found out about what I was up to with his sister. He came round one time, saw me there, and when I told him the story, boasted about it, well, the look on his face was worth everything. Not even Dutch could top a scheme like this. But it wasn't Dutch that finished my career, he kept quiet about it, his sister made him promise.

Melvin, Fiona's old pimp, had been thrown into prison for beating up some bloke in the pub. Beat him up something terrible I heard, so it wasn't him that finished my career, he was out of the picture.

No, it was me that finished my career as a Junior Pimp.

It was a quiet night, a Tuesday. Fiona and I were in the flat alone, the other girls not needing me that night. Fiona didn't want to go out, she said, because nothing ever happened on a Tuesday. I said that she had to, because I was the boss, wasn't I? It was just a game between us in a way, but she really was treating me like her boss by then, she usually followed orders. We were sitting in her bedroom, with her lounging on the bed and me in the armchair. She was still in her scruffs, so I ordered her to get changed into something sexy, she had some outrageous gear, let me tell you. She stood up and pulled off her T-shirt, and then undid her jeans, rolled them down her legs. I was just sitting there watching her, thinking maybe I should get my sketchbook out, when something happened to me.

Do I have to spell it out? I hope it's all right to say the word erection in a family newspaper. Anyway, that's what happened, I got an erection. I got excited. I slid down the chair to hide it, but the more that Fiona dolled herself up, the bigger it grew. She looked over at me, saw something was wrong, and asked me what it was. I said, nothing, get ready. But then I said, no, don't get ready, let's just watch tele tonight, it's a Tuesday, nothing ever happens on a Tuesday. But she wouldn't listen, said that she'd got ready now, she wasn't going to waste it, no way.

So she went out to find a punter.

I was left alone in the flat. I was thinking about what had happened, trying to understand. I was tempted to get it out, my thingy I mean, but I didn't. I was scared, wasn't I? Scared of what might happen. Would I still be able to protect her now, with a stiffy in my pants? Anyway, eventually I heard Fiona coming back up the stairs, so I slipped into the living room, as usual. I heard her going along the corridor to her bedroom. It was quiet out there, no talking. Some punters are like that, they don't like talking.

So I waited as I always did, trying to read a little, but my mind couldn't stop imagining what was going on behind the wall. And the more I imagined, the worse it got, my excitement I mean. All these dirty pictures flashing through my head like a cinema show. Adults only.

I was hoping that nothing would go wrong tonight, but something did, because after about ten minutes I heard Fiona calling for me. Not wanting to, not really, I made my way slowly to the bedroom. My thingy was still tingling in my pants. I pushed open the door. Fiona's bedside light was on, all nice and glowing red it was, and the man had tied her to the bedposts. I could never tell with Fiona when things were bad, because sometimes she had to be bad just to keep the punters happy and coming back for more. But if she called, that meant it was really bad, not just pretend bad.

She was screaming now, and the punter was kneeling fully clothed astride her naked flesh and he was hitting her across the face again and again, like he hated her or something, like he hated the whole world and Fiona was unlucky enough to be on the end of it.

My excitement died like a squashed fly.

Of course I recognized the punter straight away, even from the back.

Dad, I said, real slow and quiet, like I couldn't quite believe it, which is certainly true. Well, that stopped him, as you can imagine. He turned to look at me, and his look of surprise, the shock on his face, well, I shall never forget it. Trouble was, it just made him even angrier, the surprise I mean. I tried my usual trick, with the innocent face and the smile and everything, but of course that didn't work any more, especially now. I mean, that was my own dad in there, the dirty so-and-so!

He jumped off the bed, and came straight for me, his hand raised to strike. He was screaming something blue at me for being there, as though I was to blame for his stupid randiness. But then I saw the look in his eye, the real look, which was kind of blank. And it came to me in a second, the so-and-so didn't recognize me! His own son, and all. He must've been out of his head with anger, or lust, or maybe both, most probably both. Or perhaps he was just denying me being there at all, out of guilt for instance.

Anyway, I tried to dodge away but he had me already, by the scruff of the neck. He picked me up, and I'm sure he was going to throw me against the wall. I'm sure of it. So I just screamed his name out loud, as loud as I could, not his real name, I mean I just shouted out DAD!!!! DAD, STOP IT!!!! Like that, as loud as that.

And he stopped. He stopped sudden like, still holding me aloft, like a baby. Then he let me down slowly. He walked back

PIXEL JUICE

to the bed, more or less just collapsed on to the bed actually. My dad put his head in his hands, his head dropping down to his hands, and his body shrivelling to almost nothing. And then he started to cry.

WRONG?

Well, as you can imagine, that was the end of my career as a Junior Pimp. I didn't know what to say to my dad, so I didn't say anything. Instead I undid Fiona, and she got dressed. I had no excitement left in me, none at all.

Then my dad came over all apologetic and begged me not to tell Mum about him visiting a prostitute. I promised I wouldn't, just to get him to shut up, and to get him out of there. After he'd left, Fiona and I sat on the bed together, not saying hardly anything. My dad's money was lying on her bedside table, and she actually offered me my usual cut, can you believe that? Of course I told her what she could do with her money. Then I said goodbye to her.

When I got back home my mum was overjoyed to see me. It was like being smothered in kisses! Horrible. Of my dad, there was no sign. Mum didn't know where he was, and she didn't care, that's what she said. I wouldn't have told on him, I really wouldn't have, except that Dutch finally stuck his big foot in it by telling some stupid journalist about me. That caused a right stink, with questions in the papers and people going on about me as though I was the end of civilization or something. That's why I've decided to tell this true confession of my time as a Junior Pimp.

Anyway, it's all finished now. I'm living at home again, with Mum and Tango. Mum and Dad are getting divorced. I'm back at school as well, doing my best to catch up with the lessons I missed. I want to be an artist. The authorities are still trying to decide if I've done anything wrong. What do you think – have I? I don't know, sometimes it seems like it never happened, that I never was a Junior Pimp. But then I remember what I've seen, and what I've done. Seen more and done more than any other boy in the school, even those that have actually had sex, or so they claim. They all look up to me now because I'm famous, especially the girls. Some psychiatrist expert type woman has said that it's going to affect me for the rest of my life, and I certainly hope so.

SHED WEAPONS

Just about the best thing about being a kid is that you get to have hobbies. Hobbies are not graded according to how educational they are, and not even by how interesting they are; no, a hobby is deemed good or bad by how many *gadgets* it involves. Stamp collecting for instance, although undeniably educational, has only the album, the tweezers, the hinges, the magnifying glass, and that's about it. According to the gadget quota, by far the best hobby of all time is angling.

Your average boyhood fishing trip involves hooks and weights, and floats and lines, and reels and rods, and landing nets and keepnets, and strange apparatus like the little tool that gets the hook out of the fish's mouth. And all this paraphernalia gets a carefully allotted place in the various plastic trays that slot neatly into the wicker basket, the basket that also doubles as a canalside seat.

But the best gadget of all, in fishing, is the bait. By this, I mean specifically, the maggots.

You could buy these little creatures by the ounce, usually from the local pet shop. As though a maggot could be a pet. They came in a rainbow of colours, which means that somewhere on Earth, some kid is being asked, 'What does your dad do?' and he can answer, quite proudly: 'He's a maggot-colourer.' You would give the shopkeeper your sixpence, or whatever it was, and he would open the big tub and there they all were, millions of them, wriggling like crazy. The man would scoop out your portion, plop them into a brown paper bag. The bag was warm in your hand, and pulsated slightly, and from there you transferred them to your baitbox, which was plastic, with a lid. Sometimes they would show a natural history film on television, a speeded-up film in which these very same creatures could be seen devouring a dead rabbit in seconds. It took a while to get over the fear.

But pretty soon you did, especially after piercing a few with the fishing hook, right through the belly. And there was so much you could do with them. For a start you could throw a bunch of maggots on to the water, around your luminous, bobbing float. This was supposed to tempt the fish towards your hook. Even better was to put a handful in a catapult, and use this to disperse your bait. Of course this led on to more exciting pursuits; like using the catapult to fire maggots at your friends. Then there were competitions to see who could eat the most maggots. And the best thing of all was to put maggots down the back of girls' dresses.

Of course, angling soon went the way of all hobbies, as you got older and moved on to more grown-up pursuits. And when that happened, all the gear – the rod and the basket, the reels and the nets and the baitbox and all the little gadgets, most of which, truth be known, you had never ever used – all of it went into the garden shed.

The garden shed was traditionally the repository of lost hobbies, and not just yours, but your father's too. It was stuffed to the roof with rusting tools and old bikes, and broken-down lawnmowers, moth-eaten overalls, a spade with no handle, a handle with no spade, unwanted presents, cricket bats and airless footballs, jam jars full of nails and screws, and piles of rotting magazines, and all the useless souvenirs from the holidays in Blackpool.

Discarded dreams.

My father kept his weapons in the shed. When I was growing up, it was still close enough to the war years for memories of the conflict to be constantly on people's minds. The comic books we loved to read were filled with pictures of storm troopers shouting things like 'Gott in Himmel!' and 'Englisher Swinehunt!' Our favourite game was play acting the great battles, and I was secretly ashamed because my father had actually been on Germany's side in the war. I knew this because the weapons in the shed were marked with the dreaded symbol of the eagle, and any words on them were in the German language.

Of course, I know now that my dad must have stolen these off dead bodies.

There was a gun, a Luger I think. And a bayonet, a pair of binoculars and some bullets, about half a dozen bullets. Sometimes I would creep into the shed to play with these weighted, magical objects. The binoculars I lost on Blackpool beach one time, and for that I was severely punished. The pistol and the bayonet were handed in when the government called an amnesty on any old war weapons. But for some reason my dad didn't hand over the bullets, the six bullets, I still don't know why.

A few weeks after this, it was Guy Fawkes night, and long after the last stragglers had left the glowing embers of the communal bonfire, my father went up there alone. I don't know what he was thinking of, I really don't, because a few minutes later there were some terrifying explosions from the site of the fire, and my father comes sprinting down the street, waving his hands madly in the air.

He'd only thrown the bullets into the embers!

And in the morning, all along a wooden fence, we found the blackened punctures. I think this is when the people in the street really started talking about my father.

Infected as he was now with the cleaning-out mood, one day he attacked the shed with a vengeance, saying he was going to throw out all the rubbish once and for all. He was in there for hours, and the pile of junk grew in front of the door. Us kids soon grew bored with all this, until we heard a sudden cry of alarm from the shed. My father came running out, followed by a cloud, a black cloud of buzzing life.

He'd opened the baitbox. The baitbox that had slept in the shed for weeks, with the maggots turning first into hard-baked pupae, and then into the ravenous cloud that swarmed for a second around my father's startled face, before taking off at last. Scatters of ash, floating away into the sun.

HOMO KARAOKE

Operate all mechanisms! I am Girlforce 7 of world-famous PERFUME SWORD team. With my special gadget handbag I am best ever invincible. Especially note my deadly poison love ballad! Play game with me. Together we save Moonchester from all contagious evil.

Tonight, the city wears dirty slut perfume and matching outfit. The rain has stopped, leaving the streets with wet greasy hair, strands of pulp blocking the drainage. All the flyers of every party of all time have gathered at the plughole of life. I'm standing on the balcony of Dubtek's nightclub, holding my hand over my mouth. High above me, projected from the roof, lasers paint a dark cloud with colour, chameleon to the beat. I've come out for some air, but even the music has got a serious hygiene problem and there's no escaping it. It's my first ever gig in Manchester, and the place is one giant filthy arse-wipe loudspeaker, zero panache. There's no sign of my challenger. When I walk to the edge, look down, waves of people are streaming out of the club, epileptic under stuttering lights. A purified canal runs back of the club. Some tables, chairs, a couple of sun umbrellas, all wet and soggy but no matter; it's the small gaps between the rain that count, and learning how to live amongst them. Clouds of cheap, shop-bought hormones lift from the young bodies. A girl screams. Another flings her drink at a waiter; the liquid passes right through, creating radio shimmer. Some boy falls in the water. It's all very flesh-core, very human-human, and it's all I can do to stop from retching.

'Would sir be requiring assistance?'

'What?' I turn round: a waiter is grimacing at me.

'Is it the humidity, sir?' His face is twitching badly, struggling like a bad flow diagram.

'I'm fine,' I say.

'A drink? To calm the nerves, perhaps? Courtesy of the management?'

'Leave me alone.'

'Young man, I wish you luck tonight.'

Yeah, right. Put the emphasis on *man* there, why don't you? A final nod and he's gone, flickering on and off a few times before he manages it. Shit, there's still some bugs in the system, all I need. A gang of lowlife casuals stagger on to the balcony. I'm feeling pent up as it is, and I can't shake the mood, I mean, this is supposed to be the VIP zone, DJs only. The kids are crowding in, pressing close, laughing at me about how I'm gonna be a pile of melted vinyl when the killer housebass gets a hold of me. One of them hits me, a hard testing blow to the shoulder. I wouldn't mind but I'm the same age as they are; just another kid from nowhere. I look up at the opposite roof, over the canal, trying to catch a glint of corporate security, let's have some freezer-beams down here! but the cameras are blind and all the goons on locoweed. More system-glitch. Or else the whole place is against me. There's never any shit when you need some, plenty when you don't. Stick that on my gravestone if I lose tonight.

And the rain falls once more.

Operate all mechanisms! I am M.O.R.phine of extra famous PERFUME SWORD hero squad. With my special loudspeaker eyes I beam out E.Z. listening rays of Muzak power. I will dull all supervillains this intriguing Death Lounge way. Play game with me. Together we fight off evil Skinvader menace.

Getting into Manchester only this morning, pitching up at the Piccadilly Hotel, rooms paid for as promised, everything laid on. Separate rooms. Leave it be, for now. Margo celebrating with a gym workout, sauna, massage, the works, and a serious noontime session in the bar, everything on the club tab. Knowing what the drink would lead to, but like I said, leave it be. Me, up in my cell, going over possible tunes for the night, checking all the ghosts are happy, checking the weapons.

Ten past one, I look in on Margo. She's flat out, buried deep in the fog. Beside the bed, the usual nasty gear. And all the broken promises. I kiss her lips. Like smoky bruised peach, the smell of her breath. She stirs at the kiss, opens her eyes, softly.

'It's good here, isn't it?' she whispers. 'Here in the city?'

'It's fine, Margo. Just fine.' She's never even left the hotel yet. 'You get some sleep now.'

'Lullaby me, one time.'

What the hell; I sing her favourite number, all about the physics of angels, and the weight of the clouds, and when it's done, she says, 'Don't forget the deal, Perfume. Do it good.'

And then gone with a slow, slow smile, back down into limbo.

Sure thing, the big deal: Margo driving the car, Margo making decisions, finding gigs, doing the talking, counting the money. Margo getting dirty, me keeping clean. But what about the deal with the heart, eh Margo? The stupid, unsigned deal with the heart. How much longer has she got? If I can only come good tonight, collect the winnings . . .

Yeah, and all the other promises.

We're supposed to be at the club, two o'clock, for a sound-check. I really need to make it, because the decks will be way beyond my usual span. I call the desk, arrange a four o'clock alarm call for Margo, and then set off walking, alone across the city. Through the crowded heart, some rain decides to fall.

This is the start of it.

The club's on Whitworth Street, half redbrick, half-chrome. Just the pink word, *Dubtek*, in discreet turned-off neon. Discarded flyers litter the doorway. I see my face there on the ground, handfuls of my scattered eyes, blurred by the rain already. Me, with my tiny satellite talents, OK, pitched against the house on DJ-it-Yourself Night. Nineteen years old, loose at the edges, only the music keeping me glued.

Becoming pulp.

Some guy lets me in and straight away I know something's wrong. A frazzled technician is running around with sparks in her hair. The faltering lights, popping like broken stars, and the stench of burning flesh hanging over the empty dance floor. And the shiver, like the building's sizing me up, making fun of me, moving in. The technician comes close; I tell her who I am, and what I'm here for.

'Soundcheck?' she says. 'Oh, I doubt it, not at this rate.'

'What's the trouble?' I ask. 'It's not a virus?'

'Get out of here. Sweet as a virgin, we are. Nah, just a technical thing, be clear by tonight, sorted. But like I said, no soundcheck, buddy. You'll have to fly blind, eh? What's the name again?'

'DJ Perfume Sword. Four times champion of my local league.'

She looks at me as though I'm smalltown-dead already. 'Well, we do things a bit different in the city. No-one's ever beaten him, you know? No-one ever. Skinvader's a maniac. He'll swallow you whole. Still, always a first time, eh? Always a first time.' And she laughs like crazy. 'Got work to do.' Leaving me alone on the edge of the floor, with the air turning heavy around me, tracking my heart.

I should have left right then.

Instead . . .

I mean, the size of the floor, the circumference and the haze and the far horizon of the floor. I step on to the boards, kinda fearful, feeling the expert suspension give gentle breath to my weight. All around me, hanging from the walls, the projection system glimmers with wanting. Somebody tries a record out, making a hole in the air where the bass prowls loose. Hits in the stomach, like a deep-sea memory; bells in the head as the treble makes wing-glitter.

'What do you reckon? Bit better than Blazer's, eh?'

It's Margo, of course, bending close to whisper above the music. Always makes it, doesn't she? Taxi-sealed, looking like she's never been away. But how can I speak? Blazer's Nite-spot was where I learned my trade, spun my baby grooves, called up my first ghost. The bleak suburban long dark disco of the soul.

To which this is the mothership. Under the spasm-lamps, inside the music, which breaks into sick, dark crackle even as Margo moves closer still to kiss . . .

Operate all mechanisms! I am Lizard Ninja Tongue of PERFUME SWORD DJ acrobats. With my mercury poison repartee I shoot sticky death to all known enemies. Skinvader will be mere housefly to my exterminating hip hop tongue tactics. Play game with me. We bring plague by poetry.

Tonight, the same floor is a temple of sweat, noise, crush, sweaty noise crush, flavour beats, heartache, naked flesh, head fog, spilt beer, tarnished love. I'm forcing my way through the miasma, the wet flesh of dance, getting sticky with it. People recognize me from the flyers, which is more than I do. It's somebody else they're clawing at, calling fuck-off names, some stranger hanging loose inside this prickle of skin.

The warm-up DJ is playing floor-fillers only, no adventure, and strictly human. Every so often and just for a second, the lights dim, the music cuts out, leaving the crowd in quantum jerk mode.

Shit!

I should never visit the floor before a gig, especially one this big, and me the visiting team. Margo's out there, jam-dancing amid the crowd, her face a miles-per-hour glaze of bliss, when she's supposed to be looking after me. And there's one too many stabbing hand, one too many bad name screamed out, it's getting so I can't see the good way forward any more, so I'm turning . . .

Turning around, trying to make it to the big doors to the doors trying to make it to the doors being dragged under trying to make it to the doors dragged under when a bouncer beam swoops down on waves of ice and all the dancers around are stuck sudden on full freeze and I'm caught in the same cold crush jungle slow-motion overload and running now like tepid flesh smoke *too much fucking glitch in my system!* straight into the arms of corporate security with the MC's voice booming over the speakers . . .

It's soundclash time!

Operate all mechanisms! I am called Metal 6-String Boy, belonging to PERFUME SWORD. With my special Guitar Ghost powers, I eliminate all known Moonchester madness on one thousand riffs of steel. Together we six-string strangle evil Skinvader Deathbeat Squad. Play game with me. Make sonic graveyard explosions!

They're strapping me into the DJ machine. It's dark in the booth, and the world closes in. My challenger is a blur of movement in the chair across the room, spinning away from me. No Margo. I'm feeling lost without her, because it's lonely going under and without a hand to hold, no matter what it's made of. The twin faces of the turntables come up to meet me, already speeding, so that even calling out Margo's name does nothing to stop my hands moving on impulse to caress the slip and slide of the grooves. The visor clamps down on my eyes, as my fingers merge with the spinning, then my hands fully, sinking into the soft, melting plastic and I'm through . . .

. . . into the music, projected from the one thousand speakers.

Operate all mechanisms! I am Godzilla Bass member of PERFUME SWORD fighting-beat maniacs. I walk on orbital legs, heavy pregnant with Ultra Low Reverb action. Play game with me, feel Mighty Earthquake inside deepest stomach, BOOM! BOOM! BOOM! Together we destroy all lesser-known monsters of music!

All is calm, floating, prepared, on a tremble.

Below me, miles away, the dance floor; a boiling of faces, stretched-out arms, jeering voices. I'm suspended above them all, giant in my shape, made out of intersecting beams of knowledge. I sweep down a magnified arm; it moves through the crowd like a wavelength. Some of them fall back, others just let the illusion pass through their bodies, defiant. What do I care? I am the almighty Godzilla Bass, of the Perfumed Sword. There's no sign of Skinvader yet, the floor is mine, so I start a growling riff that gets them dancing; a charge so deep, they just have to move, even to the opposition. The club lights fuse and pop, a tiny darkness, split-second followed by a stutter to the beat, before the system kicks back in, and there I am, scouring the air with blades of bass, loving the flash of it all.

A cheer goes up, battle drums sound. A bass answers my own, only deeper, rivered with teeth. Shovelling the noise, Skinvader comes alive; fierce dark drenched information. Slow pounding drumbeats taking shape; a vast heart pumping. Bloodsonic caress. The club shakes with fury. Nightblack wings sprout from each side of the heart, floating dragonbass high. And when the heart splits open, showering me with stars, it's a melody of daggers. Pain floods me, like sunjuice. Staggering, I call up Metal 6-string Boy, scratching twisted funk on the ghost guitar. Drop da funk, hope to bomb the rhythm. Skinvader mutates; fogburst of psychedelic squall, dissolving into whispers. Now I become the Lizard Ninja Tongue; antique Led Zep drum loop, hip hop scatter-shot maniac. Rapid fire, hard-edged words, dissing the house DJ, the club, and all who dance in her. Skinvader is turntable fog, letting the music hit, again and again. The crowd doesn't know how to handle the beats I'm throwing them, it's going cold-crazy down there. Let's murder this; calling up M.O.R.phine now, floating in on a cool, shimmering breeze of vibraphones and finger-clicks. It's nice, it's smooth. It's a charm of sleep. Skinvader melts away, seeking slumber. And with the joining of all my monsters, all into one skyscraper, I am Empire State Perfume Sword! Projected from the exterior system, I break loose from the disco. Rain is caressing my body, but my head's above the cloudline. Immense at the centre of roads and dazzle and the distant hills where once I lived my little life. But that was on a yesterday, and now all must bow to my 97 million floors!

I'm lulled by my own dream, when the enemy-bass really slithers, earthcore deep, and the drums surge into a speeding plague that travels the crowd by the veins, sucking energy from them. The noise twists again, into a swordfish locomotive, steam driven, ravaging. The blast hits my building dead centre; elemental. Expressway to the skull. Headburst. I come crashing to the ground, so now I see only the club's ceiling, all the lights ablaze with sizzle. Dancers rush through the broken rooms of my body, scattering, cheering.

It's done. So easy.

Hovering, kaleidoscoped, Skinvader hangs triumphant from the beams of light, his shape now a horse, now a hammer, now a switchblade, now a swarm of wasps, now a rocketship; each with its own, terrifying melody. Finally, a giant snake looms suspended over me, salivating with a venom song, each drop of which burns right through my walls.

Until only one person remains inside my illusion, and I feel Margo's slow, burnt-out feelings mingling with mine. But she's smiling, I don't know why. Whispering. The lights flicker once more, the beams falter, time becomes languid. I understand all things in that stretched moment, the way that failure itself has a rhythm; lights, projection, music . . .

And in the tiny silence that follows I let dissolve all my ghosts, calling up only Girlforce 7 with my last remaining strength. The music clicks back into action, time becomes ordinary, and I'm gone, vanished. The snake hisses around, searching. But I'm small, I'm petite. Angels in the dub. I'm the little girl who sings poison in your ear, when no-one is looking . . .

> *Take two clouds and thread them*
> *one on either side;*
> *fashion raindrops in your hair*
> *and the sky will be your bride,*
> *the sky will be your bride.*

Now they're dragging me, flesh naked, out of the DJ machine, what's happening? All is dark, inside and out, with a crowd screaming somewhere far away and my challenger lying on the booth-floor, smoke rising from his puny, twitching body. In this world, he can't be no more than ten years old. I'm shaking as well, so bad I can't even feel the pain as somebody hits me. But Margo's there, she's always there when needed, demanding the money, the prizes. Somebody's offering me a job; Margo tells them to go stuff themselves, and that's good, because with the new thing inside me now, alive to my every need . . .

Close all mechanisms. I am Skinvader Deathbeat, latest member of all-time best ever PERFUME SWORD music team. With my chameleon melody weapons I am ready for all warfare. Play your next game with me. We turn Moonchester into DJ Paradise. Death to all challengers!

*　　*　　*

We don't bother staying overnight, just grab the bags, check out, start driving. Margo can't stop smiling, the mouth fixed into joy as her hands move slowly on the steering wheel. We're out of the city now, following the twin snakes of light back to the hills. All is quiet outside, the night passing by in a hush of rain.

We don't talk much. Each of us caught in separate feelings, lost in the wonder. Until, as we reach the crest of the hill, Margo stops the car. 'I can't drive any more, Perfume,' she says, her voice as gentle as the moon that hangs above. 'You'll have to get us home.'

Right. She gets out of the car, ghost-frail, walks a small distance into the darkness. I follow her there, to take a hold of her dissolving hand. We kiss, under the moonlight, and I let her spirit seep back inside of me. It's a tear-stained cadence. Then I'm alone.

I walk back to the car, carrying some beauties.

DUB KARAOKE
(electric haiku remix)

all is floating calm
on tremble-haunted wavelengths
disco magnified

groove decoders
crackle-dance to fuse and pop
illusion's perfume

drumsoft mechanisms
endazzlements of rhythm
shimmering system

explode of bassjuice
the turntable's soft horizon
spins kaleidadelic

needleburst skullfire
mutating beats-per-minute
operating heartache

invisible funk
the psychesonic angel
sucking the sizzle

loading the tongue
the little girl whispering
lullaby poison

radio tearstain
transmission of fragrances
lost in the edit

kisses of remix
dissolving all ghosts unknown
married to the sky

PART TWO

INFECTION'S COURTSHIP

BUG COMPASS

Z*zzzs!* Like the taste of the sun on the tongue of the young, the bright lick of fire that sparked from the belly of the candle bug. The brief, short flame that was made from its underside duct. *Zzzzs!* A warning sign, a mating call, a weapon also, and a fine thing for a couple of boys to catch, summer golden as they were, and light-headed with endless holiday. All that summer, as I recall, we would stalk the crackle of ignition and the tiny explosions that haunted the shoulder-high grass.

Zzzzs!

'Here! Quick! Here!'

'No. Gone. Missed it.'

'Damn!'

And drifting through the long days when the season hangs forever on the tips of the smoke grass, when school is a thousand hot miles away. Three weeks, four days, fourteen hours away, a time so carefully counted even as it disappeared in the heat haze. We said it was hotter than a hummingbird's armpit, and we laughed; but hottest of all was the fire that sparked from the candle bugs' arseholes. With two kids of seven and ten, imagine, running crazy with net and jam jar, to chase the plumes of smoke that drifted gentle and sunwise.

Finding was easy, reading the smoke trails, the spark and flash, and the heady scent. Gathering was hard, landing the bugs just before they cracked their wing-cases open, let spring the folded treasure, took flight.

Zzzzs!

'Here! Here!'

'No. Here!'

'Got it! Yes!'

Eliot was a whole three years older than me, and a wounded veteran of these fields; his hands already scarred with count-less burn marks. His jar was forever filled with fire, mine only with a spark or two, and I didn't mind one bit, happy to play tag to his shirt-tail. We both lived on the nearby Shakespeare Estate, and to there we would descend, two grass-stained warriors, carrying our booty. I don't know, I guess this all sounds like kid's stuff, but I couldn't help feeling it would all soon be over. Eliot was already talking about girls as though they were something special. There was one girl, this Valerie he was always going on about. I guess I was clinging on to something, keeping him interested in the bug hunts.

Eliot's uncle would buy the candle bugs off us, so many pennies a bug, depending on the exchange rate. Uncle Slippy, Eliot called him, I don't know why; just that he never seemed to be where he was, I suppose.

'OK, how many you got today?' he would ask.

'Fifty-seven,' Eliot would answer.

'Five,' would be my reply.

'You lose, Scribble,' says Eliot. 'You'd better buck up.'

'Leave him be,' says Slippy.

It was Eliot that started calling me Scribble, ever since I'd shown him some of my nonsensical rhymes. Bad move, I know, except that I wanted him to realize I was good for something at least. It was one of those things, I liked it when he laughed at me. And it was strange that he made up nicknames for everybody, everybody except himself. It was a way of staying in control, I suppose, but that's only me looking back.

'Here's your money, boys,' Uncle Slippy would then say.

'Cheers, Uncle.'

'You both go on now, get out of here.'

We never wanted to go, of course. Uncle Slippy lived alone, in this becurtained old house at the end of our street. He seemed to live in just one of the rooms, a bedroom. It was full of assorted wonders, most of which had no explanation or purpose, I'm sure of it. He was a collector: of broken alarm clocks, and of exotic birds' feathers, but mainly of insects. An entomologist, he called himself. It was the best word I'd ever heard. Some of his prize specimens were mounted in glass cases on the walls, vividly painted monsters from all over the world. Others, the live ones, he kept in various murky fish tanks. I would press my face against them, better to see the mysteries involved. The dark flutterings, the sudden movement of what you thought was a leaf, say, or a flower head. Sometimes he'd tell us stories of the insects, and their strange powers, and how they were quite the most beautiful and intelligent species on the planet.

'I thought I told you two to get out.'

'What's this one, Uncle?'

'That one? Oh, now that's the Compass Bug.'

Once we got him started, you see, he just couldn't stop.

'The Compass Bug. It's a male. I've been looking for a female for years now. Want to breed them. I tell you, if you ever find one of them for me, my, would I be generous!'

And then he'd laugh out loud, as though we'd never catch anything that brilliant, not in a thousand years. So we'd look in the tank, at this hideous beetle. Must have been at least two inches long, coloured black and orange, with the black in the shape of a cross on its back.

'You find one of them,' he'd say, 'you'd never get lost, not ever. You'd be on the needle, my boys!'

So we'd ask why, but the lesson would be over for the day. Sometimes though, if we were lucky, if Eliot had brought in a good batch, Uncle Slippy would give us a candle bug of our own to keep, a tame one that is. He had a way about him, a secret way of making the bugs do what he wanted. That's how he made his living. He clipped the wings of the candle bugs, but that wasn't all, there was something he did to them that made them burst into flame only when you wanted them to.

Eliot and I would take this bug with us, and the money we'd earned. Usually we'd buy ciggies with the money. Then we'd go back into the field, and we'd use the tame candle bug to light a ciggie each. You had to hold them just so, between the forefinger and thumb, and squeeze, and then the fire would come out of their arse. And you could light a fag with them! That's what Slippy would sell them as: living cigarette lighters. He made a nice little profit out of them, and Eliot was always going on about the money *we* could make, if only we got to know the secret of taming the bugs ourselves.

'How do you think he does it, Scribble?' he would ask, sucking on his fag.

'Don't know.'

'I reckon it's something to do with them feathers.'

'What, the birds' feathers he keeps? Why's that?'

'I reckon they're Vurt feathers.'

'Vurt? No way. Not Vurt.'

'Got to be, I reckon. What do you reckon?'

'Don't know what I reckon. Not yet.'

We'd read a whole lot about these Vurt feathers in the papers, how they were supposed to be the best recording medium ever, even better than fractal cassettes. How music sounded more than alive on them, how they contained the best games of all time, how you could record all kinds of knowledge on them, knowledge that nobody yet knew about, even. There were loads of rumours about them. How you had to put them in your mouth, just to get the feathers to play back. So they said, anyway, the papers. I don't know, it all seemed a bit silly to my mind, but Eliot was always getting hooked on crazy rumours. Anything to get out of his head, and into some other kind of dream. He was growing up so quickly.

'But they have to be blue, don't they?' I'd ask him. 'Vurt feathers, I mean. That's what I read anyway. And Slippy ain't got any blue ones, not that I've ever seen.'

'Nah, they don't have to be blue.'

'They don't?'

'Nah, that's just the legal ones.'

'You mean there's others?'

'Sure. Black ones, for instance. Don't tell me you've never heard of the black feathers.'

'No.'

'Black ones are the best. They're pirate copies. Illegal, like. Real snazzy. And Slippy's got loadsa black ones, hasn't he?'

'Sure, he's got loadsa black ones, doesn't mean they're Vurt feathers though. Vurt feathers aren't even on the market yet, not unless you've got a ton of cash anyway. And Slippy ain't got that kind of money, no way. Where's he gonna get a Vurt feather from? I reckon they're just normal feathers, like a blackbird's feathers for instance.'

'You reckon?'

'Yeah, that's what I reckon.'

'Well I think they're Vurt feathers, and I think that's how he gets to control the insects.'

We were just two kids with nothing better to do than lie in the long grass, smoking fags, listening to the candle bugs popping all around us, and playing with our very own tame candle bug, making its arse catch fire again and again until it was all used up. Just two kids talking about stuff we knew nothing about.

I guess I shouldn't have been that surprised at what happened next, knowing how Eliot's mind worked. And knowing how he didn't mind stealing things now and then, like comics and stuff, copies of the *Game Cat* magazine for instance, fags and stuff, or even, on one occasion, a pin-up of Interactive Madonna, just peeled it off the wall, rolled it up, walked out with it under his arm. But that was from shops, I never thought he'd nick things off his friends or his family.

So when he told me to meet up with him, about two weeks later, with the holidays nearly over and everything, I was expecting one last bug hunt before school started up again. I even turned up with the net and a jar. I guess I was right, in a way.

'You nicked it?' I said.

'Sure I did.'

Eliot had taken his shirt off. It sure was hot, that summer.

'Off your uncle?'

'Yeah, right out of his bedroom. I went round, asking if he

wanted anything from the shops. He said he'd make a list, and while he was doing that, while his back was turned, I just nicked the first feather I could find.'

'Bloody hell! Let's have a look, then.'

'Careful with it.'

Eliot handed me the feather, the black feather. I held it by the tip, as though it was alive, or something, like it was dangerous. I spun it around, and the warmth of the sun seemed to catch in the flights, glittering.

'You see the way it sparkles?' Eliot asked. 'The colours? The pink bits?'

'Yeah.'

'It's not just black, you see. It's got stuff added to it.'

'Just colours, is all. Just a tiny bit of pink in it, is all. What does that mean, pink in it?'

'Don't know. But that's where the knowledge is, in the colours. Didn't you read that?'

'Yeah, I read that. Doesn't mean it's a Vurt feather, though.'

'Only one way to find out.'

'What? You mean . . . ?'

'Let's do it.'

'Put it in our mouths? No way!'

'You scared, is that it? Scared of a feather?'

'That's not it, no.'

'What is it then?'

'You shouldn't have nicked it. Slippy will kill you.'

'So let's do it then, before he finds out.'

'OK, but you do it. You do it on your own. I'll just watch you doing it.'

'No. You're not supposed to do Vurt on your own. Didn't you read that?'

'Yeah. Yeah, I read that. Don't do it on your own.'

'So?'

'You reckon this will tell us how to tame candle bugs?'

'That's it, Scribble.'

'OK. But you first, then.'

'No, you first.'

'Why me first?'

'Because I'll do it, and then you won't do it.'

'How do I know you won't do the same?'

'Because I want to do it. Do you understand?'

'I understand.'

'Good. Give it here, then.'

So I give the feather back to Eliot. He tells me to open my mouth, which I do. Wider, he says. I open wider, wide as I can, just to get it over with. And he takes the feather, and he lays it against my lip, and it touches my tongue.

And all around the candle bugs are going wild. And the sun, the sun is beating down, like I can taste the sun on my tongue, and the tall grass is filled with wanting. And for a tiny second I think, Thank God, it's just a blackbird's feather after all, and then the sun bursts into flame, almost burns itself out.

Sudden.

And I slide away, sideways and down . . .

It's night. Somewhere in the world, it's night. I wake up in my bed. I can hear my mum and dad shouting at each other from downstairs. Maybe I should go and visit sister's room. Desdemona doesn't mind if I wake her up sometimes, just to talk the night away, especially when Mum and Dad are arguing. So I get up. For some reason I must have gone to bed with all my clothes on, but it doesn't bother me. Then there's a knocking at my bedroom door. I say to come in, thinking it must be Desdemona, but it's Eliot who comes in. He says, come on, Scribble, we've got to find them bugs now, they must be living in your house. I think, of course, of course they are. We planned this earlier, this bug hunt, I must have forgotten until now. So we go downstairs, real quiet. I can't hear any shouting any more, only my captured breath, Eliot's whispered instructions, the slow chime of a clock. We get to the kitchen. It's dark, I want to put on the light, Eliot says no, we use the torch. He's brought a torch with him. I've got the net in one hand, the jar in the other. I can't remember when I picked them up. In the kitchen, tiny scrabblings can be heard, like ice cracking say, or gravel moving. It's coming from the sink. There's a pile of dirty dishes in there. Eliot tells me to get ready, he's going to switch on the torch. I stand poised with the net raised. The light, when it comes, seems as bright as the sun, and it dazzles me. And the sudden rush of a thousand pieces of orange, as the beetles scatter for darkness. I'm scared. Eliot yells at me to strike, so I bring down the net, just bring it down indiscriminately, crashing into the pots. What a noise it makes. But a slow noise, a coloured blue noise. Did you get one? Eliot asks. I say, Yes, I got one. I hold the net closed around the Compass Bug, as Eliot brings the jar over. We transfer it, seal the jar. It's done. The house has not stirred to our noise. What now? I say. Come on, Eliot replies, back to your room. Once there, sitting on the bed, we examine the beetle in its jar. It's beautiful. So orange, and the black cross on its hard casing. We did good, didn't we, Eliot? Yeah, Scribble, real good. He's sitting on my bed, his shirt off, then he lies down, so I can put my hand on his chest. It's hard, all bone. I stroke him gently and he lets me. He smiles. I let my hand move tenderly towards his belt buckle. He was proud of that buckle, it's in the shape of a twisted snake. I start to unwind it . . .

Shit!

What was that?

Some movement to one side of me, my body being forced away from itself, like a whiplash, and sideways and up and sudden.

The sun comes on.

I'm lying in the field. I'm lying on my back, and Eliot is standing to one side, dragging on his shirt. He's still holding the feather, except its not black any more, it's cream now. A dull cream.

'Fuck!' he says.

'What was that?' I ask. 'What happened?'

'Nothing.'

His voice is tight, controlled, on the edge of anger.

'Nothing happened, do you hear me? Nothing!'

'It was a dream. It was like a dream.'

'Yeah, well, it wasn't my fucking dream.'

'Whose dream was it?'

'Shut up!'

'Whose dream was it?'

'Fucking Uncle Slippy! I always knew there was something up with him. Fucking pervert! This never happened, right? This never happened.'

'It never happened.'

I get up. My head is still buzzing with a distant colour. Eliot is already walking away from me. I pick up the net and the jar, to follow him. It's only then that I notice.

'I ought to have you two shot,' says Uncle Slippy. 'Do you know what you're messing with? You are messing with crazy stuff. Fucking kids! I wouldn't mind the stealing, long as you know what you're stealing. You're stealing my fucking pleasures!'

'We brought you the beetle, didn't we?' says Eliot. 'Brought you a Compass Bug.'

I hold up the jar for Slippy to see. He takes it off me.

'Stupid kid!' he cries. 'That's a male. I've got a thousand males. It's the queen I'm after. Males don't find nothing but females. It's the queen that finds the treasure. You won't get nothing off me for this. Nothing!'

'But . . .'

'You know the rules, do you? You know the rules of Vurt? Everything you take out of there, you have to give something in return. What did you give, eh? What did you give?'

I'm looking at Eliot, but he won't look back at me, he just won't.

'Nothing, Uncle,' he says. Says it quietly.

'Well you did. It's the law. And you'll find out one day, God help you.'

He hands the jar over to Eliot.

We don't see much of each other after that, not for a few weeks anyway, and with school starting and all that. But it's more than that, of course. It's an unspoken thing. I know Eliot is angry at me, like it's my fault. Maybe it is, I'm not sure. When I do bump into him, he's hanging out with lads his own age, and usually this Valerie girl is with him. He puts his arm round her. Kisses her. It's good. I'm glad. Maybe I can start my own growing up now.

One thing I notice, he's still got the Compass Bug with him. It's dead, of course. Beetles don't live very long, do they? He keeps the dead thing in a matchbox. Keeps it in his pocket. He says to me that he's never going to throw it away, not ever. He reckons it's his way forward, his pointer. He says his needle is really spinning now, spinning fit to burst. That's good, as well. That's something. I can understand, or at least, I can say I do.

And all his new friends, and this Valerie, they all call him the Beetle now. That's his new name. The Beetle. That's good, isn't it? It suits him.

'Come on, Beetle,' says Valerie. 'Let's go do that feather.'

Eliot pulls a feather out of his jacket. It's a blue one. He waves it in my face. He's laughing at me. I don't know where he got it from. And they set off together, him and his mates, and I don't know whether to follow or not.

FETISH BOOTH # 7

Having experienced various exasperations both personal and professional in the past year, none of which this narrative need dwell upon, a certain Janus Fontaine, former pop star, decided to end his life. Being of a famously dramatic nature, he chose a special date and time to stage his denouement: the stroke of the year's final midnight would be his orison, the cheers of a drunken crowd his mourning song.

He had no specific means of removal: no loaded gun, no carefully knotted noose, no dissolving of pills. Nothing so crude. Rather, he would lay himself open to circumstance. Somehow or other, the New Year's Eve celebrations would finish him. That's all he knew.

Apart from the ending, Fontaine's final day was well planned. At nine in the morning he awoke, heavy with last night's wine. He had a sliver of beef lodged behind a molar, which he niggled at with a furry tongue. Ten o'clock found him showered and shaved, and sprucely dressed as though for a business appointment or a romantic assignation. He took a late breakfast (full English with extra toast) in the dining hall of the Hotel Abyss. It was the first meal he had eaten outside his room.

He had arrived here from Manchester, only a week ago, and had refused all calls from the housekeeping staff, saying he could not be disturbed, even for a change of sheets. The occasional meal was to be left outside his door, along with copious amounts of alcohol.

As you can imagine, the sudden appearance of the guest from room 417 caused much speculation. He seemed normal enough, as he sipped his coffee and perused the morning's news. Some of the older staff remembered him from his better days, when the hair wasn't so thin, nor waist so thick, nor eyes so dim, and the voice not so bereft of song. One of them even approached him for an autograph, which was gladly given. Fontaine then paid his bill in full at the desk, and ventured forth. He had no luggage with him.

Informed that the occupant of room 417 had now left the hotel, the unluckiest cleaner in the world was assailed by a terrible stench of decay. The hotel room as battleground: all the towels were stained with excrement and blood; the bed-sheets thick with dried semen; the obligatory watercolour landscapes hacked to ribbons; the screwed-down television smashed to pieces, as were all the mirrors. Broken wine bottles glittered the carpet; cigarette smoke mapped every drift of air. A slew of pornographic magazines covered the bed.

Ten thousand pounds, in loose notes, lay on a bedside table, with a brief letter thanking the staff.

By this time, Janus Fontaine was pushing through the crowds on Tottenham Court Road. London town, the seething city. A palpable expectancy that was easy to get lost in. The people were too busy buying cameras, camcorders and dicta-phones to recognize him. Janus was captured on a thousand lenses as he walked along, but only as just another face on that momentous day.

He wandered along aimlessly, allowing the crowd to carry him into the maelstrom of Oxford Street. He visited five or six stores during this period, spending some time in each one. He didn't buy anything. The longest time was spent in one of the larger record shops. Only two of his seven albums were represented, and those only in the 'Rock Bottom' bargain section. Eventually he reached Marble Arch and Speakers' Corner; he listened, for a while. Then he took a light lunch at one of the better hotels on Park Lane, using a tiny sliver of the large roll of cash he had folded in his pocket. His last resources. The waiter couldn't stop looking at the lone diner, and even-tually got up the courage to ask if he really were 'Janus Fontaine, the pop star?'

Janus smiled.

'Oh, my mother will be thrilled when I tell her.'

A time to take stock.

The *Encyclopaedia of Popular Music* has little to say about Janus Fontaine, unable even to give his real name. He was born in Manchester. His first single, 'Plastic Flowers', was a number-one hit around the world. As was the follow-up. Even the third single did well. Following a marketing scandal, his fourth single, 'Pixelkids Come Out Tonight', reached only number ninety-five in the charts. His fifth, 'Sooner Than Summertime', along with the album (his second) of the same title, disappeared without trace. Nothing was heard from him for ten years, when he started a long, arduous come-back campaign, this time as a serious, adult-orientated artist. He made a series of critically acclaimed albums for a small, obscure record label. None of them sold very well. Current whereabouts unknown.

Whereabouts unknown? Alive or dead?

Hyde Park, where Janus was enjoying the dead trees and the skipping children and the dogs and the scent of love in the air. He watched a group of young women walk past, but not with any feelings of lust; just the smiles on their faces brought him joy, of a kind. A kind of joy that quickly palled. Also, it had started to rain.

He retreated into the Serpentine Gallery.

They were showing an exhibition by a young artist he had never heard of; all melted plastic and broken glass. This charmed him a little, and he spent an hour studying the work. Most visitors left in a minute or two, especially when it stopped raining. Janus Fontaine was still alive enough to appreciate the finer points of contemporary art. Living off his small royalties, his shrewd investments, his careful savings.

A life saved up, by degrees. What was the use of it?

Four o'clock found him lightly sleeping on a bench in the park, like a down-at-heart tramp, working off the alcohol. Upon waking, he noticed a small dog sniffing at his leg. Shaking the creature off, he set out once more on his journey.

He wandered along Constitution Hill, towards the Mall, in a slow daze. When was it going to happen? Darkness was slowly covering the world. The trees of St James's Park, to his right . . . all covered with darkness; the children still running . . . covered with darkness; the dogs, the tramps in the park, the posh folk to his left, in Marlborough and Pall Mall, the people gathering . . . all covered with darkness . . .

His short nap had left him feeling more than tired, and the day seemed to stretch out for ever in front of him. He needed to get drunk again, and not in public, so he booked into the next hotel he came to, a grand place. Paying cash in advance for a single night's stay, he spent an hour raiding the minibar in his room. That brought on the jitters. He lay down on the opulent bedspread, only to calm the monsters in his head. Instead, he fell sound asleep.

He awoke to the sound of the telephone. Confused, he let it ring, in and out of his half-grasped dreams. Finally, he realized what it was, answered it. 'Your alarm call, Mr Fontaine,' said the voice.

'What?'

'It's eight o'clock, sir.'

'Oh. Right.' Janus looked out of the window, trying to gauge the light. 'In the evening?'

'Yes, sir. As you requested.'

'Thank you.'

Strange, that he couldn't remember placing the alarm call with the reception desk. Groggy, he washed his face, got together his few things, left an overgenerous amount of money on top of the minibar. Stumbling out of the hotel, for a few minutes he couldn't place himself on the streets. Where was he? A surge of people carried him along, into Trafalgar Square. The place was packed already, alive with manic expectation. Janus realized he was still carrying a large amount of cash and, fearing pickpockets, he clutched his coat tightly around him.

Eventually he found an offshoot crowd, a tangential flow that carried him northwards, towards Cambridge Circus. Dragged along and pressed in, as he was, it made him calmer; now at last he felt a victim of fate. The city was moving to its own internal rhythms. Where would it lead him? A sudden hunger, a drunken loneliness, gnawed at his guts. Sensing a sudden sway in the crowd, he took advantage of the slight give to move towards Chinatown. Here the crowds were less manic, moving in blocks rather than streams. And the smells, and the look of the foodstuffs on display, all made him ravenous.

Of course, every restaurant was fully booked, but the ridiculous amount he was willing to pay, even for the plainest meal, soon got him a table to himself. He ate long, and heartily, in the banquet style, savouring every mouthful. He abstained from more alcohol, thinking it wise to keep his wits about him, now the end was in sight. But so very lovely was this, his last ever dinner, he would like to eat a thousand more. It was not to be. It could not be. The decision was made.

It was approaching eleven when he let himself be pushed into Soho. Crushed by a river, a river of flesh. The celebrating flesh, filled with photo-flash and camcorder-whirr. Flinching from the cameras, as though still world famous, Janus moved from the fashionable area to the seedy. Here, beneath the lurid displays, and surrounded by cries and entreaties, he knew for sure it would happen. It felt right, that it should take place amid such desperate, cheap pleasures. Loud, brazen music was pulsing from the beaded doorways; raucous voices promised specialist delights; realms of squeezed flesh offered themselves to him, demanding his attention. The narrow, dirty streets were blurred with the rain that dripped off bare neon, and coloured like a downmarket rainbow. Most of the clubs, the strip joints, the exotic cinemas and the live bedshow emporiums, were doing good business, as people threw aside their usual fears. Men and women were taking advantage of the sudden loosening as the end of the year approached, and the stench of pheromones was languid on the air. Queues were forming outside the more palatable establishments. The atmosphere was heavy, overwhelming, caustic.

A tramp, seemingly blind, was holding out a battered tin

cup. Janus took some money out of his pocket, a random amount, and stuffed it into the cup.

Then, ducking down a dingy back alley, he found himself entering a strangely peaceful world. The alleyway was tiny, barely wide enough for one person to squeeze down. A series of locked steel doorways studded the walls, the locked fire escapes of the various strip joints. Rubbish bins overflowed with mounds of pulpy detritus. Halfway down the passage, a beaded curtain clacked sullenly below a sputtering neon sign that had once spelled PARLOUR OF FETISH, but now spelled LOUR OF FETI.

Janus looked back to the end of the alley, where the people thronged and sang and waited for the bells to ring. All of it seemed distant, and of little import as he turned back to the doorway. The strung beads swayed slightly, as though inviting custom. Quickly, before he could change his mind, the former pop star entered the parlour.

'Mr Fontaine, I presume?'

All was darkened purple within, and the thick scent of incense hung over a deeper, more rancid smell, barely cloaking it. Janus waited for his eyes to adjust. 'Do you recognize me?' he asked of the voice, whose owner could not yet be seen.

'No. I assumed it was you.'

Now a figure, a man, an old man, emerged from behind a low counter. He was carrying a book, a ledger of some kind. 'You have made an appointment,' he announced, in a voice as smoky as the room.

'Appointment? No . . . I . . .'

'Oh, it's all down here.' The old man had opened the book, was running a finger down a page. 'Mr Fontaine. Eleven-thirty p.m. You are slightly late, but never mind. Shall we choose?'

'Look . . . I . . .'

'Quickly. Which shall it be? One, two? Three, four? Five or six?' The man was gesturing in turn to each of six doorways, all of them hidden behind velvet curtains. 'You have the payment, I presume?'

'Yes, I have it here.' Janus took out his wallet. Once again he felt the pull of circumstance. 'How much will it cost me?'

'Well that depends, of course, on which booth you choose. Each is quite delightful, in its own way. And together they offer every possible desire. Will it be submission, or domination? The English vice, perhaps? Bondage is always popular, whereas the animal is a more select taste. Or else you are a user of criminal devices? Which will it be, I wonder?'

Janus looked at each of the booths in turn, trying to make his mind up. His eyes, filled with the incense, started to water. The room seemed to revolve slightly, as though on a slow treadmill. Another doorway, another curtain appeared beyond the first six.

'What's behind there?' he asked.

'Ah, booth number seven. You truly are a connoisseur, Mr Fontaine. Perhaps it is beyond your means?'

Janus opened his wallet, took out all the money that remained. This substantial roll of cash he silently handed over. The man smiled, gently, as he flicked through the notes. 'You have chosen wisely. Please, enjoy . . .'

Janus walked, slowly, over to the seventh booth. Distantly, as though from another country, another time, he could hear the chimes of midnight, the cheers of the crowd, the dull whiz and pop of fireworks. Hesitating only for a second, he pulled back the curtain, and stepped through.

PIMP! — THE BOARD GAME

This is by far the most complete of all the items on exhibit at the Museum of Fragments. It was dated and copyrighted in 1997. All of the more obscure terms can be found in any good dictionary of the late twentieth century. (See addendum* for further, more speculative remarks.)

(text begins)

CONTENTS

∎ 1 game board, depicting a stylized map of the Soho area of London; 4 playing pieces (Pimp, Prostitute, Punter, Pig); £100,000 in play money, of various denominations (not to be used as legal tender); 30 assorted Pleasure cards; 30 assorted Punishment cards; 30 assorted Fetish cards; 4 Sexual Stamina Charts; 2 dice (six-sided, twelve-sided); 1 instruction leaflet.

INTRODUCTION

- The game of Pimp! is to be played by four players, who choose by luck of the draw to play either the Pimp, the Pro, the Punter or the Pig.

- Each player has a different objective, which they may undertake alone, or by forming alliances with other players.

- Movement around the board is governed by the throw of the dice, or by utilizing any stamina points they may have won during play.

- The winner is the first player to reach their given objective, or to find themselves the last player alive.

RULES OF PLAY

- Players begin the game at their designated starting locations, as marked on the board: the Pimp at the Pad; the Pro on the Street Corner; the Punter at the Pub; the Pig at the Police Station.

- Each player starts the game with the following amounts of money: the Pimp receives £100; the Pro £50; the Punter £200; the Pig £1,000. The rest of the money forms the Bank. Money can be lost or gained during play, depending on the skill of the player. If any player's resources dwindle to zero, they are deemed to be out of the game, unless they can persuade any of the other players to lend them money.

- All players receive 6 sexual stamina points to begin with. These may be supplemented by certain Pleasure cards, or else gained by visiting the Drug Dealer's pad. If a player's sexual stamina drops to zero, they are deemed to be out of the game.

- All players receive 2 Fetish cards to begin with. Others may be gained during play.

- Pleasure and Punishment cards are to be taken up whenever a player lands on the designated squares (the telephone booths), or when forced to take them by another player. All actions described on these cards must be undertaken immediately, unless the player can 'buy' his or her way out of it. Fetish cards, however, can be used as desired, as long as the player has the required sexual stamina.
- To successfully complete an objective, the winning player must get back safely to the correct starting location.

OBJECTIVES

- The Pimp must take all the money off *all* the other players, without being arrested by the Pig. The Pro must not leave him; the Punter must not beat him in combat.
- The Pro must get through the night with her initial resources intact, and without being arrested by the Pig. She must not fall in love with the Punter, or get beaten up by the Pimp.
- The Punter must have sex with the Pro, without being arrested by the Pig. He must try to get the Pro to fall in love with him, thereby not having to pay her. He must not be beaten in combat by the Pimp.
- The Pig must arrest the Pimp. He must receive a bribe off the Punter. He must have sex with the Pro, without paying.

EXOTICA

- Sexually Transmitted Diseases: if infected, a player will lose an escalating number of stamina points each turn. Cures can be found at the Drug Dealer's pad, or from the All-Night Chemist's.

- Sex without a Condom card increases the risk of disease by ten points.
- Various illegal drugs can be purchased from the Drug Dealer. If a player experiences a Bad Trip, two stamina points are lost. Poppers increase the strength of Pleasure cards by five points.
- Any player caught in possession of drugs by the Pig loses 6 points, unless they give the drugs to the Pig as a bribe.
- If the Punter is spotted by his Wife, he loses 5 points.
- The Pimp must be male. The Pig must be male. The Pro may be male or female, or transsexual. The Punter may be male or female. If the Punter is male, and the Pro is male, the Punter is deemed to be Homosexual. Homosexuals play the game at greater risk.
- If the Pimp is killed, any other player can become the new Pimp, except for the Pro, for whom there can be no escape.
- The Pig may never be arrested, not even for murder.
- Any player surviving Fetish Booth # 7 is deemed to have won the game, even if their overall objective is not yet reached.

(text ends)

* *Addendum.* The actual 'game', to which the above leaflet offers instruction, has never been found, nor any mention of it. This has led to certain theories stating that the game was meant to be played 'for real' on the streets of Soho. Some commentators have even speculated that the instructions refer not to a game at all, but to real life.

CHROMOSOFT MIRRORS

(V.4.2)

The dramatic rise and fall of the Chromosoft empire has already been expertly charted, especially the part that Mirrors version 4.2 played in the short and dramatic end. I offer the following story as a more human addendum to the official history. It may illuminate a dark passing, if only with a single beam of truth. Concerned as they are with the bigger picture, none of the extant histories have managed to reveal the actual person responsible for the final, terrible error. It was, of course, Chromosoft's policy that all mistakes be veiled by collective responsibility.

My grandmother, Elisa Gretchen, died before I was born. Any knowledge I had of her life came through borrowed memories, until my discovery of her private journal. I need not go into the details of this discovery, except to say that the primitive nature of the recording medium necessitated the expensive purchase of an antique cd-rom player.

Elisa was on the famous skunk team that came up with the original idea for the Mirrors technology (code-named the 'Alice' project), and was active during all stages of its development and demo-testing. Later on she was assigned to the troubleshooting team, which suffered heavily during the fretful launch period. Version 1.0 was riddled with bugs, and the new interface itself so strangely inhuman that the critics were quick to predict the company's demise, especially with its main competitors riding high on the 'back to nature' campaign of the fashionable DOS revival. Version 1.1 ironed out some of the problems, and v.1.2 introduced the new feedback loop dynamics. It was the major relaunch, with v.2.0, that really kick-started the product's unprecedented success. With a brand-new interface, greater thought-recognition software, and an inspired marketing campaign centred around the slogan, 'Chromosoft Mirrors – *where's your head today?*', the whole world turned to gaze in on itself.

The problem with Windows – the most famous interface prior to Mirrors – was that the more advanced it became (version 491.7!), the more difficult it was to use. And for all its increasing complexity, still all you ever did was *use* the technology; it never *used* you. Thus was the Mirrors project initiated. A new simplicity was called for, something beyond windows, beyond the blinkered one-way gaze. Although my grandmother makes no claim to inventing the actual concept, she does write that the name 'Mirrors' was her invention. It came to her in a flash, one evening in a Parisian hotel bathroom, 'after a rigorous bout of continental-style lovemaking', as she puts it in her journal.

It wasn't the first system to use thought recognition, of course, but the first to successfully marry it with a usable feedback loop. Put simply, previous attempts allowed you to change the screen by thinking about the changes, but only Chromosoft allowed the information to redirect your thinking in turn. The Mirrors system really was a new way of working, a new way of being.

Where's your head today? Gone downloaded.

As it did with the invention of the typewriter and the word processor, a new type of creation emerged from the mirror. Suddenly, 'speed of subconsciousness' novels were all the rage. Punctuation mutated into mere rhythm, narrative dissolved, symbols became deeper, more dreamlike, more dangerous.

Version 3.0 introduced the concept to a network. Version 3.4, to the Internet. These were radical upgradings, with long-lasting social effects; because, although it wasn't strictly true that we were all telepathically linked, it certainly felt like it. The Internet's long-promised 'revelation of the global soul' suddenly seemed less of a pipe dream, more of a God-given right. Version 4.0 added little that was new, merely a cosmetic repackaging to fend off the latest clones. 4.1 was another tweakjob, and it was this version that became the standard for the next three years.

The public will always find its own use for technology, and usually in secret. Nowhere in the Mirrors manual did it warn against remaining connected whilst asleep. Nowhere in the manual did it even mention that such a thing could be done. And nowhere did it mention the effect this could have on the human psyche: the ability to get up in the morning, simply to access the correct document, and then to view, or rather review, your dreams of the night just gone. Could the company have seen how this would lead to a possible madness, a knowing of one's self that was too deep, too far-ranging?

Where's your head today? Why, it's playing with the

burning giraffes, dancing with a turquoise lobster on the top of a grand piano, thank you, Mr Penguin.

Many were affected by this dream-knowledge, and many did not make the journey back from the twisted, inner world.

I can now reveal that it was my grandmother, Elisa Gretchen, who developed and introduced the *disable dream* switch to version 4.2 of the Mirrors system. Approximately 6 per cent of the world's population activated this facility, before the dangers of it were realized. Could Chromosoft, could my *grandmother*, really have so easily forgotten the feedback loop in the user/device interface? Her journal mentions little of the moment of invention, and even less of the subsequent events, except to note the 'burning sense of shame that welled up within me, a shame that persisted even after the corporation had taken control of all responsibility'. Her last recorded entry reads simply: 'I can do no more.'

Chromosoft Mirrors was taken off the market by government order, and all existing devices were recalled, and trashed. By then it was too late for the 6 per cent who had already succumbed to the censoring loop. Those darkened, veiled unfortunates, who would never dream again.

I need hardly add that my grandmother was one of those unfortunates.

CLOUDWALKERS

Scattermasked, working the all-night leisure zones, keeping check on the flotsam and jetsam that played the cheap graveyard rates. It was the end of a five-night shift and some dumb-arse flot had got himself hooked on a pirate trans. By the time we got there the game was frozen solid and overlaid with these stupid dancing prawns. Low-level broadcast, most probably from Beenie's Fishorama over on Level 5. There was no slogan, no slugline, just the prawns. The advert was in the image, and by now the desperate need for some seafood would be implanted in the kid's head. Another two kids, bystanders, had also got caught in the thrall, which was what we called this state of freeze, and a girl standing nearby was saying, 'Best do the deed, lady.' Gumball came up then, saying he'd got a warning bleep from HQ, a nasty on line. 'Come on, Muldoon. Leave the flot till later, eh?' And he pulled the gum out of his mouth, a livid blood-red it was, stretched it full size, and then snapped it back in with the practised tongue-flip.

'No. Only take a minute. And get that mask on.'

'I was only renewing the flavour.'

'That's an order.' I had the spoiler gun out, checking the load and the flush on it. Some of the flots were still unholed enough to notice the noise, and their eyes were bleary and game-fried as they watched me handle the weapon.

'Muldoon, what's wrong with you these days?' Gumball had his scattermask back down, his voice muffled by it. 'You want to lose a big score?'

'Get the van started, Gum. I'll be there.'

Finally I swung the spoiler over to the screen, took aim, fired. The game-screen seemed to melt for a second, turning pixelshima, and then came back online with a hard reboot. The prawns were dead adverts, and the game was back in play. The flotboy jerked into action, fingers jabbing automatic at the duck-and-dive buttons, too damned slow. Screen death. 'Shit! How did that happen?' His freshly thawed spectators laughed some, till they all noticed me standing there, mask down and the needle in my fist.

'Oh shit!' said the player. 'What did I get? Say, my friends, let's go catch some seafood.'

I went to jab them, but Gumball stepped in, caught my arm. 'We'll catch the flot in Beenie's later, give him the spoiler shot there. Come on now. We got a nasty. Big prizes!'

I came out of it then, this voodoo mood I was in. I felt like I'd come unfrozen myself, and that made me shudder. Got me thinking about Parker again. I pulled up my mask to get some air. It was safe, now the advert was dead. Most of the flots had gathered around the action, and some jets in there as well, slumming it. Flotsams were those that society had thrown aside; jetsams had left of their own free will. And all of them had eyes for the spoiler gun hanging from my belt. I could see them clocking up imaginary scores, dreaming their brains away with thoughts of getting their sweaties on such a piece. One of them in particular, the cheeky young jetgirl that had been telling me my job earlier, she had this look of complete 'shop' on her face, the illegal kind. Gumball had seen the look as well. 'So join the commcops, knucklebrain,' he spat at the kid, 'you want some good leisure.'

A minute later we were back on mission, riding the jeep through the shopping lanes, towards the up-chute. Gumball, jaws hard at it still, had switched to manual drive. I swear I never saw a man put so much into chewing gum, it was like an art with him, and never a word was said without it coming round the sides of a sticky lump of Gob Spectrum. He claimed it made his head slick, and he sure drove like it; crash-wired and genetic, with the siren singing hosanna and the usual darktime shoppers screaming wild to get out of our flight path. Meanwhile, I pulled the new job-stats out of the dash.

Incident: rogue campaign
Location: Dollberg's, Unit 1572, Level 10
Product: unknown
Transmission Source: unknown
Range: unknown
Public Reaction: 15 frozen, 9 at risk
Code: APXC

'Will you look at that!' shouted Gumball. 'We got us an Apex rogue. Didn't I tell you this was a big scorer? Bring on the bonus!'

We were in the up-chute now, floating up past levels six and seven. Apex was copslang for the APXC coding: Approach with Extreme Caution. And there were too many unknowns in the printout, and all I could think about was . . .

'What's wrong, Muldoon? You don't want some bonus?'

I realized that Gumball had been talking all the while. 'What?'

'Jesus, you're out of it tonight, girl.' He snapped his gum, hard, driving with one hand to do it.

'Just get us there, Gum. And quit the girl stuff.'

'Sorry, ma'am. Officer Muldoon. Janet, my dearest.'

'Will you—'

'Oh . . . I get it . . . it was an Apex that got Parker, right? The staircase. Doesn't mean this is the same one.'

'I want full effect on this, Gumball. You hear me? Mask on at all times, and no go without my orders.'

'Sure. Hey, that was bad, I hear, with Parker. Some of the guys were talking about it. You were with him, right? What happened? I mean, really.'

'Will you shut the fuck up!'

'Right. Touchy. Sure thing.'

We were on Level 10 now, and turning into Lane 29, where the Dollberg unit was. Another commsvan was already pulled up outside the store, with a bunch of cops standing around, looking nervous. We pulled up hard, and when I got out, it was Chief Inspector Brendel in the other van. Scattermasked, of course, but I could tell her from the shape; no-one that fat ever got to work the patrols, strictly desk-job. She called me over, and I did the salute, and she did the greetings, then she asked me to get in the van with her. She leaned close, till our masks were almost knocking together. 'Officer Muldoon,' she stated, 'I don't want you in there.'

'But—'

'It's too soon. This is a bad one. I can't afford to mess up again.'

'It's the same one? The stairway?'

'Never mind what it is. Officer Drane, here, will handle it.'

Drane, a big strapped-in guy, was looking over at me, that stupid smile on his face. It was difficult to tell him apart from the still-dancing autodolls in the store window.

'No way! This is mine. Parker, he—'

'You're excused. Thank you, that is all.'

'I know this rogue. Who else does? I can handle it. Drane can't handle it. He doesn't know. It does things to you. Makes you want to—'

'Janet . . . please.'

Here we go. It was always bad when Brendel called you by the first name. The switch to casual meant a dismissal in no time, unless you backed down.

'Ma'am. Of course. Please forgive my speaking out of turn.'

'Granted. High stress, no doubt. And too personal. You know how that messes up a job.'

'Yes, ma'am.' I was speaking from a distance, as Drane and his team prepared to enter the Dollberg store.

'Never get too close, Muldoon. And this is woman to woman, OK? Colleagues are not for loving. You understand? I'm sure you do.'

'Right.'

I walked back to the van, where Gumball was loading up. 'We're off this one, Gum,' I said to him.

'Off it! Shit, it's our call. Apex call.'

'Let's go check out Beenie's for the infected flots.'

'You do that. I'm staying.'

'You stay, Gumball . . . it's your last job.'

'Ma'am.'

We climbed back in the van. Gumball drove on empty for a while, but I stopped him around the first bend. 'OK, we watch from here.'

'We do? What is this?' He was raising his mask.

'No. Keep it on.'

I had a bad feeling, you see, and I knew Brendel was at a loss on this one. And when we walked round the corner, I could already hear the cries and the screams from the store, and see the chaos that the commcops were thrown into. Brendel was struggling to get out of her van, and even from the end of the lane, the look on her face, the fear . . .

'Jesus! What the—'

It was Gumball's voice, and I swear he actually took the gum out of his mouth to say it. But what could I do? He was all set to run, to give help, but I called him back. I wanted to tell him how bad it would be, and how hopeless and if only people listened to me, once in a while, wouldn't life be better, easier, more long-lasting. But the mood of before, the distance from the world had come upon me again, folding like a stranger's shadow.

Later, I went with Gumball to visit Beenie's Fishorama. I guess we were, the both of us, hiding our despair behind the workload. First of all we rounded up Mr Beenie himself, told him the usual about transmitting illegal adverts, confiscated his broadcaster, slapped another fine on him, his seventh in that year alone. Then we found the flotboy from before, which was easy; him and his friends were tucking into plate after plate of spicy prawns. I gave him the spoiler shot, which he had to receive by law, and of course, a few seconds after the stuff had entered his veins, he threw up violently. The jetgirl was there as well, the one who had been fixed upon my spoiler gun. This was strange, because flots and jets kept well apart usually, and anyway, she wasn't eating, not having seen the prawn advert up front. Again, she was all eyes on me, on the uniform, the upraised scattermask, the gun, especially the gun.

Meanwhile, Gumball had succumbed to a plate or two of prawns himself. 'I must have got a glimpse,' he said. 'Never mind, eh? I'm hungry anyway.'

'No, you're not, Gum,' I answered. 'I told you, mask on, all times.'

I didn't eat, myself, still too strung out from the Dollberg incident. But we sat together, and I watched Gumball tackle his meal. His chewing gum was stuck on the table beside him, for later use. It was a sickly green this time, the colour of a bad moon. And between every mouthful, my new partner was full of spittle and talk.

'What about Drane, eh? Thank Christ we didn't go in. Hey, I should thank you for that. Jesus! What'll happen to him, Drane I mean? The same as Parker?'

I shrugged, keeping the mood cool. Really, I just wanted to finish this shift, get some sleep.

'You were close to him, weren't you? Parker, I mean. So the boys tell me. I mean, you had a thing going on, right?'

'Wrong.'

'Wrong? But I thought—'

'Look, Gum. Shut up, will you. Eat the prawns.'

'Sure I will. Nice prawns, these. What happened?'

'What?'

'You know, with you and Parker, and this . . . what is it? This staircase advert thing. I mean, what's so fucking bad about it?'

'You've read the reports.'

'Official-line bollocks? Never touch 'em. I want the truth,

Muldoon. I mean, don't I deserve it? Nobody wanted to take Parker's place, you know? You're down as a bad deal.'

'You think I care?'

'Do I fuck think you care. Ain't that why I like you?'

I didn't tell him everything, of course. I left out the worst part. But I kept it truthful, and I kept it cool and neat, because telling it like that, like a story that had happened to somebody else, well it brought a calmness to me. It started, as most of our jobs do, after the beginning. It's double-bonus time if we catch an advert before it's affected anybody, especially the killer thralls. Usually, we're too late to save the first victims. We're just the cleaners, really; we go in after a bad show, we make it safe again for the taxpayers. Apex jobs are a recent trend, and the Stairway trans was my first. Parker's last.

He was only a kid really, Parker, and I should've looked after him better. He'd been my partner for about two months when the trouble started. I knew all about the locker-room gossip, of course. There's still only a few of us women in charge of teams, and Brendel's decision to set me up with a kid ten years younger than me, well . . . let them talk. But we had a thing, you know, a way of working together that was good. Parker respected me; it wasn't the constant battle of wits, like with Gumball and all the rest. I really should've looked after him.

We first got word of the trouble when a too-high proportion of people started killing themselves. Lobjobs, mostly, and usually off the top of prominent buildings. It was a public display, a grand exit. It was fairly obvious that an advert was to blame, but tracking it down to source was proving difficult. The adverts they've got these days, it's not just buying the latest gizmo; they can make you do anything. That's why we have the strict controls; that's why we're here, the commcops. Someone should've realized that bad people would get hold of the technology, because don't they always? So, we'd had killer transmissions before, but never this successful, and never this prominent. It was the number one job on the crime sheets, and we were getting nowhere on it, until a victim came forward.

This guy was in a right state, babbling mainly, and screaming about a stairway, 'a golden stairway, endlessly . . . endlessly . . .' Eventually, we got some sense out of him. He'd been sitting at home, quite peacefully, watching a game show on television. His wife was with him. The children, thankfully, were upstairs at the time. They missed the advert. The advert that came out of nowhere, just sitting in between all the other adverts that plagued the TV that night, and nothing strange about it, just this image of an endlessly rising stairway. No words with it, no slogan, but that was the norm. The usual freeze. The freeze and the thrall. Legal ads were low-level interference, and you could easily resist their temptations with a little will-power. So they'd thought nothing of it, this man and woman, except they both dreamed that night of the stairway, and of going up it, and what they might find there.

The next day, two in the afternoon, the wife had thrown herself out of the top-storey window of the office where she worked. That was five days ago, and distraught as he was, and full of suffering for his lost wife, how could the husband not want to join her? This is when he read about the spate of similar suicides. God knows what resources he had conjured up to get himself as far as the commcop station.

Brendel wanted to place him under arrest, for his own safety, but the authorities would have none of that. So we filled him up with the maximum dose of spoiler juice, and then let him go. He lasted two days. Of course, we had a cop on his tail the whole time. Did no good; he shook the cop off, just for a minute.

A minute's a long time when you're falling . . .

Things got bad then, because the story broke loose. The media were hounding us, and Brendel was on a sharp edge. She cancelled all leave, tripled the bonus for the Apex score, got the lab boys working full-time on the transmission source. The only good thing they could find was how the stairway ad would only ever appear on one receiver at a time. What we call a narrowcast. It would turn up on a private TV, a computer screen, an arcade game. Never on a public system, like a cinema screen. As though the advert was picking people off, one by one. Sniper mentality. We tried putting out our own adverts, warning people not to watch, or play, or in any way to have serious leisure time. We did the usual pointless appeal to the TV and game companies, asking them to suspend all transmissions. Like, yeah, sure we'll cut off our money supply, just on some unsubstantiated claim about a killer ad. Get out of here. So we distributed free scatterglasses, cheap and nasty ones, which is a bit like getting flotsams to wear pinstripe suits. No deal, and you can't reach everybody, not all the time, so I guess we all got to feel like warriors, us commcops, naked on the streets against this invisible, deadly enemy. How else explain what Parker did, what I *let* him do?

It was a Sunday night, quiet time in the all-night arcades. The usual flots and jets to unfreeze, no big deal. Parker was getting bored, and itchy. He was expecting more of the job, of course he was, young like that; I was the same. Pretty soon you get to find out that being a commcop isn't quite like the recruiting images, and I tried to give him the real package. Stupid kid wouldn't listen, going crazy he was, with fighting talk about how he was gonna take this stairway fucker out, once and for all. He was hot for it, and I couldn't help but get a secret pleasure, remembering mainly, remembering how it had been when I first started out.

We found a group of flots gazing full on at a game screen. Locked solid they were, and as we came up, I was dreading seeing the stairway there. This had been my fear, the last few weeks: coming across a spectator in thrall to the killer. Luckily, it was just a slowly rotating pair of plastic trainers up there on the display, saying in secret, 'Buy me! Buy me! Buy me now, you stupid suckers!' Easy game, because this had all the design flair of a camel's arse, and was obviously a trans from Minskey's Muscle, a sports shop only two blocks away. Parker was mad keen to shoot the trainers himself, he had the gun out and loaded and everything, so I said, 'This one's yours, kid', and went off to slap the fine on Minskey.

Big mistake. Because it took longer than I thought, what with Minskey putting on a show, and his pumped-up sales assistants hanging round in sub-pensive mode. All around me were banks of screens playing out the same commercial, and variants thereof, and here this guy was, claiming he 'didn't never have such bad adverts, no ma'am, not never. See now, these good adverts, clean adverts, no nasties. No freeze. See?'

All the time I was hoping Parker would hurry up. I needed the back-up. What was the kid doing? Surely he'd done the deed by now, come on. In the end I had to walk out of there empty-handed, which pissed me off. So I was all set to give the grief to my so-called partner. I was acting mad for my own failure, I know, and maybe the kid was having trouble, it's just that I can't stand not making a clean case of a job. And by the time I get back to the arcade, the place is deserted, all the games standing empty, forlorn with abandoned play. No flots, no jets, no Parker. So I'm looking round and getting worried, when I hear this noise from the next aisle, a kind of screaming sound. Like human, through the mincer. Straight off, I should've called for back-up. Instead I was just running over there, towards the bad sound, because the sound got me in the guts. Bad reaction getting to me. Round the corner, I see a bunch of people going crazy outside this one shop. The screaming coming from them. OK, get up close, and slow down, slow down, check the situ, play the book. The shop was a dark-eye, shut for business. Abandoned, read the slashed-on sign across the window. The door thinly open. OK, what's the score here?

'My sister! My sister! Help her! My sister!'

One freaked-up flotboy, coming right on at me, making me sweat, so desperate. And someone else, saying, 'It's the stairway thing, pretty sure it must be.'

'She's in there?' I ask.

'Get her out!' screams the boy. Keeps on screaming.

'Where's my colleague?'

'Uh?' Voices.

'The other cop, where is he?'

'He went in.' Voices all round.

Shit.

I look around the crowd, most of them quiet now and just looking at me, as though I could save one of their kind, but all I was thinking about was Parker, that stupid fucker, going in alone. I think that's when I got round to calling HQ for the back-up van, Apex coding. Of course, I didn't wait, how could I? Instead, pull the mask down tight, load the spoiler, kick the door wide, step through.

Dark. Dark in there. Only the faint buzz of colour through the scatter, vapour from some screen, way back. No sign of Parker or the girl, and what the fuck was a television doing on, in this dump? Moving through, beam on, I see signs of cheap habitation, spread duvets, camping stoves, pots and pans. Flot squat. In the dark my beam flashes on something, a rolled-up duvet or something, then I see it's a kid, a young girl. She's lying on the ground, all cradled up in herself, gently rolling, back and forth, back and forth. And when I bend down, turn her over, and she opens her arms for me, I see this amazing thing – she's got a mask on.

A commcop mask.

'Jesus, I didn't know that,' said Gumball. 'You mean . . .'

'Yeah. Parker took his mask off, gave it to the girl. He saved her life.'

'Jeez!' He'd finished his prawns by now, and the gum was back in his mouth, and he was chewing on it, but slowly. 'That's fucking brave!'

'It's stupid. But yeah, brave, I suppose. I found him there, stuck fast in front of the television. He had the gun out and everything, and he was pointing it at the screen, and I swear he was trying to shoot, even with the thrall on him. He had tears . . . tears on his cheeks, frozen. That's when I heard the back-up sirens. Too fucking late, course they were.'

'Hey, don't blame yourself, Muldoon.'

'Why not? You got someone else handy?'

'So . . .' And here he stretched the gum out of his mouth in a long line – a dirty yellow this time – and then let it snap back. 'So what did it look like?'

'The advert? Well, I had the mask on, so I was only getting the filter. Just some stairs, nothing special. Animated, so that they kept rising upwards, and never ending. Looked kinda cheap, really. You know, amateurish.'

'That's it?'

'That's it.'

'Jeez!'

'Yeah. Let's clock off.'

But when I started to get the gear together, I saw this kid looking at me from the next table along, listening distance. It was the jetgirl, the one with the hard shopping eyes, and away from her flottish friends now. She was smiling at me.

'What's up with you?' I asked her.

'Nothing much, just listening.'

'This is cop business,' said Gumball. 'Get the hell out of here. Bloody flots!'

'I'm not a flot. I'm a jet. How dare you?'

'All the bloody same. Nothing better to do than play stupid games all night long.'

'They're not games. It's an art form.'

'Yeah, right.'

'I'm good at them. I get to cheat, you see. It's a secret, cause the cheating's built into the art. You have to discover it, then you progress. The next level.'

Gumball stood up. His mouth worked at the gum like a machine, a rainbow machine. 'I'll progress you!' he snarled, and when he spoke, you could see all the colours inside, caught in the change.

'Sit down, Gum,' I said to him. 'Just a kid, that's all.'

'You're not telling him everything, are you?'

She'd said this directly at me, with a look in her eye, a knowing look.

'What's that supposed to mean?'

'Tell him about the mask.'

'What is this?' asked Gumball.

I ignored him, kept my eyes on the girl. She looked so young, nine or ten, although you can never tell for sure, not once they're on the street. 'What do you know?'

'Stuff.' And she smiled again.

'What's your name, girl?' I asked.

'Lucy. What's yours?'

'Never mind that. You'll have to come with me, I'm afraid.'

'Smashing. Will I get to be a commcop, please?'

So I sent Gumball on his way, clocked off with HQ on the bleeper, and then offered to buy the jetgirl some breakfast. This she readily agreed to; not prawns, just coffee and biscuits would do. She sat there, slurping away. I took a look at her; quite good-looking, incredibly slim, like I could pick her up like a feather. And well-dressed like all the jets were. Compared to the flots of course, who were trash personified. I asked her why she'd left home, and she said that home was for the lonely, and I could connect to that. I was a commcop, wasn't I?

'I can look at adverts,' she said, with a crunch of biscuit. 'Bet you can't.'

I remembered, then, that she'd been hanging round real close to the action this morning, and maybe she had seen a glimpse of it, I couldn't be sure.

'I've got the mask, haven't I?' I said back at her.

'I don't need a mask, me, so don't think that's why I want to join up, just to get a mask and a gun, cause I don't need 'em, well, the gun would be nice, but just for kicks like. Why do you think I don't want prawns? Adverts mean nothing to me.'

Now I knew there were a few people out there that were immune to the messages. The marketing men called them the Blind Consumers, the Unresponsive 6 Per Cent. And I knew that Brendel would love to get her hands on this girl, this Lucy, subject her to a million lab tests, extract all the scattering out of her. I wasn't keen on the procedure, because I'd seen what the extraction did to the immune. It made them go hollow.

'What should I have told my partner about the mask?' I asked her.

'You took it off, didn't you? When you saw the stairway advert. Am I right?'

'No. I mean . . . I wanted to . . . it was . . .'

'It was trying to make you, right?'

'Yes . . . I started to . . . started to lift up the mask . . . I couldn't . . .'

'How much?'

'What?'

'How much?'

'Just a bit, a sliver, not at all.'

'You haven't told anyone?'

'Look, what is this? Nothing happened.'

'And now you're scared. Scared that they'll take you off the streets. Am I right?'

I looked away. The flotboys had all left now, and another bunch of diners had taken their place. Maybe these were people with real hunger, maybe they were artificially induced, there was no way of telling, not without the proper equipment.

'You've seen it, haven't you?' I said to the girl.

She was quiet for a time, and then she started to cry. Not tears of pain, or anger or frustration even. She nodded her head, said nothing. Just cried.

They were tears of loss, I'm sure they were.

Later on, when really I should've been home and in bed, I took Lucy out to the commcop station. She got over the tears as soon as she got in the van, and the journey through the streets had her smiling, especially when I turned the siren on, just for her. Anything to take her mind off what was happening, because I wasn't sure about what I was about to do; I had no way of knowing the reactions that I would get. Luckily, Brendel was off duty as well, and the high-security cells weren't her natural habitat anyway. I signed in with the guard down in the cellar, put a tick next to 'Officer in Attendance' and another against 'Family/Acquaintance' and got Lucy to sign against that.

'It's breakfast time, anyway,' said the guard. 'I was going to take this in.' He was holding a plateful of mush and a spoon. 'You want to do it?'

I nodded. Took the plate and spoon – plastic plate, plastic spoon – and then waited as the guard unlocked the door. 'Be careful in there,' he says.

The occupant of cell 945 was asleep as we came in. At least, I thought he was. It was dark, and the faint light from the door fell only on a bulky shape lying on the bed. I put my fingers to my lips, but Lucy was quiet anyway, and too nervous even to breathe out loud. I felt the same, and when I put on the small and well-protected overhead light, and the figure on the bed stirred slightly, it felt as though I was waking the dead. There was a draw of breath at last, and a gasp as Lucy saw what Parker had become.

Become.

Reduced.

Victim to.

It was the first time I'd come to visit. Maybe guilt had kept me away, or just the sense of helplessness. He was tied to the small bed. Strapped down. I hadn't expected this. It must've been bad. Still bad. Shit. I could hardly think of anything at all, and when his eyes opened, and it took him a good long moment to recognize me, well, I was on the edge of turning away.

Parker's head was propped up slightly on a pillow, and this was the only bit of him that could move at all. The bastard only smiles at me, doesn't he? Then he says, 'Muldoon, you came. Is it breakfast time already?' I come forward with the bowl, and I scoop some of the mush out of it with the spoon. I place it against his lips, he opens them, chews the stuff, swallows. After about six of these mouthfuls, he shakes his head for no more please.

'You caught it yet?' he asks.

I shake my head.

'Keep working,' he says. 'Don't worry about me.'

I can't believe how peaceful he sounds.

'Muldoon?'

'Yes?'

'A favour, please.'

'Anything, Parker. Anything.'

'Undo these straps. Just the ones on my arms. Just my right arm will do. I want to eat my own food. I can't stand being fed like a baby. Will you do that?'

I look around the cell. Then at the door. Lucy's standing there, and she nods at me.

'Come on, Muldoon,' says Parker. 'What am I going to do?'

I lean over his body, to get to the strap. It comes loose with a strong tug, and Parker's hand strokes my face, just for a second. 'Thank you,' he says. 'Thank you.' Then he picks up the plastic spoon, and starts to feed himself.

'Who's this?' he asks.

'Her name's Lucy,' I reply.

'I can answer,' says the girl. She comes closer to Parker, but stops a few steps away from him. 'My name is Lucy Bell. I'm ten years old, nearly. Adverts mean nothing to me. And I've seen the stairway.'

Parker stops eating. 'You've seen it?'

'Yes. It came up on a game I was playing. I was alone, luckily. I've seen a million ads in my time, you know what I mean, and nothing gets me frozen. Sometimes I think I'm the unlucky one, because it must be nice to be really affected by something. Usually I just move to another machine when the screen freezes, but this was different I could tell, but I couldn't tell why. Something about the stairway, the way it goes on for ever . . .'

'Yes,' said Parker. 'For ever . . .'

'And it made me really sad to watch it going upwards like that, with nobody on it.'

'Yes. Sad.'

'It made me put my hand out. I couldn't help myself. I put my hand against the screen. It was cold, the screen, like the machine had broken down. But it was nice, just to let my fingers rest against the steps. I felt like I was walking up it just by touching. And I was so sad, I started to cry. I don't know why, so don't ask me.'

'I know,' said Parker. 'I know.'

'And ever since, this sadness . . . it won't leave me alone. I feel like I've missed out on something. Inspector Muldoon tells me you were brave, that you saved a flot by giving her your scattermask.'

'No, it wasn't brave. The staircase made me take the mask off. I could see the girl hadn't seen it yet, she was doing her best to look away. I only gave her the mask because I didn't need it any more.'

'Well, I still think it was brave. And I was thinking, maybe I should volunteer for being tested, or something. Because surely there's something inside me, something strange that adverts don't like. And I know all the normal stuff, the spoiler drugs and all that, I know they don't work on this stairway thing. Maybe I should—'

'No.' Parker came up as far as he could. 'I've heard what happens to people when they extract it. It's not good. Not good. You just work with Inspector Muldoon here. Maybe you can find out where the adverts are coming from, eh? Working together?'

'I'd like that. I'd like to be a commcop one day.'

'You will be, kid. You will be.'

I was watching all this from one corner. I wasn't sure what I was aiming at, bringing these two people together. This young girl, barely out of childhood, and having already witnessed and survived what amounted to a murder attempt; and this poor young man, this rookie cop, who had become just another victim. A young man strapped to a bed, and with a plastic spoon in his hand. They seemed happy together, at least. Parker then called over to me, 'You keep Brendel away from this girl, OK?'

'I'm doing that already.'

'Good. Now leave me, please.'

He pushed Lucy towards me, his face suddenly hardened into a frown. 'I'll get you strapped up again,' I said. But Lucy was in the way, and I was walking around her when a sudden choking noise frightened me into stillness. It was Parker. Right in front of me, he had stuck the plastic spoon down his throat. He was jamming it, again and again, deeper and deeper into his mouth. For a good few seconds I couldn't move; the look in his eyes, the sheer pleasure of submission that played there, it rooted me to the spot. Coming out of the freeze, I simultaneously called for the guard, pushed Lucy aside, and rushed over to the bed. With one hand on his face, and the other forcing his mouth open, I tried to make him breathe, to breathe, to breathe again. His right hand had squeezed around my throat. Where the fuck was that guard? Behind me, somewhere behind me, and far, far away, Lucy was screaming.

I got home at eleven, dead beat and frazzled. Lucy was with me. She was showing all the tagging skills of a jetgirl. I shoved her down on the sofa. 'You sleep there,' I said. 'Don't think I'm giving up my bed for you.'

'I don't want to sleep,' she answered. 'It's the daytime. Will Parker be all right?'

'What's all right? We're keeping him alive against his wishes. Is that all right?'

'Maybe we should let him . . . you know?'

'Don't even think that, right? I mean it, girl.'

I took off my gun and mask, and it seemed like I was taking off my skin, so long had I worn them.

'OK,' said the girl. 'This is a nice place. Wow, you've got a TV.' She said it like she'd never seen one before.

'It's off limits,' I told her. 'And I've got the password.'

'Sure. You live here alone?'

'Yes.'

'No husband?'

'I'm going to bed.'

'No boyfriend? Girlfriend?'

'Bye.'

I carried the mask and gun into my bedroom, stripped naked, fell slowly, blissfully into bed. I don't know what I dreamed of. It had been a long, bad night and morning, and I wish I could leave it at that, the night and the black sleep and the end of the story.

Some things you just can't wish for.

I woke up feeling worse than when I'd gone to sleep. I don't know what time it was. I had to shift through several layers of reality until I got the noise fixed in my head, the sound of a television far off in the distance. At first I thought I was fighting some killer ad along the shining pavilions of a golden arcade, Parker at my side; then I was thinking it was all a dream, and how glad I was at that realization; then I heard the sound of my spoiler gun firing in a long continuous burst of static, and I was back in the arcade once again, but only for a second as I caught the last thread of reality. The noise was coming from the living room, chased by a terrible howling.

The blind sight of my mask was staring at me from where I'd left it hooked to the wall, but the gun was gone. That stupid girl . . .

I burst the door open, naked.

That stupid fucking girl was just sitting there, right in front of the TV. She had the gun in her hands, and was still firing it at the screen. The howl had gone from her now, replaced by a whimpering cry. I don't know how she broke the password on the set; that girl always was a mystery. And still she fired. Fired and fired at the golden stairway that travelled ever upwards, unrolling on the screen like an escalator to the sky.

Just kept on unrolling, right through everything the girl could hope to spoil it with.

Yeah. I saw it. I was naked, straight from bed. And the mask was still hanging from the hook in the bedroom.

'Don't look! Don't look at it!'

Those were the last words I heard, and they seemed to freeze on the air like drops of ice. Everything froze. Everything froze for me.

'I'm sorry,' said Lucy. 'I tried to . . .'

'What?'

'Come back to me, please!'

Moving through slow ice that melted, I came alive with my eyes tight on the screen, where a dancing elephant played gaily. There was no sign of the stairway. Everything seemed normal, perfectly normal. Me, a young girl, a television set. Almost a family. There were no feelings inside me, nothing I could touch.

'Oh God, I'm sorry.'

'That's fine.'

'I was trying to kill it.'

'I said it's fine.'

I realized that I was naked in front of the kid. Walking slowly back into my room, all I could think about was getting dressed. I even put on the mask, I don't know why. I put it on first, as though it could still protect me. I went back into the living room, took the gun from Lucy's clutched hands, just as my bleeper went off.

'Muldoon, that you?'

'Yes.'

'You heard?'

It was Gumball, and I could hear his voice clearly, no sticky chewing sounds. I knew it was bad then. 'It's Parker?'

'Yeah. He found a way. You'll want the details, right?'

'No. No details.'

'Right. Look . . . erm . . . shit, I'm no good at this stuff. I'm sorry. Oh shit. Look, they got a partial trace on the killer trans, it's coming from the Ancoats area. We're doing a house-to-house. You up for it?'

'No. I'm going to the arcade.'

'The arcade? You're not on tonight. Are you all right, Muldoon?'

'Fine. I'm fine. Goodbye.'

I broke the connection, just ripped the bleeper off my belt, wires dangling. Lucy was looking at me scared, as I took up the spoiler gun, reversed it, and with the reinforced butt smashed in the TV's screen, killing that stupid poor innocent elephant dead. 'Come on,' I said, grabbing the girl by a skinny little forearm.

'But where?'

'Shut up.'

I wasn't sure when it would kick in, the suicide impulse. Some cases had taken at least a week for the urge to strike, others felt it in seconds. So time was everything, making me drive like a madwoman, swerving the jeep, a crazy snake through the traffic. I wasn't even sure why I was going to the arcade, but it was my natural hunting ground, after all. I had this intense feeling that I was needed there.

'I thought we were going to the commcop station,' said Lucy.

'Not yet.'

'But miss, what if you . . . ?' She couldn't finish the sentence.

'This is between you and me, kid,' I said to her. 'You understand?'

'It's a secret?'

'Yeah. A secret.'

'OK.'

I looked at the girl; she was small and slight, making herself even smaller by pressing back into the seat. Her eyes were blank, fixed on the badly lit road ahead, the arcade that loomed suddenly over us now, all twelve storeys of it almost bending down to receive me.

I drove into the service entrance, through to the underground park. Another commcop car was there, and Gumball was leaning against it. He called out my name, but I just swerved away from him, heading for the up-chute. I could hear his starter engine growl and echo in the hollow space, the screech of tyres.

First storey. Second. Now he'd turned his siren on, as though I should care any more. Third storey, fourth, fifth. I was burning the curves of the building. Six, seven, and Lucy was screaming at me to slow down, to stop, to just please stop now please. I couldn't. The storeys were unfolding, upwards, upwards. Eight, nine, ten. I think I lost Gumball around there. I lost everybody. There was just me and the girl and the stairway leading me on. I had to get to the top. If I could only get to the top, I'd be OK then. Something good was waiting for me there. Eleven, twelve. I jammed the car against a barrier, smashing the bonnet flat. Electrical sparks rose from the engine and the girl was crying now as I bundled her from the vehicle.

'Please! Don't—'

I didn't have anything to say in reply. Grabbing her by both wrists, I dragged her to the metal door that led to the roof. With a kick I released the locking bar, banged it open, pulled the girl through behind me.

Release! I came to, out of some dumb freeze. Felt like I was breathing, for the first time in hours. The whole trip upwards, a superzoom of quick fire. But how fine everything was now, standing on top of Manchester. All this was mine – the black spaces, the glittering lights. Chill breath of air, first spots of rain, the child at my side, barely struggling.

'Let me go,' she said.

'Not yet,' I answered, throwing the gun to the ground. 'I need you still.' And tearing off the scattermask, throwing it down as well. So much spent trash in my life. A glimmer to my right turned me around. There, oh there! The stairway continued, ever upwards, made out of cloud. It was simple, and so clean, and all I needed to do was carry on climbing. There the pleasure awaited me. There it waited, and what else was there to do? With a violence that shocked me, I gathered the girl off her feet, lifted her up into my arms.

'Please. What are you doing? Stop it, please. Please stop it!'

She had a weight, but it was nothing really, a mere shadow. And the words of the shadow were but textures in the night. Only the staircase mattered, only the golden way. I started to walk towards it, towards the edge of the building. I took a few steps, and the girl was struggling, but nothing I couldn't handle. Within moments, out of another freeze, there I was, balanced on the tip of the night. Below me, and all around, the silent, pained city lay so distant it barely shimmered.

'Muldoon!'

A voice from behind, the clang of a metal door.

'Muldoon! It's me, it's Gumball. What's going on?'

'Stay away.'

'It's the stairway!' cried the girl in my arms. 'She's seen the stairway!'

'Come away, Muldoon. Come away from the edge. We're moving in on the trans. Muldoon, we've got a trace.'

'Stay away, Gumball! I have to do this.'

'Put the girl down, then. There's no need to—'

'Shut up!'

I looked ahead. The girl had gone quiet now. It was a cruel and terrible thing to do, and I don't know what passion drove me there. Only the need to challenge, I suppose. I had to set myself up against the advert, see who was strongest. It could make me kill myself, that was easy. Could it make me kill another, an innocent?

Gently, so gently, I put my foot on the first step. The cloud shivered. The girl held on tight to me, and it was all I had left.

The rain hit me.

Hit me cold.

I stepped back. Unfroze. The stairway shivered again, then became a mere gust of wind and the droplets of the rain, vanishing.

I got the girl safely to the floor, where she ran into Gumball's arms. I picked up the gun and the mask.

'OK, Gumball,' I said, moving towards the door. 'Let's go find the bastard.'

BLURBS

I was only five images old when I got my first Blurb. Mummy Wave bought it for me, a present for my first ever press conference. Oh, she was so proud! Her only daughter, the youngest girl in the street to achieve a press-con.

Imagine the headlines. The in-depth analysis: YOUNG GIRL WITNESSES VICIOUS MURDER! ANGRY MOTHER DEMANDS PUBLIC RECOGNITION FOR GRIEVING CHILD. NEW VIRUS INFECTS GAMEWORLD™. AUTHORITIES AT A LOSS TO EXPLAIN THE KILLING.

This is how it happened: Tommy Smart was my best-ever friend, and I miss his tactics dearly. We were playing Corporate Sleazeball™ on the Game-Pimp™. Tommy was so good, he'd already scored seven freebies, five perks, four liquid lunches and two complete takeover bids against me, easy pickings, before the bad thing happened. At first it was just a whirling shadow at the very edge of my game-vision, like a mild intrusion from reality, nothing to be scared about. Perhaps our collected mummies were calling to us, to come eat?

Before I knew quite what was happening, the shadow shape had pounced on Tommy, hard and fast. It splintered his game-play into a million pieces and then sucked his image clean away. I pulled out of the Pimp, double quick and falling . . .

Into my mother's arms. Back to the Real World™, as Tommy's image drained away to zero before my startled eyes.

Marketing disaster!

Zero-image is a kind of slow death. Tommy didn't really die, he just became a nobody. I couldn't bear to play with him now that he had no flaunt, no flourish, no publicity value. I guess that being privy to his erasure made me too famous, far too quickly. Whatever, the Commcops™ soon came knocking, and I was hauled off to give the press-con. I had to give this tear-stricken speech about what a noble player Tommy Smart had been. The news hounds asked me a ton of questions about the monstrous virus that had wiped Tommy's image off the map. I said it was a twisting whirl of data-smoke, dark and brutal, like a tornado, only more fashionable. I was already learning how to work the media.

The next morning's editions were full of screen-prints of the Twister Wipe™ virus, and how it was going to kill all the game-pimping children unless caught quickly. Thus was my fifth image-change achieved.

From 'Media Virgin' to 'Grieving Witness', all in one easy move.

Mummy Wave was so pleased with my press-con that she bought me the pet as a reward for being so open to notoriety. Blurb Worms were rare and expensive in those days, but Mummy had sold my story to one of the more downmarket news hounds.

So, my very first Blurb. I called him Scoop™.

Scoop was only three inches long to start with, and a pale cream colour. I kept him safe and warm in a glass tank filled with earth and sawdust. Following the instructions in the user's manual, Scoop's first meal consisted of five metazine articles about my witnessing the evil Twister Wipe at his play, a mating pair of Vids reproducing my press-con, and the complete series of howlings my mother's exclusive had produced from the newshound.

Mummy Wave threw a launch party to celebrate my exploits, inviting all of the street's residents. I allowed Scoop out of his tank for the first time. By now the Blurb had completely swallowed my hot news story. He'd grown an inch in size with the info, and his once-naked body now sported the colours of my new brand image, my very own logo. TINA WAVE ENTERPRISES™, ran the letters along his spine. The Blurb Worm sat lovingly on my shoulder, beaming his messages of goodwill:

Important Press release! Tina Wave is currently recovering from her traumatic experience at the hands of the Twister Wipe. She will not be giving any further interviews until after the publication of volume one of her memoirs.

That was my street name: Tina Wave. Short for Christina Waverly. Just like Blurbs is short for Bio-Logical-Ultra-Robotic-Broadcasting-System. Just like the commcops are really the Communication Police. Because this is the Golden Age of Appearances™. We don't even call them *names*, really; rather we have logos, or corporate identities, or else brands or trademarks, copyrighted designs, slogans, tags or communiqués.

Nothing is real, and that's how we like it.

Meanwhile, more and more kiddie players were twisted to

zero-image. The Wipe-out rampant. The commcops could only patrol the games, like the useless watchdogs that they were, discovering zero, zero everywhere.

My sixth image was 'Lone Vixen'. I retired to my bedroom, and stayed there a whole season, writing my memoirs and formulating my game plan for the public life ahead. Scoop also went into hibernation, enfolding himself in a cocoon of secreted commercials. Everything slowed down; kids world-wide were leaving the Game-Pimp machine alone, egged on by horror-struck parents. Of course, most of the kids really wanted to have a go against the Twister, relishing the image they would gain by killing it. But the parental advice prevailed, and the kids went AWOP: Absent Without Official Play. The Big Pimp's profits took a graph plunge.

Sometimes Tommy Smart came round to see me, but my mother never let him inside the house. I would watch from my upstairs window; his thin, weak, almost transparent body disappearing into the afterglow. But what could I do? After all, he had no commercial value.

By my seventh image-change I had acquired another five Blurbs, including a rather lovely female specimen I called Gossip Monger™. My latest image was 'Petulant Brat', and the Blurbs actively promoted that labelling throughout the street. Scoop had meanwhile outgrown his wormhood; he emerged triumphant from his shell, his new wings fluttering madly to dry themselves. Two hours later he was airborne. Scoop became a Flier™, reproducing my image joyfully over the entire village.

Press release! Tina Wave is now open for business. Read her memoirs. Let her manage your campaign. Become as famous as she is.

By the time I was ten images old (CRAZY ALIEN KID ON

PLANET EARTH BY MISTAKE!) I had a hundred or so Blurbs flying around the whole city, and a hundred more waiting to hatch their messages from cocoons. Mummy Wave didn't need to buy the worms any more. Following Scoop's courtship and mating with Gossip – and the birth of the first of their larvae, Blabbermouth™ – the other Blurbs were soon hard at it, making their own baby adverts. But Scoop was the official King of Blurbs™, and I was the Queen of Publicity™. The famous Tina Wave, the young girl behind the release of winged logos. I should have realized the problem: I was becoming famous for being *famous*, not for actually perpetrating any new major stories. I was making a handsome profit from my marketing business, thank you, but nothing stupendous had happened to me in the last few months. I was becoming a media ghost, fed by past glories only.

I really should have realized.

Image number eleven: 'Sullen Bitch-Kid'. I had a thousand or so Blurb Fliers surrounding my body by then, thanks to Mummy's desperate attempts to over-extend my public life. She had started to feed the Blurbs with Junk Mail™. Designed by the engimologists, Junk Mail was a nasty subscription hormone that made the adverts go sex mad. They birthed a buzzing halo wave of publicity. They worked as one, this new swarm of logos, arranging their bodies into a collective display. Hanging over the city like a cloud of desire.

Press release! Buy Tina Wave's latest output! Volume two of her memoirs, now out! Learn the secrets of her publicity drive!

It seemed that the whole world must know about my exploits; but really, it was only publicity about publicity. Self-replication of the Image, which is a kind of inbreeding. The Blurb Worm manual was very strict on this point: 'Lack of cross-pollination can lead to mutated images.' You bet! My twelfth image was 'Psychotic Juvenile!' And the Blurbs were becoming ever more hungry: 'Info! More info!' they buzzed in ragged formation. 'Feed us! Feed us major stories!'

Myself and my images were becoming clichéd and malformed, thanks to the limited meme-pool. 'Do something, Tina!' cried Mummy Wave from her sunken armchair. She was slowly dying from the lack of reflected fame.

Shrinking.

By this time, a lot of the other kids had Blurbs of their own, and the pitched battles between the various publicity campaigns left the streets covered in media corpses. My poor army suffered dearly for its victories. I found my beloved Scoop, and his wife, Gossip, lying dead in the street, and their first-born son, Blabbermouth, crying all over the remains. I buried the two press warriors in a grave of obituary columns.

Here lie Scoop and Gossip. Long may they propagate.

The Blurb Wars gained me some blessed new publicity, but pretty soon that died away, taking Mummy Wave to the very edge of zero-image: 'Do something drastic and stupendous, Tina! Save the family's brand identity! Save the logo!'

Mummy met her deadline. So sad.

A few days ago I heard that Tommy Smart's body had been found. He'd killed himself, hanging his emptiness from a street lamp. One final streetvert, his second death. No life beyond the image.

The Blurb Wars, the deaths of Scoop and Gossip and Tommy Smart, oh yes, and of Mummy Wave: these events all raised my public profile slightly. I came to realize that death was the ultimate advertisement.

So now, I prepare my final press campaign. My final image. Believe me, you will hear about it. Believe me you will.

All my Blurbs will help me.

DUB BLURBS
(press release twister remix)

Exclusive! Tonight, in a death-pool beaming machine, desire tactics were cloud-swallowed. In-depth girl analysis revealed images of naked juvenile wave. Witnesses saw meme swarms pimp from reality. Imagine liquid killing. Murdering fashion!

Public bought child user's virus, injecting recognition. Pollination inbreeding mutated loophole desire, causing ultimate trademark feedback. Meta-corporate game howlings take over our collected shadowzine loss. Sunken, the colours reflected fame-value deadline. Emptiness street.

'Eat sleaze!' gossips cliché-incorporated larva mouth. Manual blabbervert feeds vision game, shapes a million hot-data smoke-map designs. Virgin brand-plunge logical, given transparent fashion for hormone buzzing. Cops imagine flaunt-worms flourish.

Discovering zero tornado, everywhere system-sex

hounds wiped the whirl. 'Reproducing is nasty,' robotic marketing specimen cocooned at news disaster. Erasure campaigns labelled info too female. 'Dark brutal naked little logo!' messaged public-life junk alien. 'Too much worm-hood propagates downmarket mating.'

Comm-twister wings broadcasting to splintered scoop vid: 'Publicity, sell your ultra!'

Logo bio death. Falling media slogans secreted zero-media. A nobody image. Malformed afterglow infected final shadow. Body sported commercials; copyrighted slow graph disappearing down to sub-subzero. Hatches new instructions: infection's courtship, unfolding.

Meanwhile, world halo-shrinking conference editions change of sucked ghost.

TWEEDLES

.
.

The company flew me back to England for retraining, my first visit in years and, as always, coming back made me long to get away again. But what the hell, it was Christmas, and the guilt finally got the better of me. So I'd got the train up to Manchester. Christ, the place reeked. 'Remember me?' I asked my mother. 'Here, have some perfume.' She sniffed at the gift, like it was alien drool. We made some awkward conversation, until she astonished me with the news that Oswald Peel was still living in the same house down the street, still living with his parents. 'But the guy's my age,' I said. 'What's he doing living at home?'

'You should visit him,' my mother replied. 'He's working for the weather.'

So Christmas morning found me calling round at the big old house. His father didn't recognize me at first, until I nudged his memory. 'It's Billy, Mr Peel. You remember? Billy

Sunset, from down the road? I've come to see Oswald.'

The mother was frozen in brandy, trapped by the television, smiling away at the twenty-four-hour weather channel. They were predicting snow. 'Oswald's in his room,' the father said. 'Shall I call him down?'

'No, no. I'll go up.'

The bedroom was dark, the curtains drawn against daylight. The latest telescope was peeking through the curtains, fixed upon some distant, unseen star, no doubt. Oswald was sitting on his bed, reading a book. It could have been years ago. 'Hello Ozzie,' I said. 'Happy Christmas. Look, I've brought you a present. Take a sniff. How you doing?'

He put the book down, got up from the bed.

The first thing I noticed was how well he was looking, for his age. I mean, I've lost a little hair myself, and grown a stomach in the passing years, but Ozzie was hirsute and trim-lined. The bastard, I thought, it shouldn't be allowed.

'Who are you?' A voice from the past.

'It's Billy. Remember?'

'Billy Sunset?'

'That's right. I've brought you some aftershave. It's what I do these days. I sell smells. What are you up to? I hear you're a meteorologist.'

'Yes, for the television.'

'That's brilliant.'

'You think so?'

Well no, actually. I would have thought Oswald worth much more than that. But I didn't want to mention such things. Instead I said something even more stupid:

'I was sorry to hear about Junior. Do you hear from him?'

Oswald just looked at me. Then he moved to the telescope. It was a bad thing to say, of course, about Junior I mean, but the years of selling have frozen me solid, I suppose, especially in the heart. And I was dragged backwards to another Christmas morning, ages ago, when I wasn't yet so cold.

Ozzie was the neighbourhood kid you just had to hate. I mean, there was the stupid name to start with, and the fact that he somehow managed to have two parents, which was one more than any other kids on the street could ever manage. And they were posh and rich of course, these parents, with two incomes and a nice house and two vintage cars, never mind the pedigree dogs and the goddamn loving relationship, whatever that was. Also, he received every little thing he could ever desire, this spoilt little brat, which was every little thing more than I could hope for. The latest model kit, the gun that saved the world, a telescope, pointed towards the stars.

Really, I should've hated his guts to the toyshop and back, but somehow I fell half in love with him, much to the downmarket taunts of my other friends. I was nine, Oswald ten, and we wasted some time together, talking about the moonshot and the effect it might have upon the atmosphere, and fantasizing about what presents we would get for Christmas. I was pinning my hopes on a new football, or some such small-fry dream, compared to Oswald demanding the latest model Tweedle Boy from Santa.

I laughed at him, of course, because Tweedle dolls were *the* toy of choice that Xmas, ever since the Only Child Law had been passed, and how could even his well-to-do parents afford such a luxury? But sure enough, that week one of the antique cars vanished, likewise one of the pedigree dogs, both of them sold to the same collector of oddities. Two days later Oswald was taken into hospital.

I didn't get to see him until Christmas morning, when I paid a call to show off my new Air UK football, my mother having also made a few sacrifices. 'Fancy a game, Ozzie?' I asked, but he claimed he was too weak still from his operation. 'What? You mean it's really happened?' I was dumbfounded. 'You've really gone through with it? Didn't it hurt?' I was shuddering to imagine my own bone marrow being excavated.

'Nothing much,' he answered, quite slowly. 'It's only a little DNA, after all, and I've got lots to spare.' Together we went up to his bedroom, where his number one present was sleeping in a specially designed cot. It was the first time I'd ever seen a Tweedle, for real I mean, not on television. I must admit I was disappointed at first glance, mainly because the adverts had painted the Tweedles as these marvellous objects, exact copies of their owners. But this sleeping toy was only about a foot long, rather chubby and quite blank in the face, hair and eyes, rather like a blindworm. 'But it looks nothing like you, Ozzie,' I said.

'Give him time.' Ozzie picked up the doll from its bed. 'He's called Junior, by the way. He's my younger brother.' The poor thing stirred in his arms, and started to gurgle.

Well, the holidays were soon over, and we all went back to school. Oswald turned up five days late for the new term, clutching his Tweedle close to his chest. He sat the doll on his desk during every lesson, where it got some looks of course, and all those kid jokes that cover jealousy. And maybe you're thinking, what's a ten-year-old boy want a doll for anyway? The thing is, Tweedles could be monsters, if you wanted them to be. Some tough tried to steal it off Ozzie once; maybe the kid hadn't heard about the security devices, or was just too stupid to care. Whatever, there was an almighty flash of light, a shower of sparks, and a scream from the tough. I tell you, he wouldn't be playing the guitar for a living.

Oswald turned eleven, passed all his exams with ease, and went on to high school. He dragged the Tweedle along with him, which was over two feet tall by now, with a twisted reflection of its owner's face. The thing could even talk a little, a mutated impression. I followed along as best I could, giving up the football to concentrate on learning. But, you know, Oswald became reclusive round about then, preferring the company of his Tweedle I suppose, rather than real people. I must admit I was jealous, to see Oswald and Junior growing up together like that, growing closer. The thing had these special growth hormones, and pretty soon it was catching up with him. I suppose other kids had the dolls, but they weren't hanging out together all the time, you know? Not like Ozzie and his brother.

By the age of sixteen the two of them were more or less the same size, and quite inseparable. Oswald did brilliantly in the exams of course, getting into the University of Manchester, no problem, studying physics and astronomy. And the better he did, the worse I got. Sixteen found me leaving school too early, with a couple of bad results. I landed this job with a local menswear shop, the start of my glorious life in sales. Anyway, it gave me the money, and the freedom, and pretty soon I had enough to rent my own place. I was itching to get that small-town stench out of my veins. It didn't take long. A year later I was taken on as an apprentice with a big London firm, selling the smells. I went round to Ozzie's, to say goodbye. Yeah, he was still living at home, despite the charms of the student life. No girlfriends or anything, not for Ozzie. Not for Ozzie and Junior.

I hadn't seen them for a while. Ozzie opened the door to me, said hello, gave me his congratulations, all that, gave me a hug, just about the first we'd ever managed. I don't know, there was something about the lad; maybe the skin was too cold, or else too warm. I can't remember exactly. Just something, you know. And then I felt the crackle, electricity under the skin. I pulled away from his clutches, just as another Oswald came up behind this one.

Even I could no longer tell them apart.

The current was still running through my fingers as I followed them both into the house. Their mother was all over the two of them, already mashed on the brandy, as though she had actually given birth to twins. If anything, she seemed to have more affection for Junior than her real son. And why not? The Tweedle was more handsome than the original. The poor lost father, meanwhile, he just looked on with a spooked-out expression, as though there was nothing he could do about it.

I got out of there as soon as I could. And carried on getting away, all the way to London. On the train I covered myself with aftershave, masking the smells of home.

And that was my exit.

For a couple of years I kept in touch with mother, just by answering a few of the many letters that followed me around the country. Occasionally she would have news of Ozzie, and even more about Junior, but nothing good. It seems the brother was turning out bad, causing trouble, getting into fights, running wild. I'd heard rumours that some of them got like that, as they grew older. Some kind of bad reaction to being second best. The last I heard, the Tweedle had taken off. Climes unknown.

I hope he found what he was looking for. That's all I could think, and that Oswald didn't take the desertion too badly.

Everything comes around. And here was my answer. A lonely, forty-year-old man still living in his parents' home; days and days in a darkened room, looking through a telescope.

'Come on, Ozzie,' I said. 'Speak to me, please. You must still think about Junior.'

'Nothing much,' he answered.

His glazed expression was still indented with the shape of the telescope's eyepiece, the reflection of a star. Distant objects were more appealing, obviously. And then I thought, what's he doing looking through that thing, middle of the morning? There's no stars out now. What's to see? I put my eye to it. A circle opened up, on a house across the way. A bedroom window. A half-dressed woman was walking across the vision.

There was a noise behind me, a dry choking sound; and then a hand being placed very gently upon my shoulder.

I felt the crackle.

PRODUCT RECALL — MARILYN MONROE

The Celeborg Company has discovered a slight fault with their Marilyn Monroe 729 model. The product concerned is stamped CC729–45X on the frame, and is painted *Hollywood Pink*. These models should be returned immediately to the nearest point of supply.

Celeborg pride themselves on their commitment to service. We present the following information to assure our loyal customers of this commitment, and to dispel any rumours that may be circulating in the press or elsewhere.

A virus has infected Marilyn Monroe.

We believe this to be the first of its kind: a parasite that lives off biotechnology. It appears to have entered our manufacturing process through an infected batch of RoboVaz, which was unfortunately applied to a small number of models. Usually the virus lives and breeds within the oil, in no way affecting the excellent performance of the host. It now appears that a new strain of the virus has evolved, which can move around the models at will, living not only within the oil but also in the special paint used on the latest Marilyn Monroes. Gradually the voracious appetite of the intruder will eat away at the celebrity. There is a slight risk that under certain circumstances this model may collapse whilst in use, putting the consumer at risk.

For this reason we are recalling all the Marilyn Monroes, and would ask our customers to keep these models away from other celebrities, to prevent cross-infection. Our JFK and Bugs Bunny models are particularly susceptible to this danger. There is no truth in the rumour that the virus is in a symbiotic relationship with the model. It does *not* make the celebrity more charismatic.

A new 'guaranteed pure' Marilyn Monroe will be supplied, free of all charges.

Please make love safely.

XTROVURT

Mr Alan Cooder, a salesman specializing in children's accessories, was dismayed to find upon arrival that the airline company had managed to lose his baggage somewhere between Manchester and New York. He still had with him a small briefcase that contained his passport, catalogues and credit cards, and the clothes he had lost could easily be replaced. Unfortunately the missing suitcase had also contained his feed supply.

He had argued with the baggage check in Manchester that he could not possibly travel without feeding himself; only to be reminded of the recent air crash in Germany, whose cause had been traced to 'one of his kind' eating during a flight. Apparently the necessary act had interfered with the aircraft's control systems. He had been told that his supply would have to travel in the hold and that he should stock up now, while in England, with enough energy to get him over the Atlantic.

Reluctantly he had done just that, visiting the Gents to do so, because he was still ashamed of feeding himself in public.

Now he found himself alone in a city he had never visited before, and already his last meal was wearing off. He could feel himself slowing down, even as the taxicab dropped him at his pre-booked hotel. His room was small, hot, and a playground for cockroaches. They never mentioned insects in the guidebook, and he shivered at the sight. Trying his best to avoid them, his first act was to cover all the mirrors with the bath towels, turning his gaze aside whilst doing so.

Alan Cooder never could stand the sight of himself when hungry.

Really, he should be preparing for his first appointment; instead he went down to the registration desk and asked for the nearest reliable supplier, hating the look of distaste the clerk gave him. He was informed that 'the best place for such things is right here on Times Square. A general store. Walking distance.'

'Only be careful, sir,' the clerk added with a sneer, 'there's some nasties around.'

Indeed. It seemed that all the world's ugliness was concentrated in this small area. Only a few steps into the glare and bustle brought him offers for pink and wet dreams, the street sellers waving their feathers at him like magic rattles. An old black guy was slumped against a wall, a feather stuck in his mouth and his body twitching with whatever cheap, dirty dream he was flying. Walking fast and keeping his head down, Alan Cooder bought a pair of cheap sunglasses and a pocket map from a stall, and then tried to follow the clerk's directions. The map must have been printed upside down, because within fifteen minutes he was lost in the maze. It was midday, the heat packed tight between the buildings. He checked his watch, only to find he'd forgotten to adjust it to the new time zone. His eyes felt like pinpricks, his stomach aching with need, and no sign of a specialist shop or even a general store. Retracing his steps in a fever, he found himself somewhere else entirely, a small thin street without name or number, overshadowed by crumbling façades and filled with the smell of overused flesh.

It was at the end of this street that Alan Cooder found a dingy little shop calling itself SLICK CITY. Underneath the dark, cracked neon a smaller sign, hand-painted: 'You want it, we got it. No high too far.' Underneath that, a scrawled sticker: 'Robos, no problemo'.

Welcome sight, even if Cooder hated the word Robo, even if the shop's window was covered in black paint and the door marked, 'Strictly Adults Only! No browsing!' He went inside.

The shop was small, more like a passageway really, with the two walls filled floor to ceiling with boxed-up feathers, a counter at the far end with a large woman squeezed behind it. There were two other customers, carefully avoiding each other and the new arrival. Cooder looked around for a second only, his nostrils clogged with the thick smell wafting from the merchandise, before heading for the counter.

'What is it?' asked the woman, wiping her brow with a rag.

'Do you have anything . . . anything for . . .' He hesitated, English and ashamed, despite his desperate need.

'Aw! Love the accent, mister!' the woman squealed. 'English, so sexy.' She laughed, ripples of her flesh hanging over the counter. Her blouse was too small, stretched to the last button over her gross stomach. Cooder couldn't bear to look at it, knowing full well already what lay behind there.

'Hey, buddy!' the woman shouted over Cooder's shoulder. 'Read the fucking sign!'

Cooder turned. One of the other customers had taken a

feather out of its box, and was just about to stick it in his mouth. Above him a printed notice read: YOU WANNA SUCK, PAY THE BUCKS! The customer placed the feather back on the shelf and quickly left the shop.

The woman turned her attention back to Cooder. 'You're one of us, mister,' she said. 'I can always tell. And . . . aw! You're in a bad way! I know that smell. Here, let me show you what we've got.'

Showing was just pointing, because the woman seemed to be wedged in place. Cooder followed her fingers over to where a section of wall was marked out as being for 'Robots Only!' Hundreds of feathers in boxes. He'd never seen so many kinds before, none of them familiar, none of them AutoBuzz, his usual brand. The boxes were illustrated; a sickening display of illegal dreams, overwhelming.

'You after something special, mister?' the woman called out, and Cooder, embarrassed, walked quickly back to the counter.

'I just want to eat,' he mumbled. 'None of this . . .' gesturing to the shelves.

'You don't want a pink one?'

'No. I don't . . . I mean, I never . . . I just want to eat, please.'

'You want a purple?'

Cooder nodded. 'I want some AutoBuzz, do you have it?'

'Is that English?'

'Yes.'

The woman made a smacking sound with her lips. 'Can't get hold of it, love nor money. We got this in last week.' She pulled a box from under the counter. The box was plain white, with the word XTROVURT stamped across it. Cooder picked it up. There were no other words on the package: no instructions, no recommended dosage, no country of origin or even manufacturer's name.

'Xtrovurt,' he said, more to himself. 'I've never heard of it.'

'It's nice. Take a look.'

Cooder opened the lid. Inside lay at least a dozen purple feathers. He held one up to the smoky light. 'It's not pure.'

'Course it's pure. We don't sell anything but.'

'No, look – it's got some pink in it.'

'Let me see? Nah, that's just a design feature. Look, mister, I've been using the stuff for the past week. No problemo. Special promotion, isn't it? Sample stocks, pre-market. Good price, too. Cost a packet in Macey's. You want some? Try some here. We've got a back room. Private booth.'

'No, no. Thank you. I'll take it. One, that is. I'll take one. How much?'

He'd brought out a credit card, but the woman looked at it as though he'd slapped something dead on the counter. In the end he'd paid cash for it, a fair sum, but he was desperate to get out of the shop by now, keen to get air, clean air, his hotel room, get the stuff inside him. His stomach felt like it was caving inwards.

Strangely, once out on the street, with the single feather tucked safely in his briefcase, he felt better already. A young girl (think she was young, think she was a girl) called out to him, 'Hey, Robo! You want some licky licky?' but he hurried on, no trouble. No trouble finding his way back, and no trouble seeing a general store he could hardly have missed the first time, close to his hotel. In this clean, well-appointed place he found a whole rack of AutoBuzz, at a price less than half of what he'd just spent. He bought six completely pure feathers, all the deep rich purple he had grown to love. And back at his hotel, a message saying the airline had found his missing case, it was being sent over by a courier.

Suddenly, the trip was happening. He would ring his

first appointment, excuse his lateness, but first . . .

Cooder closed the curtains, turned on a bedside light. Using only this light, shining through the bathroom door, he stood by the sink. He found the courtesy jar of BodyVaz, opened it up in readiness. He pulled the towel from the mirror above the sink. His briefcase was open, resting on the closed toilet seat. A cockroach was crawling across the floor; Cooder moved aside to let it pass. From the case he pulled one of the best-looking AutoBuzz feathers, its fine covering of powder gently clouding the air. Looking in the mirror, he started to unbutton his shirt. Just before the last button was popped free, he looked again at the feather he had chosen, and then at the briefcase.

The Xtrovurt feather was lying there, nestled among the others, the usual, the normal, the everyday affairs that governed his life. The strange feather that sparkled with traces of pink from the bed of purple. He picked it up, looked at it more closely.

What was he thinking of? This lonely salesman, a man without adventures, holding such a thing in his hands.

Alan Cooder: Autogen No. 279954XY. The truth spelled out on his passport.

How he hated the word 'robot'. He wasn't a robot. People were so cruel, did they think it was easy, having to feed yourself dreams every single day, just to pass as human? They should try it. No wonder Autogens stuck together. Maybe later that night he would find a club, a meeting place; surely New York of all places was home to thousands, if you knew where to find them. He had read stories in *Autogen Monthly & Lifestyle Choice*.

Goaded by this image of the Land of the Free, Alan Cooder did something he had never done before: he took a chance, a small chance.

He smoothed a handful of Vaz grease on to the Xtrovurt feather, and then opened his shirt fully, exposing his abdomen.

The mouth was there, waiting. It gasped.

It was funny, he never could feel it was a part of him, despite the fact he had been hatched with it there, the mouth in his stomach. The pair of thick red lips that parted now to be fed, the barely wet tongue that licked and tickled, tickled and licked, longing for food.

A woman's mouth.

Cooder rubbed some Vaz on the dry lips, and then slowly pushed the purple and pink feather into his abdomen. The lips closed around it, taking it deep, sucking deep to get every last drop of the dream.

Cooder fed himself.

He woke up five hours later, sprawled out on the little bed, with a bloated erection. A roach was crawling over his bare chest. He crushed it, quite easily, between finger and thumb. He pulled the used-up feather from his stomach. The deep purple of the flights had drained away to a dull cream. Empty. Swallowed. Pausing only to button up his shirt and throw on his jacket, Cooder left the room.

At the registration desk the clerk tried to get his attention, saying something about a suitcase and a telephone message. Cooder ignored him, stepped out into the New York night, flashes of the dream still racing through his body. Visions of a female of the species, a lovely man's mouth in a soft, hungry stomach, where they kissed and nibbled and stuck their tongues in each other's bellies for hours on end.

The city cried beautiful around him, swirling with life and noisy colour.

A young couple were hailing a taxi; Cooder stepped in front

of them, climbed aboard the yellow vehicle. 'Where to, bud?' asked the driver.

'Downtown,' said Cooder, 'where the Robos play.'

'Uh-huh. Would that be female robos, or would that be male robos?'

'Whatever.'

'Oh my. Hang on tight, buddy.'

THE PERFUMED MACHINE

By their very nature Autogens are doomed to a patho-
logical shyness bordering on a terror of the purely
human. This has led them to form into various cabals and half-
hidden sects, and to make their homes in self-made ghettos,
most famously 'Toytown' in Manchester, England, where the
first of their kind was created.

It is in this strange, quasi-suburban theme village that the
esteemed Professor Kalk made his best-selling study of
the autogenetic reproductive system, *The Perfumed Machine*.
That the Autogens themselves hate the word 'machine', when
applied to their own bodies (as they do any word – robot,
automaton, artificial being, biomechanical – that reminds
them of their invention) never seems to have worried Kalk or
his many readers. Also, the fact that he actually posed as an
Autogen in order to research his work, whilst adding intensely
to his promotional image, could not fail to stir the subjects of

said research into a vengeful anger. Certainly, the sentence that most incited them – 'autogens are nothing more than a laboratory experiment gone wrong' – can be seen as fatally provocative.

But it is not the purpose of this short treatise to excuse murder, or to promote the rights of autogenetic citizens; rather, it is to set the record straight once and for all regarding the sexual habits of the so-called 'perfumed machines'.

Autogens, whilst vigorously denying their machinehood, have never claimed full humanity; their only goal, it seems, is to be seen as a separate and distinct species, and to claim the rights appertaining to any such group. It must be remembered that the crime rate for their species is far below that of the purely human, and that the National Council for Autogenetic Affairs has publicly chastised the perpetrators of Professor Kalk's death.

Be that as it may, we can only imagine the surprise of the murderers when they discovered that Dr Chandra Kalk was not in fact an impostor, but a fully formed autogenetic male! If the killers had seen the mouth in Kalk's stomach prior to their vicious act, perhaps they would have shown mercy. We shall never know.

The twisted logic that led the professor to pretend to be human for so many years has been the subject of much debate. It may well be that only by doing so could he overcome the prejudice that allows only 5 per cent of Autogens to enter the scientific community, despite their natural ability in that area. Perhaps some other factors, psychological for instance (from which Autogens are known to suffer more than most), can be blamed for his dissemblance. Whatever, it certainly explains his success at pretending to be one of their kind during his research!

Did he, I wonder, try to 'be himself' at the final moment? Or was the professor so lost in the layers of disguise by then that he could not find his way out in time?

The final pretence concerns his work itself. *The Perfumed Machine*, a book which established in the public's mind the exotic lifestyle of the Autogens, has now been shown to be a tapestry of lies.

Was this, finally, the cause of the murderous revenge? That Kalk had made a vast fortune out of nothing more than his own twisted imagination?

Here then, are the facts: Autogens are capable of three different kinds of reproductive activity, each of which leads to a different kind of offspring. The first (which Kalk freely admitted to) is a rudimentary copy of the human sexual practice, where a male and a female between them create a child. Following the natural process, this baby receives half its genes from one parent, half from the other. This technique is used in times of affluence, when prospects allow for the nurturing of a long childhood.

The second type of reproduction (which Kalk merely hinted at) is used more in times of slow economic growth. This is the autogenetic process in its purest form. The female of the species reproduces without the need of the male. This produces a child more or less identical to the parent, one who very quickly (a matter of four years or less) grows to full maturity. These offspring are always female, and can be 'stacked up' in the womb; that is, a foetus may already have a foetus of its own inside it, and so on, down to an undiscovered break-off point.

The final type of reproduction (of which Kalk said nothing) is concerned with the so-called stomach-mouths in relation to which the Autogens suffer their greatest prejudice. It seems that the purely human will always be disgusted by this aspect of autogenetic physiology, and not without reason. The female has a male mouth in her stomach, the male a female one. Each mouth has a tongue, sometimes known to be over eight inches long, and a rudimentary set of teeth. Kalk claimed that the act of 'kissing stomachs' is merely an intimate greeting, or else a form of foreplay. It is now known to be the most desired and most difficult of the reproductive methods.

The female's stomach-tongue is placed within the male's stomach-mouth. It is believed that the female's 'sperm' is present in her saliva. It is the male that becomes pregnant. A small egg is formed in the stomach, which becomes a kind of male womb for the process. The egg is ejected, again by use of the stomach-tongue, and then taken over by the female, who warms and protects it (outside the body) until the hatching takes place. This can take up to two years. The resulting baby is always male, and takes fully thirty-five years to reach puberty.

This strange sexual process has a 98 per cent failure rate. Of those successfully conceived, many die within the egg. Those managing to be born are always weak and sickly; many more die before becoming fully grown. For these reasons the 'hatched' are considered more precious than the other two kinds of Autogen. Their very existence can bring about intense feelings of jealousy within the more 'normal' children. The hatched often become figures of power and authority, despite the fact that they are the most prone to psychological problems. Then again, they often become criminals or outcasts.

There now seems little doubt that Professor Kalk was such a child.

INSTRUCTIONS FOR
THE USE OF

The following incomplete document (from the Museum of Fragments) has been provisionally dated as belonging to the early twenty-first century. Although various theories have been put forward regarding the nature of the 'device' referred to, none of them has yet gained universal credence.

(text begins)

1c. The device is not to be used by children under the age of fourteen, or adults over the age of thirty-nine.

2b. If device is to be handheld, click button B to 'portable'.

2e. If device is to be shared, activate 'protection' mode.

3a. Device to be used only four times a day, unless authorization granted.

3b. Any one session not to exceed sixty minutes, or the onset of auto-shutdown by device, whichever duration is the shorter.

3c. Do not attempt to use device after auto-shutdown, unless a period of at least thirty minutes has passed.

4d. Special dispensation required for use of device in public place.

5b. In case of such breakdown (see 5a), owner of device completely to blame.

5c. In case of legitimate breakdown, device should be removed from body, and returned to point of purchase.

5d. Under no circumstances should corrupted device be left attached to body.

6a. Under no circumstances is device to be left unattended during 'dispersal' procedure.

7c. Unprotected dispersal can lead to infection of receptacle.

(text ends)

PART THREE

POISON'S FLIGHT PATH

GETTING HOME SAFELY
(in the mix)

Gone two in the morning and a gang of us were leaving a Megadog gig at the Academy on Oxford Road, Manchester. There was me, and four people from the bookshop where I worked, and some strangers we'd got talking to. Eight of us in all, trying to get a taxi, but none would stop for such a large number, so we all start walking down the road towards the Royal Northern College of Music.

It was a Saturday night and the streets were crowded with people trying to get home. When we get to the college, the taxi rank is buzzing. I think there must have been over a thousand people in the queue. Now I don't know if you've ever seen the taxi rank that they've turned the College of Music into? The taxis leave from the basement, and the queue starts on the roof. From there you have to walk around the outside edges of the building, dropping down layer by layer till you reach the basement level.

I think we're on the second level down, in this long curving snake of people, when I look over the balcony and see my friend Rikki on a lower level. Now Rikki used to live in Manchester, but he moved to London about a year ago and I haven't seen him since then. So I tell the party I'm with that I'm going to go see my friend.

I climb down the side of the building. Eventually I reach him, and we chat for a while. I look over the balcony again, and this time I see Ian, another friend who also moved to London. I haven't seen Ian for at least fifteen years, and he was my best friend way back then. I don't even have his telephone number, so I'm desperate to get down another level to see him. I set off climbing, but somehow climb too far, so that now he's above me, looking down. He throws a paper towel down towards me. It blows around in the wind a bit, but I catch it easily and it's got his number on it. By now I'm worried that I've lost my original party.

The next thing I know, all eight of us are in a taxi, heading for Levenshulme where I live. We're going very fast, way too fast for a taxi ride. And when I look through the window I see we're going through Droylsden, where I was born. This is wrong, because you don't go through Droylsden to get to Levenshulme.

Then it hits me. I'm in a dream!

I tell my party this news, but they all laugh at me, and say that I'm drunk. So I set out to prove it to them. I tell them that there are eight of us in the taxi, when only five are allowed to travel in one. No way would the driver let eight of us in. This doesn't convince them, so I remind them that the College of Music is not a giant taxi rank, and thousands of people don't queue for taxis all at the same time. I tell them that we're going through Droylsden, which is the wrong way home. I tell them that I've just seen two friends I haven't seen for years, both in the taxi queue. Too much of a coincidence. Then I start to hear voices . . .

(for my seventh birthday)

But my friends are still laughing at me. (for my seventh birthday I asked me dad to steal us a bike) So I explain the feeling I'm having, the sudden realization that it's a dream. A very specific feeling, you only get inside a dream. (not any old model mind) You never get that feeling in real life. This finally gets their attention. (Boomerang Mountain 509) Some of them are looking worried, others are getting angry. I think they're starting to realize that it's my dream, and that when I wake up, they'll simply vanish. They don't want to vanish. They're fighting against it. Still hearing these voices . . .

(not any old model mind, Boomerang Mountain 509)

(not any old model mind, Boomerang Mountain 509)

I offer to prove it to them, once and for all. I tell them I'll open the taxi door and step out, even though we're moving at top speed on a very busy road. (steal us a bike, steal us a bike) I tell them that no harm will come to me, because it's only a dream.

(hearing these voices, lost in the mix)

So I open the door. (pixel face boomerang) The road is just a speeding blur. I prepare to put a foot down on the road. As I step out I see a large truck hurtling down towards me.

(Boomerang Mountain 509)

Nonetheless, I do step out, only a little scared . . .

PIXEL FACE

For my seventh birthday I asked my dad to steal us a bike. Not any old model, mind, but the Boomerang Mountain 509. Mustard-cloud finish, all the trimmings. The forty-seven Japanese gears, the bolstered Californian frame, the Great British air tyres. Fractal steering.

'I can't locate that shit,' he says. 'How about a new computer?'

I tell him I've got two already and if he doesn't deliver the bike, I'm telling the cops about him.

'Give Melvin what he wants, you useless twat,' my mam says.

I like my mam, she can swear.

'You get to work,' my dad says to my mam, 'before we all go starving.' Then he turns back to me, saying, 'Steal your own fucking bike, you want some flash. Haven't I taught you good enough?'

Anyway, he gives in to my wishes eventually, with Mam's help, but only to turn up with a lilac-finish, nineteen-geared Wombat 207! Put stabilizers on it, I couldn't be more embarrassed.

'Well say something, you fucker,' says my dad.

'Thanks, Dad,' I say, but thinking really you should get arrested for stealing such shit.

'Happy birthday, Melvin,' says my mam. 'Go on now, you'll be late for school.'

But I had my own wheels now, and the school could go fuck itself. So I ride myself over to the old biscuit factory on Hamlet Road. It was raining like forever and the factory looked great against the sky, like a hollow skull with a thousand broken windows for eyes. My dad had his last real job there, making tons of custard creams and bourbons and digestives. But now that place didn't make crumbs, even.

Anyway, there's this waste ground behind the factory. Where they pulled down the hospital and didn't put up shit to replace it. There used to be a pond there but that got drained and now there's just a hole.

Just a fucking great hole in the ground. Absolutely!

The crew was out there, circling the hole, making a noise and riding down into it like crazy stuff off a vid game.

I hang around the edges for a while, thinking it's now or never and then *whoosh!* Activate burners! Check co-ordinates! Commence manual override! I'm making like *Xterminator 7* meets *Whizz & Chips* in the *House of Krazy Mak Robokat*, down down down! I'm shouting something loud and stupid, I can't quite remember what.

Fucking floating, man! Aye, I bet that's what it was.

Shit, the Hang 5ers think I'm the cops! They scatter like chickens till they realize it's only me. Then they get angry. Dazzle and Spike start laughing at me.

'Pouf bike or what!' says Dazzle. 'What is that? A Wombat 205!'

'207,' I answer, trying to make something of it.

'Looks more like a pram!' says Spike, and Matchstick starts to laugh and twitter along.

Matchstick was a loony. He hardly did nowt but laugh and twitter.

And then the whole crew's laughing except for Flute, who's a girl and Dazz's girlfriend, so she just hangs back, saying nothing. But even Flute has got a better bike than me, so I'm like totally embarrassed.

'What you after?' says Dazzle.

'He's after getting twatted,' says Spike, swinging his dad's hammer.

'I wanna be a Hang 5er, Dazz,' I say. 'I wanna steal some stuff.'

'Let's see that pram go ride!' says Spike, making faces.

Dazzle and Spike live on the same street as me, King Lear Walk in the Shakespeare Estate, five miles out from Namchester. A right dump, Shakespeare is. No big shakes and certainly no spears. Just a slagheap or two, some dirty sparrows and a mangy blackbird. All the streets are named after stories by this William Shakespeare guy. Dazzle taught me that fact, not that he'd ever met this William Shakespeare or anything. He was quite kind to me, Dazzle, when he wasn't hanging five with the crew, and I was always after joining.

'You're too fucking young,' he says now.

'I'm seven today,' I answer.

'You've gotta be eight to join.'

'I've got a bike,' I say.

'Wowee!' says Spike. 'It's the fucking Melvmobile! Wobble on it!'

'Fucking wobble!' says Matchstick. Which is a bit much, coming from him.

'Shall I take him out, Dazz?' says Spike.

'Enough,' says Dazzle. 'Let's do the biz. Hang 5 alive!'

'See ya around,' says Spike, laughing.

'Around and around,' echoes Matchstick. He was seriously in awe of Spike, and all he ever said was just a slight copy of Spike's curses.

The crew pull down their hats, tug up their collars, pull down their hoods, adopt their balaclavas, ride on out of there.

Alone as forever, just the rain and the biscuit factory.

So I ride over to school, figuring I can make some excuses for being late. Of course, I never quite make it. Instead I head for the Caliban Mall. I spend the morning there, eating crisps and watching the free shows in the TV shop. *Krazy Mak Robokat* and *Xterminator 7*. Watching television in a shop window is much better than watching it at home, because the TV shops have like loads of machines all tuned to different stations, whereas my dad only ever has the racing on, or else the porno on cable. Of course, you don't receive the sound in a window, but who the fuck needs to listen to *Whizz & Chips* to get the message?

Anyway, I'm happy just hanging out in the mall, until some woman sits down next to me on the bench, spoiling the pleasure. 'You not in school today, Melv?' says this woman and it's only when I look that I realize it's Jackie Flint sitting next to me, eating a ham and pickle sandwich.

Jackie is Dazzle's older sister, like eighteen years old. She's the white sheep of the Flint family, because she's actually got a job. Not a job like my mam's got a job, down at the bingo hall, I mean a real job. She was working at this techno shop in Caliban Mall, selling videocams and computers and cd-rom players and such.

'The teachers piss me off,' I reply, nonchalant.

'Why's that, then?'

'They don't teach you the real stuff.'

'Fair enough.'

I often thought Dazzle's mam must have shagged someone else to produce Jackie, because she was so brainy. Jackie had a ton of computers and various gadgets, up in her bedroom. It was great, cause she could always break into the latest rom-game to give us shortcuts. She could break any code going.

Anyway we both just sit there, watching the silent TVs for a while. It was Jackie's dinner hour. A security guard comes along and tells me that bikes aren't allowed in the mall. Jackie says it's all right, I'm with her, which makes me smile out loud, and the ape gives in to her straight away. I just knew that he was fancying Jackie something rotten, and why not? So would I if I was old enough.

I'm thinking how easy it would be to nick stuff from the shops in the mall, maybe that would impress Dazzle enough, when Jackie says to me, 'You best go now,' and she turns to kiss the guard, mouth still stuffed with ham and sweet pickle.

I can't understand why she's doing that, but I leave them to it, because what else can I do? It's too late for school now, and what does a day lost add up to? Nothing much, so I ride around town for a bit, just getting the hang of the bike, making the best of a bad wheel job.

I get home at the right time, just like I've been to school, and the next day I turn up at the hole again, but this time I keep away until the Hang 5 crew actually ride out of there. Then I follow behind, keeping my distance just like in the films. They head for the Pitstoppers garage on Macbeth Street. I watch them all getting into position.

Dazzle's the leader. He was old, like nine already. Almost past it. He was itching to get a drug-runner job with the Namchester lads. Out to prove himself worthy. He never did any stealing any more, he just directed the traffic.

A posh car drives into the forecourt, parking behind a dingy red Mini.

Matchstick was the decoy. He was eleven years gone, but going on four. The poor kid was totally out of his mansion, which made a good diversion. Now the loony is wobbling into the forecourt, on-bike and singing a little song.

A posh guy gets out of the posh car, moves over to the pump. He turns to look at Matchstick as he trundles by, howling wild. Good sign.

Flute was acting as the lookout. Eight years old, a real good-looker in a tracksuit and a balaclava. Dazzle liked a girl who could handle a bike, and this was a beauty. She's no doubt got one eye on the securicam, the other on the bloke behind the counter. Hopefully, he's busy dealing with another customer, the one from the red Mini.

I see that somebody is still sitting inside the beat-up Mini, looks like an Indian guy, or a Pakistani, could cause problems. But then he actually gets out of the car, and goes into the shop, maybe to get some cigs or a chocolate bar, but this is the best thing – he's left a window wide open!

Meanwhile, the posh guy at the pump is smiling at Matchstick.

I'm watching all this from above, with my new wheels perched on a slagheap. Well, it used to be a slagheap, till the council grassed it over, called it a theme park. Slagworld. I pull down the hat, tug up the collar, pull down the hood, adopt the balaclava. Actually, this wasn't an official Hang 5er balaclava, but the balaclava that my dad used to wear when he was a young biker thief. I stole it from his bottom drawer.

Flute gives the signal to go, and Spike darts out from behind the garage on his Boomerang 509, supercharged! Spike was the second-in-command, almost nine. He rides over to the posh car, smashes the window with his dad's hammer, reaches in.

The posh guy turns at the sound. No doubt the joker behind the counter turns as well, startled. Maybe even the owner of the Mini car turns around. I'm watching all this from the grass, perched to fly. By which time Matchstick has vanished and Spike is flying away with the posh guy's case, stolen from the car.

Easy meat! and then I'm flying too, scooting after leftovers. Into the forecourt even as the guy is rushing to his car, the securicam is whirring, and the bloke behind the counter is calling the cops. But there I am, sliding up next to the Mini. Window open, I look inside, where a stupid little handbag is just waiting for me. Excellent! The brown guy is running out of the shop now, a young woman with him, but way too slow because I reach in, grab the bag, and then out of there! Fucking great stuff. Flying home!

It took all my knowledge to shake off the Mini, and I was proud of that.

So we all meet up down the hole, and Dazzle lays in straight away, telling me off for being so stupid, for going in so late. I tell him I got summat, didn't I? I got the woman's handbag. What did Spike get? Only a fucking attaché case.

'There's fucking over a hundred quid in here, you twat!' says Spike, throwing the case at me. 'You nearly blew us wide!'

'But I didn't,' I say.

'That's right,' says Flute. 'Nobody got caught. Let's see what the kid got.'

'You fuck off, girlie,' says Spike. 'Like who asked you?'

'Enough,' says Dazzle, opening the handbag, pulling some stuff out of there. Some tampons, a wallet with £15 in it, a beef sandwich in polythene, a computer disk, a photograph of a puppy dog, an A–Z map of Namchester. Nothing much else. Oh yeah, a bird's feather, don't ask me what that's doing in there. Green-and-yellow coloured. But then the eyes light up on Dazzle. He pulls out a piece!

That makes the crew go quiet, let me tell you, even though it was only a tiny, girl-friendly model.

'Jesus bike!' says Spike.

'Is it loaded?' asks Flute.

Click, click. 'Sure is.'

'Jesus mountain bike!' says Matchstick, laughing and twitching.

'What's a lousy handbag carrier doing with a gun?' asks Flute. 'What was she protecting?' But nobody answers.

Dazzle tucks the gun and the wallet into his rucksack and then hands the bag and remaining contents back to me. 'This is yours to keep, Melvin,' he says. And then, 'The Melv is in. But only on a trial basis, OK? We'll give him seven days.'

'Absolutely!' I shout.

'Oh fuck,' says Spike. 'The crew is doomed.'

'Crew super-doomed,' echoes Matchstick.

'He found us a gun, didn't he?' says Flute, and I'm sure there's a little smile between us, but most probably I'm just thinking there should be.

So Dazzle gives us our next job. Hang 5 alive! During which I perform the lookout duties like a trainee Nam United defender. I do OK. Another three jobs after that, then we call it a day. Dazzle gives us our share of the takings. I get the lowest except for Matchstick, who would only spend it on sweets or something. I tell Dazz that the gun must be worth hundreds. He tells me to fuck off, that he's the manager and that he has to sell it first. This is on account, he says.

I get £45 for the trouble. The most I've ever had. And when I get home I give my mam a tenner for the housekeeping. My dad starts to warn me about messing about with kids like Dazzle, but my mam says he's only jealous and way past it.

I like my mam. She's had a hard fucking life bringing me up, and I don't blame her. Also, she's got tattoos. And she said that I could hang around with the gang as long as I didn't neglect the studying too much, which I promised not to do.

Anyway, that's how I got to join the Hang 5 crew.

That night I go up to my bedroom early, in order to examine the handbag. I eat the beef sandwich, throw the tampon and the photo of the puppy and the stupid bird's feather into the waste-paper basket. I look at the computer disk. Maybe it's a game? I slip it into the computer, and this title screen comes up, FLIGHT PATH 5.02 it says, and underneath that, DEMO VERSION. Must be an air-sim with a name like that, and there's no real interface or anything, just these lines of techno stuff. Says it's been programmed by somebody called Celia Hobart. Maybe Hobart was the stupid woman in the Mini car, leaving her window open like that, doesn't she know there's some right bastards around? And I'm thinking this must be a pre-market copy, when what should happen but a PRESS-TO-PLAY icon comes up.

I mouse on over and do the old clickety-click.

The screen lights up with a feather, yeah an animated bird's feather, just like the one I'd thrown away, sparkling with a million greens and yellows. I'm kind of pulled in by the sight, like I'm on drugs or something. I should be so lucky.

But nothing else happens, just this feather floating around the screen, like forever. No matter what keys I press, it just stays there, turning slowly. So I'm thinking I've stolen a bloody screen-saver, when a PASSWORD PLEASE message comes up. Straight off I try the usual suspects that Jackie taught me, GOD, JESUS, SECRET, PASSWORD, MOTHER, FATHER, but none of them work, and after the six bad choices the password window vanishes, like I've used up my options, just leaving the feather, still spinning and there's nothing I can do about it.

I'm thinking that maybe I should send a net message to Dazzle, just to tell him that the disk has got a password, but that would make me look stupid, wouldn't it? Anyway, it makes me feel tired, just watching the feather, like I should lie down and sleep. Before doing so I grab the real feather from the basket and lay it on my pillow, I don't know why, and the smell of it makes me drowsy, and the spinning, spinning on the screen, the spinning, the spinning, and I didn't even know that feathers had a smell . . .

The next day I turn up at the hole, all excited for my second day's adventures, but nobody's there. I'm wondering what's up, like maybe they're avoiding me on purpose. I check out the Pitstoppers garage again, but there's no sign of action there, and I don't know any other places that the Hang 5ers patrol. Instead I ride over to the Caliban Mall, to see if Jackie knows where Dazzle's riding today, and to ask her about the disk I've stolen.

It's hours before her dinnertime, so I head for the shop where she works, which is called YE OLDE COMPUTER SHOPPE. Jeez! The guard from yesterday is hanging around outside, obviously wanting another kiss, so I tell him to mind my bike, cause I haven't got round to nicking a lock for it yet. He wants to argue, but already I'm inside the shop and looking for Jackie.

She doesn't know where her brother is, so I ask her if she'd have a go at cracking a password for me. I take the disk out of my bumbag, but not the feather, yeah I've brought that along as well, don't ask me why. It's quiet just then, so Jackie slots the disk into one of the shop's best computers. The title screen comes up, and then the pixel feather, but nothing else. 'Where's the password window?' Jackie asks.

'It vanished. I tried six words, and then it vanished.'

'Right. It knows you're not the owner. I'll take it home, have a look.'

'Thanks.'

Just then there's some kind of commotion going on outside, and who should come in but Dazzle himself, followed by the stupid guard, who's looking pissed off about something, maybe the fact that Dazzle has actually ridden his bike into the shop! Wish I'd thought of that. He rides his bike all round the displays, laughing like he's on something wicked, obviously thinking to cause his sister some trouble, it was like that between them sometimes, and the guard is jogging along trying to keep up, but not doing very well.

Jackie is shouting at him to get out, and that brings the manager out from his office, and then they're all making some noise, Jackie, the guard and the manager. I'm the only one that's keeping quiet, mainly because I can see that Dazzle's not got his balaclava on, which is strange, but maybe he's not up to big trouble today, just messing about. Maybe that's why he didn't wait for me, the job wasn't big enough for it. Aye, that must be it.

But then there's more noise, from outside this time, and Dazzle does an absolute spin-turn, glides past the guard easy, and then gone, through the door and racing!

I'm outside in a second, because what the hell is happening?

Dazzle is speeding across the mall, and I get on my bike to follow but the Wombat 207 is no match for the Boomerang 509. Then I see the trouble. There's a raid going on, over past the dried-up fountain. Alarms are doing the noise thing, and there goes Flute racing for the nearest exit, and Matchstick more or less going round in circles, and then Spike careening out of a music shop carrying some booty, looked like a handful of promo T-shirts. They were all masked up as per regulations but Dazzle wasn't. I could see he was pissed off at the raid. Spike must have gone in on a whim, which Dazzle always hated, just like I'd done yesterday. At least I'd got away with it, because a trio of security guards were chasing Spike and Jackie's boyfriend wasn't far behind. Spike made a nice move, managed to find a gap, sped off after Flute. Matchstick wasn't so fast. He'd fallen off his bike somehow. Dazzle had reached him, and was trying to help him up when the guards moved in on them.

Dazzle did something then, let me tell you. He pulled out the gun, the one that I'd stolen, forgotten all about, but I was proud of that, very proud, especially when he aimed it at the nearest guard and started shouting wild things, top-shelf abuse.

Abso-fucking-lutely!

The guards backed off, and so did I, because it was suddenly too deep for me and too crazy. I hid behind the fountain, watching from there, and Jackie came up beside me, cursing at her brother for being so stupid. Dazzle had managed to get Matchstick back on his bike and the kid was racing out of there, under cover of the gun. Dazzle was all set to follow when we heard the copcars wailing and it was time to make with the quick exit, *Whizz & Chips* on a sesame bun style!

I didn't know where to go, but school was out and so was home, so I went down the hole and sure enough Flute and Spike and Matchstick were there, all screaming at each other, well Flute and Spike were, Matchstick was just lying in a folded heap, crying his eyes out. 'They've got Dazz!' he was saying, over and over. 'They've got Dazz! Cops got Dazz!'

Mad times.

I went up slow as I could, but Spike turned on me straight away, calling me a coward for keeping back, yeah, he'd seen me hiding behind the fountain. I guess he was just trying to shove the blame on to me, that's OK, I can see the need. Flute tried to stick up for me, but I know when I'm not wanted, I went riding, riding, riding. Riding just anywhere until I found some rain to cycle through and that felt good, hood down and getting my hair wet.

That evening, after I got home, I kept quiet about what had happened, because I didn't want my mam finding out I'd been so scared. I spent some time in my room, pretending to do some homework, but really just staring at that stupid feather for ages, like I could fall into the colours and maybe fly a million miles away.

I came down for my tea, and the tele was on as always, my dad waiting for the sports news. Then everything went crazy because it was like I was back in the mall and having to watch the trouble over and over for ever. It was just a news item about the trouble, but that's what it felt like anyway. It was all there, captured on an overhead securicam, Spike racing out of the shop and Flute racing off and Matchstick falling off his bike and Dazzle pulling the gun on the guards. The camera didn't reach behind the fountain, so I wasn't on film. Damn it, would've liked to have been. There was some tight-faced reporter going on about youth crime and that was pretty good, but the best thing of all is what they'd done to Dazzle's face. There he was being dragged off by the cops and his face had been hidden behind these special effects. OK, Dazz was captured but it didn't matter now because he was famous. Famous for being an expert biker and a fucking great captain, but most of all famous for having been pixellated. Video masked! Like covered up in these computerized little coloured squares to protect his identity.

Ultimate for ever, or what?

Dazzle's mam and dad were ever so proud to have their son on the tele, and with a pixel face at that. That night they invited all the street round to view a video recording of the broadcast. It was a real nice party. My own mam and dad were there, and so were Flute and Spike and Matchstick. Even Jackie's boy-friend, that fat guard from the mall, even he was there believe it or not, beaming at his own television appearance. Jackie was roaming around the party, filming the splendid occasion on her latest digital videocam. 'Always at my back I hear,' she says, 'time's winged security guard drawing near.' I tell her to take that stinking cam out of my face. I was still angry at not being on the tele, I guess. I'm thinking that more than anything I would love to have a pixel face just like Dazzle's: that would make me a real Hang 5er beyond all measure! Jackie says to her mam that she could maybe unpixellate Dazzle, given the tech-nology she could maybe steal from the shop. Of course, the parents refused. They liked their boy being hidden, I guess, although they did complain that he really should have worn his balaclava, as was passed down from his dear old imprisoned uncle. Nobody seemed bothered that Dazzle had been arrested, it was all a part of the family tradition.

Later on, after the booze is nearly gone, Jackie gives me back the flight path disk, saying it was too dangerous to keep in the house because it's got a homing device on it. I ask her what she means and she tells me that using up six guesses at the password had activated a signal to go through the net channels, so that the owners would soon know exactly where it was. 'It's an Exocet soft,' she said. 'And your computer's the target. I managed to hide my address just in time.'

'Can't you hide mine? Can't you?'

'Too late, Melv. They're on to you.'

I think she was just trying to scare me, because she was as drunk as I was, but then my dad says that somebody did call round this afternoon, asking for any kids in the house.

'What?' I'm trying my best not to show how frightened I am.

'Don't worry,' my dad says, 'I told them to get stuffed.'

'Them?'

'Yeah. A woman, and some Paki bloke.'

My dad's laughing at me and I think everybody is by then, the whole party, even my mam. So on the way home, riding through the rain, I drop the disk down a grid. Maybe that was real stupid of me, I don't know, but all the time I was expecting a beat-up red Mini to pull out of a side street. And when I got home, the first thing I did was erase the copy of Flight Path 5.02 from my hard drive.

I went to sleep after hours of just lying there, staring at the real feather, which sparkled even in the dark, and I had a great dream. I was riding through the mall, mask off, posing for the securicam, full tilt to rescue not only Matchstick from the guards but Dazzle as well, who made me his new assistant the next day down the hole. Flute gave me a kiss, Matchstick was copying my words, and Spike was happy to follow me. He even swapped bikes with me!

I wake up early, stick the feather in my bumbag, like I can't leave it alone.

Of course when I got to the hole, there was just Matchstick waiting there, sitting beside his bike. 'Where's Spike and Flute?' I asked.

'Don't know,' he replied. 'I'm waiting for Dazzle.'

I noticed then that Dazzle's bike lay under Matchstick's. 'Dazzle ain't coming today,' I said.

'Not coming? No. He always comes. Look, I got his bike. Went back for it after the cops took him. Did I do good, Melvin?'

'You did brilliant, Stick.'

'Dazzle can't get arrested. He wouldn't let that happen. Dazzle will be here soon. Will you wait with me?'

'Matchstick, I can't. I'm going to school.'

'School?'

'Yeah. Why don't you come with me.'

But he wouldn't, so I left the poor kid just sitting there, what else could I do? But when I got to the top of the rise, I see this beat-up red Mini driving over the waste ground towards me. I'm about to hit top gear except I suddenly can't. It's like the force has gone out of me, like happened to Krazy Mac Robokat in that episode with the giant Twister Wipe snake. I'm just sitting there astride my bike, waiting for the car to come get me. I guess I wanted to get it finished, because what else could go wrong?

Anyway, the Mini stops and I can see the woman in the passenger seat and the Pakistani guy beside her. It's him that gets out of the car, the woman just stays there like she's the big boss or something, like she's Dazzle to Spike's action.

As the man's walking towards me I hear Matchstick coming up close behind. 'Who's this, Melv?' he asks. I tell him not to be scared, get back down the hole, get on his bike. But he doesn't, he just stands there waiting.

'Where is it?'

It's the man talking. I shake my head, wipe some sweat away.

'Come on.'

'Threw it away,' I reply.

'Best not have.'

'Yeah. It's down a grid.'

Now he's angry, takes a step forward. Matchstick is gone suddenly, don't know where. It's just me and the man, and his face is right up in front of mine with his hands holding the handlebars tight, I think he's going to throw me off.

'Down a grid!' I shout. 'And I wiped it from my hard drive.'

'Not the disk, kid. The feather.'

'The feather?'

'Come here! Where's the feather?'

Now he's grabbed me by the shoulders and I'm thinking what's all this about, some stupid bit off a dead bird? So I'm shouting for him to get off and leave me alone, the same time trying to get me and the bike out from under him until he throws the both of us, that's me and bike, aside. I land with the bike half on top of me and when I get up I bring the bike with me, the whole thing in two hands, just pick it up and throw it at him.

Yes!

Hits him square.

He nearly falls. I think he will, but he doesn't. He grabs my bike, smashes it down. I can see already that the front wheel is buckled, so I'm just standing there, facing him off just like the movies. He's standing there as well, I think I've impressed him a little because he starts smiling at me. 'How about we make a deal, kid?' He's taken out his wallet, and he's waving some notes around. 'Twenty quid,' he says.

'Twenty quid? I can nick that in two minutes.'

'Fifty?'

'Fifty? Just for the feather?'

He nods, and I nod back. He wants the feather, but I want the money first. He gives it to me, and I'm thinking maybe I should just run now. But instead I unzip my bumbag and take out the feather. The woman has got out of the car, she's waiting for me to hand it over. I can see now she's only young, maybe only twice my age. 'It's OK, Celia,' he says back at her, and I suppose it is because I hand over the feather.

'What is it?' I ask.

'Beautiful, isn't it?' he says.

'Yes. It's the most beautiful thing I've ever seen.'

He laughs at that, as well he might, cause there ain't much beauty in my life to compare it to. 'Did you use it?' he asks.

'Use it?'

'Did you dream with it?'

'What?'

'Never mind. I hope it was a good one. For your sake.'

Then he's gone, back into the car, the woman beside him. I watch the red Mini till it disappears, then have a look at my bike. Busted. Matchstick has vanished, but Dazzle's bike is waiting for me down in the hole. Why not? Dazzle won't be needing it now, not for a while anyway. I'll keep it warm for him.

I think about school for a bit, I really do. I even start to ride over there, but the feel of a Boomerang 509 under me with the seat set high and the weight of the wheels is too much to resist. I spend the day in a wild spree, doing wheelies and flips, which come easy with the good bike, and checking out some possible victims for a little snatch and chase of me own.

I get home late and get my mam mad by telling her I

haven't been in to school. I tell her tomorrow definitely I'll start keeping my promises. My dad wants to know where I got the flash bike but I tell him to piss off down the pub where he belongs. My mam then says that the cops have let Dazzle out, and that something's happened, she's not sure what. So I ride over to Dazzle's house, already pissed off that I have to give up the good bike so soon and why had I left mine down the hole so easily? But when I get there all that falls away because all the gang's in, watching the tele, Dazzle and Jackie and Spike and Flute and Matchstick too. They're all bunched up round the tele, like it's the World Cup final and England are winning with ten seconds to go or something. But they go quiet when I walk in. I ask what's up, but all they do is make way for me like I'm some kind of hero or something. They sit me down in front of the tele, and it's Dazzle who gives up his seat for me. He uses the remote to restart the vid, the one showing his glorious arrest. I'm wondering why I have to sit through this again, but then I see it's not the same programme, this one was broadcast earlier this evening, some kind of follow-up report no doubt. 'Melvin, you are the bomb!' says Dazzle, and before I can ask, the reporter has finished speaking I don't know what and the security film from the mall starts rolling.

There's Dazzle on the screen just before the cops come get him, then the camera closes in on his lovely pixellated face till it's filling the screen. Then the pixels start to pop one by one like bubbles and it's not his face underneath them, it's my face!

I look around at Dazzle, who's smiling, and at the others and nobody's saying anything especially not me until Flute asks, 'How the fuck did you do that, Melv?'

I look at Jackie, thinking she's behind it with her hi-tech wizardry but she just looks at me smiling and says, 'Not me,

Melv. This is from the cop station, and the copy at the mall is the same, I checked.'

'The cops don't know what to do, Pixel!' shouts Spike, ruffling my hair.

'Cops don't know nothing about Pixel Face!' pipes up Matchstick, then they're all hugging me and slapping my back like I'm a hero, and you know what? I am a hero, I am a fucking hero!

Anyway that's how it happened, I swear. That's how I got my new name, and that's how Dazzle donated me his Boomerang 509 like for ever and that's how I became a full-time member of the Hang 5ers, except that now we're called the Pixelkids. And I don't care if you cops don't believe me because that's what happened and I can't explain it and I don't even want to.

STIGMATICA

Flute wasn't your usual low-level partaker, no cheap and greedy half-incher she. Sure, she could turn on the hard-luck fairytale bollocks when cop-cornered, how she'd been a test-tube baby for instance, and had never known a good home that wasn't made of glass, so was it any wonder she was always throwing stones? Never known no father, except for some wayward fridge specimen. Her mum was *nouveau* lesbian with hetero latents, and posh with it, well able to afford the very best in frozen goods, so there must have been a mix-up at the Spurm-U-Want, don't you think? Must have been some nasty in there, how else explain her criminal tendencies?

These were the kinds of tales that Flute could tell with her mouth closed, and the look in her eyes said you better believe it, baby, or else you'll get this here in your gob, comprendez? Yes, we see.

She'd tried to go straight a few times, just to prove how good at heart she was, once when eight, once when nine, one final time at the age of eleven. But then she'd come on, and nicked her very first pack of tampons, which kinda sealed the life of her, stained her pocketbook, so to speak. A dark streak of blood, set loose.

The next day she ran away and by the age of fourteen she was known all over as the best of her kind. All the estate boys, both good and bad, were happy to hang around. No deal. Flute was saving herself for Dazzle, some crazy kid. Some crazy kid on holiday, enjoying His Majesty's Youth Adventure Camp, and hoping to get out in a month or so for good behaviour. Until then, Flute would keep the faith, steal the day, thieve the night, purloin the moon. Whatever it took, she took. Without consent.

Always one step ahead of the cops, always on the next but one adventure of a life gone bad.

One time – July this was, last year – Flute stole a camera off a woman in a café. It wasn't much of a steal, skills-wise, because the woman was mostly to blame, just leaving her bag like that, unattended, and too busy stuffing her face to notice.

Back in the hiding place, Flute did the once over. Slim pickings really, and not much of a thing to look at; small but snazzy in its add-ons, and worth a minute's work, I suppose. Some film inside it. There was a little light on one side, which glowed yellow. Just for a laugh, Flute pointed the camera at the burned-out biscuit factory in the distance, waited for auto-focus, released the shutter.

Click!

That simple.

She panicked some then, with this mad fantasy that a cop would work out her hiding place from the exact angles of the shot taken. So she ripped the film out, exposed it. Didn't even notice, so busy with the paranoia, that the light on the side was now a deep, pulsing red.

The next day was market day, so Flute was visiting Crabtree, with a stockpile of items she'd been building up in the last week or so. Crabtree was a discerning bastard for someone so far down the feeding scale; he was only interested in prime items, stuff he could sell within a day or two. Flute wished she could get hold of his contacts, maybe get into the fencing business herself one day. Oh, she was a girl with ambition, no doubt about that. So, he took the videocam gladly, and the mountain bike; the motherboard and chips would be difficult, because they were slow as fuck since last month's update, but Flute accepted a knockdown for them. They did the business, and the last thing on the table was the snazzy camera.

Flute wasn't expecting much, enough to bump the margin up to the next level, that was all.

Crabtree wouldn't touch it.

I mean, he literally wouldn't touch it, backing away from the table like the thing was on fire. Flute asked him what was wrong. He wouldn't say, he just pointed out the little flashing red light, told her to get the fuck out of his place of work.

That night, Flute was feeling pretty pissed off, and she didn't know why. The rest of the stuff she unloaded to further fences, even further down the line. None would touch the camera; none would say why.

She woke up in the middle of a bad dream, covered in a sweat. Was she coming down with the fever? Stumbling to the bathroom for a drink of water, her eyes in the mirror, blood-shot. Her hands shaking to turn on the taps, to wet her face.

With a gasp she stepped back from the sink, out of its halo of light.

And then forwards again, first one hand, then the other, both hands back into the light as though disembodied. The hands of a ghost, pale and spectral. And on each wrist a stain of red, a small stain.

She woke, thinking it just a dream. Brought her hands up, from under the covers.

The stain had spread.

Washed and washed, she did, but the stain remained, covering her wrists now and creeping down to her palms, and on the back of the hand also, creeping down. Washed and scrubbed, and scrubbed and washed.

The stain crept on.

She wore gloves that day, and for the rest of the week, and not just to keep her fingerprints to herself. She thought a little about seeing a doctor, but Flute didn't have one, and never would, most probably. A doctor was authority, a kind of cop in a way, a body cop. It wasn't her fashion. Instead, she went back to visit Crabtree. It was market day come round once more, but this time no loot for sale, only an answer desired.

She took off the gloves, one after the other, peeling them slow to reduce the pain. And when she held up her hands, for Crabtree to see, he took in a long sharp breath. For the whole of her hands, both hands, wrists to fingertips, were burning a bright scarlet red.

Crabtree told her to keep her distance, not even to think about touching him, or any of his property.

'What is it?' she asked, with the fear in her voice.

'Don't know how it works, not yet. We're working on it.'

'But what can I do?'

'Should've noticed that little yellow light. Didn't you notice that little yellow light?'

'I saw it.'

'Should've known what it was. Don't you keep up?'

'Ain't got time for keeping up. What can I do, please?'

'You got to give yourself up.'

'No!'

'Only way. That's how it works. And they can fix it to anything these days. The owner has a code for it, but no-one else does, and you must've used that camera.'

'Just the once. Just the one little picture.'

'That's it, then. You're infected. Keep back! I said, keep away from me!'

'Please, it's not catching, is it?'

'Don't know. Just keep away from me.'

'There's got to be something . . . something you can do.'

'Only the cops can cure you now. Got to give yourself up.'

So Flute put her gloves back on, and already the redness could be seen stretching up, from the cuffs of the gloves, and creeping up her arms.

But she wouldn't give herself up.

That night she smashed the camera into pieces, and a thin trickle of liquid came from it, from behind the red light, as though from a gland.

Summer came to the estate, and the local boys, the bad and the good, were most disappointed to see that the famous Flute was all dressed up this year, none of the revealing tops of last year. What was wrong with her, usually so proud of her midriff with its cute and pierced button? And worse than that, the fact that she wasn't stealing any more. What was the use of a girl that didn't steal?

But she wouldn't give herself up, not to the cops, not to a doctor, not to anybody in command.

If anybody saw her at all, she was in the shadows, the darkness, never in the daytime. And even then, dressed up to the collar tight, even in the height of summer, and sweating.

But she wouldn't give herself up.

The next time the boys saw her she wore a hat pulled right down, and sunglasses, and a scarf tugged right up. And the make-up was thick on her nose and cheekbones. By then of course they had all heard of the curse. So they were no longer interested and they kept away, which made her glad, for she was far better alone.

And then it was time for Dazzle to be released. There was much gossip on the streets about what he'd think of this new-fashion Flute, wrapped up to the tens, and with the all-over tan. And much laughter – boy laughter, girl laughter – because Dazzle was known for his love, and let's see him love her now, eh?

There wasn't much stealing going on any more, not by anybody, not since the redhanded curse came into play, because how could you trust a videocam or a stereo system or a portable computer any more? They might turn against you, and bite you, and that would be that.

Only Dazzle kept up the stealing, more than ever he did before going off to camp, and nobody could work out why: what game was he playing?

One time he stole a portable with the accessory he was looking for, the little yellow light on the side.

He switched on the computer, wrote a brief love letter on it.

The light on the side turned red – a pulsing, flashing red.

And later that week, what a sight that was; Dazzle and Flute just like in the old days, walking out proud as you like, stripped for action, and both of them showing off with glee the colour of themselves, the colour of their arms and bellies and faces and hair even, the great scarlet spectacle of themselves.

And the boys and the girls, both, could only look on in amazement, and wish themselves so proud of their calling.

Six months later, the Stigmatica Anti-theft System was taken off the market.

AUTOPSY OF A HUMMINGBIRD

.1 *Discovery.* The body was found in a disused, overgrown garden centre in Cheshire, some few miles from Manchester Airport. According to the investigating officer's report, there appeared to be no visible wounds or bruises of any kind on the body, which was that of a young white female. She was fully clothed. From various documents found in a handbag (discovered with the body) police have named the woman as Georgina Finch. A certain amount of money (in loose notes) was also found, a substantial amount. Spermicidal jelly was found in the vagina, which also bore signs of recent congress. No evidence of sexual molestation was indicated, implying that the congress had been consensual. No sperm was found, indicating that a condom was used. The woman's handbag contained a packet of six condoms, from which one was missing. It is thought that the woman died during, or just after, having sex. Police are still searching for the condom used during this last act.

1.2 *Background*.   Georgina Finch was a known prostitute. Operating from a hotel adjacent to Manchester Airport, she was a specialist in the needs of recently arrived foreign businessmen and diplomats. Her street name was Gina, although of course she had long ago left the 'street' behind. For the last year she had been working the lucrative airport circuit. Interviews with her friends and colleagues have revealed a fiery temperament and a bright, articulate perspective on her course in life. Gina was a realist, albeit a time-hardened one. Interviews with her 'business partner', one Tony Malone, are still being conducted. He is adamant that Gina was no longer his 'property' at the time of her death, having had an argument with her over money some five weeks previous. This was not the first time she had tried to cheat him. He knew of no other 'pimp' that had taken his place in her business affairs.

1.3 *Question*.   Why did Gina take her latest (and last) customer to the abandoned garden centre? She worked the hotel bar, and always the customer paid for the room, usually one of the finer rooms. Was this change of scene at the special request of the customer? Perhaps he was known at the hotel, by colleagues for instance. Or did he wish to take her to this dark, tangled garden for a more sinister purpose?

2.1 *Oddity*.   The pathologist, upon commencing his investigation of the body, noted a long, recently stitched scar that stretched across the woman's stomach. Upon closer investigation he was alarmed to hear a quiet, low-level humming noise emanating from inside the woman's abdomen.

2.2 *Findings*.   Upon cutting open the body, a small 'machine' was found in the stomach. This egg-shaped apparatus was attached to the stomach wall, and to various other internal organs, by a series of wires and ducts. There were no discernible markings on the egg, apart from a small green light. And, despite the death of the woman, the machine was still operating; the light was flashing, and the strange humming noise was even louder now the stomach had been opened. Curious about this finding, and having seen nothing like it before, the pathologist notified the investigating officer.

2.3 *Movement of body*. It was decided that the apparatus should remain attached to the body until such a time as its purpose could be discovered. To this end a female scientist from the University of Manchester was called in. She demanded the body and its strange cargo be moved immediately to the university for further study.

3.1 *Suspect*. Meanwhile, Gina's last customer had walked into a local police station. He had seen the death reported on television (although all details of the machine were, of course, held back) and had decided it was best to come forward voluntarily. Although four days had elapsed, he was still shaken by the events he had witnessed. According to his testimony, he had arrived in England on business from New York, and, exhausted from his flight, had decided to stay overnight in the airport hotel. Here, as can often result from extreme tiredness, he had found himself in thrall to an urgent desire. He chatted to Gina in the bar, some money exchanged hands, they went up to his room. The act was accomplished.

Under extensive questioning, the suspect broke down. He admitted to forcing the young prostitute into certain acts she had not fully appreciated, at least not at the prices he could afford. He had pressed ahead anyway. During these unspecified acts he had received a shock, an electrical shock of some kind, that had caused him intense, if momentary, pain. He claimed that the shock had come from the prostitute's body itself. He had immediately leaped from the bed. His outraged demands to have his money returned met only with laughter, and when he had struggled with her, again the shock had burned through his body. He claimed that the woman had left his room then, a claim later substantiated by a night cleaner who had been working in the corridor at the specified time. The cleaner could not fail to remember the woman's smile.

3.2 *Motive*.   A colleague of the deceased met up with her in the bar after the incident described above. This source has confirmed certain details of the customer's story, as related to her by the deceased. A possible motive was supplied, when Miss Finch confided that she was thinking of getting out of the business soon, and to this end was appropriating more than her fair share of the proceeds. The friend had warned her of the dangers of cheating on a pimp. The friend did not know the name of Gina's new pimp.

3.3 *Witness*.   Miss Finch was next seen one hour later, running down the service road away from the hotel. The witness who saw this was drunk; still, his claim that the deceased was heading, in a panic, towards the deserted garden centre certainly fits in with the known facts. The witness added that, although the woman was quite alone, she had the look of someone being chased. This is the last time the deceased was seen alive.

4.1 *Lab tests*.   Experts at the University of Manchester carried out extensive research on the strange egg-shaped apparatus found inside the woman's body. X-rays were taken, but only when the machine stopped functioning (the green light went out; the humming noise stopped) was the egg actually removed from the stomach. A simple mechanism allowed it to swing open, into two half-shells. Inside were found a primitive motherboard and chip, various regulating devices (including the 'shock' device mentioned earlier), a battery (obviously a back-up in case the body died), a complex organic 'soup', and a removable recording device. This last, when played back, revealed details of all Georgina's sexual acts, or transactions, during the previous five weeks, including details of the cost of each, the amount credited, along with any 'shortfall'.

4.2 *Cause of death*.   It was determined that Georgina Finch died of a massive electrical shock. The police are treating it as murder.

5.1 *Addendum*.   Further to the above report, police inquiries have finally uncovered the makers of the device. They are now under arrest, awaiting further investigation. The device is marketed as the Proactive Internal Master and Protector ('Pimp', for short). It is recommended that all details of it be kept from the general public. The makers have admitted that twelve such devices have been sold already, including four 'male' models. We must do all we can to track them down.

FROM THE
BOOK OF NYMPHOMATION

The following document (recently donated to the Museum of Fragments) was found in the ruins of Manchester. As with all our exhibits, it raises more questions than it answers. Several attempts have been made at completing the two extant pages; we prefer it as it stands. A faint glimpse of a long-lost world. Date: unknown. Please note: The museum advises that the fragment contains information of an adult nature. View at own risk.

(text begins)

A-LIFE   *n.* abbreviation of artifaecial life; the process by which sinformation is evolved until it simulates, and is no longer distinguishable from real life; any product of this process.

AMOUR   *n.* human love for a fellow creature or machine.

ANAL-YSIS   *n.* sinformation taken via the anus.

A.N.U.S.   *n.* abbreviation of Auxiliary Nurturing System. Aurafice common to both male and female machines (and therefore seen as superior to gender-specific models) used for the introduction of artifaecial information to the body. Compare Vaginode.

APHRODATA   *n.* the female goddess input into nymphomation; also known as Intra-Venus. Lover of Zuice.

ARTIFAECIAL   *a.* not originating in real life; an imitation of life.

ATTRACTION   *n.* the measure of how much beauty a sinput possesses. Measured in attractons.

ATTRACTON   *n.* the unit by which attraction is measured. One attracton is equal to pure blandness, ten attractons equals pure beauty.

AURAFICE   *n.* an orifice in the body specially designed for the taking of nymphomation.

AUTOGEN   *n.* product of hatch technology.

BABY   *n.* the outcome of unprotected sex between a human male and a female.

BABY-DATA   *n.* the outcome of unprotected sex between a mail sinput and a femail in a nymphomatic system.

BASTADATA   *n.* an illegal offspring of two sinputs which are not properly married in nymphomation.

BEAUTY   *n.* the amount of attraction installed in a sinput in order to facilitate nymphomation. Compare with Ugliness.

BIO-PLASTIC   *n.* the material from which biorgs are made.

BIORG   *n.* a loving combination of flesh and machine.

BIORGASM   *n.* what happens to a biorg when nymphomation takes hold.

BIORGY *n.* what biorgs get up to when too much nymphomation is introduced to their systems.

BLOW JOB *n.* (*sl*) another name for cunnilogo or fellatio.

BLOW-UP DOLL *n.* an early attempt at an artifaecial doll, which allowed humans to have sex with inanimate matter.

BORBI DOLL *n.* the most sophisicated doll of the early twenty-first century. The girlfriend of RoboKen with whom she produced the baby-data called Borble.

BORBLE *n.* the first true child of the nymphomation. The child as product, where the product is the future.

(text ends)

SOMEWHERE THE SHADOW

In the bathroom, combing some grease in the hair, suddenly this blue shiver lit through me. Pointed little fingernail scratchings, back of the neck, tingles. From the street below, the noise of the crowd; gathering laughter, making blaze. And there's me with the deep skull rendezvous. Feeling so up for it so suddenly, I was in two minds to maybe, yeah, go answer the call, go fetch Dugg, tell him to bring the dark along. A shadow in the mirror, lingering smile, just behind and ten miles away. A hint of pheromone, a taste of sugar. If you can't get laid on the last night of the year, well when can you?

Trouble lies along that way, which is why. Last time I'd let him out, Dugg had gone a little wild on me, despite the promises. I was scared of him doing wrong, ruining it for both of us. He could sleep this time.

I shake off the feeling, turn around; the shadow turns with me, and then it's gone.

Vanished.

When I get to the club, of course everyone's twice-ways drunk and half-past wild already, with five hours still to go till midnight's global kiss. I was used to being the loner by now, well practised at getting off on other people's getting off, but the fever of the countdown caught me unawares and strung out. The madness was on sale and the dancers were circling each other, male and female, like animals. I could taste the sex in the air, like a blind dog can feel the moon rise. I just couldn't connect to it. I did the dance, drank the booze, even talked to a girl or two, tried to forget the incident in the bathroom. Then the cops came to get me, scouring the crowd.

Ten minutes later I was being driven towards Old Trafford, where the Monastery is, which is the street name for the sex-offenders' prisonship. Along the wet streets, people were dancing, which just made me bite down harder. The chief cop, a woman called Kinsey, had simply told me that my shadow had escaped. Then she'd shut up, left me alone in the fear, because Dugg was a peaceful little pervert usually, and nobody, as far as I knew, had ever escaped from the Monastery before.

My questions to Kinsey brought no response, not until we actually came within sight of the prison. I wanted to know how Dugg had managed it.

'You give it a name?' was all she said, and the way she said it made me ache with shame, because I know the normals just don't understand.

The Monastery ship was looming large across the river, with all its lights misted by the downpour, and a wailing from the sirens. This vast floating bulk of caged life. And as we drove over the road bridge to the other side . . .

Towards the other side . . .

Always, traversing this bridge in happier times, I had sensed the meaning of those words, and welcomed it. Now I was dreading the passage. Again I pressed the cop woman for details. 'At least tell me when he escaped,' I asked.

'Is the time important?' Kinsey replied. 'Did you feel something?'

I nodded.

Then she told me the time of his escape, and of course it was 6.35, right when I was greasing the hair, and the feel had sizzled me.

It's strange, but you always know when the darkness is feeling lonely. I might be down in London on business for instance, no matter, I can feel it. In boardrooms and offices, on trains or in taxis, wherever I am; when Dugg wants to fuck, somehow it gets through to me. It's not like I get a sudden erection or anything crude like that, because that's impossible without Dugg being there; more a feeling of being needed, deep down, like I said, in the skull. The shiver, the tingle, whatever.

'But how?' I asked. 'I mean, it's not possible, is it?'

Kinsey turned away as the car swung into the dockyard, where a frazzled guard checked our IDs. On the wall beside him someone had sprayed the words GNOMES GO HOME. Around the gateway a bunch of applicants were waiting, desolate and soaked through. The prison must've called off all hand-overs, because this sorry crowd was shouting at the guards to let them inside.

No deal.

But we went through easy, and as the car pulled to a halt, already I was feeling the guilt come over me; if only I'd let Dugg out. If only. He was allowed out five days a year and I'd only used up four of them. He was due another, and with the year coming to a halt, he must've been terribly desperate.

But escape? How could he do that? He'd been well behaved on all previous leave-days, following the rules, well except for the last one, but that was a blip perversion, nothing serious. A few more months, he was due out for good, and I know how much he's been looking forward to his freedom. Believe me, I know.

What could have made him so crazy?

In 1999 I was classified as a Class E sexual pervert, which is the weakest kind, no trouble if properly controlled. Well there you go, because one day I let the thing inside get out of hand. It wasn't a serious incident, and nobody got hurt, at least no-one except myself, and that's what I'd paid for anyway. But the act got reported by some professional voyeur, and the next thing I was dragged before a judge, who ordered the pain inside me removed.

Digital castration. Either that, or go to prison myself, which I doubt I would've survived. Not with my desires.

It was a four-year separation.

You think, straight after the operation, that you'll never get over the loneliness, because the shadow of your desire haunts you like a ghost-itch. Then, slowly, you come to terms with it, actually start to enjoy the freedom, in a way. Life turns easier, without the other person raising their snake inside you.

Stuff like that, because you start to see your lost sexuality as a separate being eventually; another, darker reason to live.

And then, sometimes, usually when the night is darkest, you get the tingle again. Being a Class E, I got the five days of freedom, and that's a way to scratch the need. But you have to ration it carefully, make sure it's a good need, not just a whisper. And of course you have to control it, once it's out, just use it for the normal stuff, the boring stuff, which they say is better than nothing. Yeah, sure it is.

But you live with it, you know. You live with it. And Dugg was good, I really thought he'd been changed by the life in exile.

Made clean.

But now . . .

Maybe it's true, what they say about prison just making you worse.

We sailed out to the Monastery aboard a rickety launch, and I was drenched to the hollow, still in my party clothes. On previous visits the ship had seemed a quite civilized place, more like a laboratory than a prison, with the guards wearing nice suits, and perfumed breath, with a gentle calming music being constantly played. All that had now been stripped away, like a flimsy skin. I was led down a long corridor past the old cell doors. From behind which came a fearsome noise, as of so many trapped animals. What I had taken earlier to be emergency sirens was mostly this caged and hungry growling.

What does the human sex look like, the nastier kind anyway, once released from the body's containment? Artists' impressions, based on 'genuine eyewitness reports', showed either a lump of misshapen flesh, as though ripped from the guts, or else a paler, more spectral version of the original sinner, a sort of waking dream or ghost figure.

One famous photograph showed a hideous, malformed monster, small and hunched, with a fixed evil grin. The image was dark and badly processed, the kind of thing you can find a thousand shapes within, whatever your mind desires to see, fitfully. From this photograph came the popular name for the sexual miscreants.

The twisting of pheromones: Pheronomes.

I suppose there was a gnome-like figure vaguely squatting there, but for myself I have always seen the interior as the fleeting, following shadow. The authorities, for their part, maintain that the sexual knowledge is merely that: *knowledge*. Pure information; a batch of digital biology imprisoned on a computer's hard disk. If this be so, then what strange creatures made the hideous noise coming from all the cells?

Kinsey and her partner more or less shoved me into the transfer room. There was another man in there, an older guy. I remembered his face from my day of separation. The prison governor. 'Well,' he began, 'this is a sorry way . . .'

Somewhere or other, I was wondering what this 'way' was, and where it was leading.

'. . . to celebrate the New Year.'

Right. I made an effort to keep myself glued together. There was a chair. I sat down. Put my hands on the table. To steady them. Asked for a cigarette. Got ignored. People talking over me. Around me. The table was wedged up against the wall. In front of me, set into the wall, the apparatus of transfer . . .

How many times had I sat at this same table, waiting patiently, excitedly, for Dugg to be transferred back into my body. Hardly thinking of it, my hands were now caressing the various switches and buttons that glinted there, almost willing the computer's screen to come to nascent life. To wake from this dream and find Dugg still living, in the lines of numbers and symbols that constituted his collected presence.

It was not to be. Usually, upon coming aboard I would feel his desire growing; the closer we were, the stronger the bond. But now the ship felt quite empty, devoid of that exquisite tension. My shadow had drifted.

Somebody was talking. The name Breakheart was

mentioned, which stirred a dark memory, and then another voice: 'That poor, poor child . . .'

'A child . . .' I whispered, turning.

Now, for the first time it seemed, the three of them, the two cops and the governor, paid me serious attention. Kinsey laughed, and then did a strange thing, or not so strange: she hit me. It was a powerful blow with the flat of her hand, with enough force to shock me back to reality. The strangest thing of all, however; the terrible, laughable thought that went through my head: that in different circumstances, earlier in my life and with Dugg back inside me, nothing in the world would have thrilled me more than to be treated in such a way by a figure of authority. A cop, a female cop! Hitting me! From such practices have I made a sorry life, and paid for it.

'You like messing with children, eh?' Kinsey asked. 'You want to mess with me?'

'But . . . but Dugg . . . that is . . . I . . . I've never . . .'

Struggling for the feeling.

'I've never been like that!'

'You may calm down, Mr Carter,' said the governor. 'And you too, Detective Sergeant. Mr Carter is innocent. The prison, that is, myself, will accept full responsibility. There will be an inquiry.' The governor's eyes were filled with a shadow of his own making, one of imminent loss, as he turned to me.

'Please tell me what's happening,' I asked. 'What is it?'

'Earlier this evening, there was a breach in our security. A serious breach. Our mainframe computer was penetrated. Do you understand what I'm saying?'

'Dugg . . .'

'Doug?'

'The name he calls his sex,' Kinsey told the governor. 'Cute, huh?'

'I see. Yes. Your sexuality was stolen.'

I was almost laughing, I don't know why. 'Security?'

'Oh, the very best. But. Well. You have heard of Breakheart?'

'Thomas Breakheart? Of course. He's in prison.'

'Unfortunately, no. He was released six months ago.'

'Released? But—'

'His sentence was shortened. It was part of the deal, I'm afraid. For volunteering.'

Kinsey banged her fist against a wall.

The governor ignored her. 'So, you see . . .'

'With Dugg inside him?' I asked, hardly believing. 'Out there?'

He nodded. 'We need your help, Mr Carter. Only you can find him. You may remember Breakheart's methods. He will strike before midnight. We have . . .' He studied his watch, shaking. 'We have less than three hours.'

Suddenly, there was a fifth person in the room. That shadow there, fleeting, or else the play of the ship upon the dark water as somebody touched the back of my neck. Kinsey, or the other cop . . .

I turned round. They were standing apart from me.

'Mr Carter?'

Who spoke then? The governor? Kinsey?

'Carter! Are you all right?'

No. The tingles. The shivers. It was happening. Happening again.

I think I said something. I think so. I must've done.

I seemed to come awake, back in the car, speeding now, over the bridge, back towards Manchester, the waves below, the waves inside me, the shadow somewhere, somewhere . . .

Other cars were behind us, lights flashing like afterthoughts through the wailing fog of sirens. Kinsey in the back with me, urging me to be strong, to keep the connection open.

To keep the . . .

'Just find that bastard,' she said.

Twenty-five years ago – December it was, and the last day thereof – a young boy of eleven was found strangled and sexually mutilated in the car park of a biscuit factory. A greetings card was left pinned to the body, actually pinned to the flesh, with the words 'Happy New Year, Billy' written inside. Underneath the message, a crude drawing of a Cupid's loveheart, where the arrow had split the heart clean in two.

Despite extensive inquiries, no arrests were made.

One year later, again on the last day of December, another victim was found, a girl this time, the same age. The same method of despatch, the same greeting; this time, 'Happy New Year, Daphne'. The same broken heart.

Again, no traces of the killer.

For the next five years, the end of year celebrations were darkened by identical murders. There was much speculation in the press, from various experts, about the patience, if that be the right word, of this curious murderer; what cold, determined mind could wait so long between the satings of evil desire?

Somewhere, the shadow . . .

Finally the murderer made his error, and Thomas Breakheart, a quiet, well-mannered computer programmer, was arrested. He readily confessed to the seven killings, saying by way of explanation that his own parents had been killed on 31 December, when he was only nine years old. This was true, and their murder was still unexplained, but it made no light shine in the jury's broken soul. Breakheart was sentenced to life imprisonment.

A few years later the first experiments in digital castration were conducted, on life prisoners only, and without the public's knowledge. Six volunteers died in the early phase; died unknown. Breakheart was the first successful result; his damaged, perverted sexuality was separated from his body, and stored on disk. This plague of information was then analysed, in vain search of warnings.

When the government finally went public with the process, there was the usual outrage from the liberal tendency, but mostly the people were behind the castrations; revenge was satisfied, at least to some degree. If the murderers couldn't be executed, at least let this happen to them, that was the feeling. A right-wing campaign led to the proviso that all Class A perverts were to have their sexuality killed.

Killed. Turned off, wiped clean.

Three years after his sentence began, Thomas Breakheart's sexuality was erased from the prison's mainframe. The man was alone, neutered, with another fifteen years to serve before his promised release, his gift for being an experiment. Fifteen years; which time he spent quietly, studying mathematics in the prison library, never giving the guards any trouble and showing all signs of the cure.

He was released, on the specified day, without fanfare, without publicity, without any word being given. In secret.

He would be fifty-five years old.

Somewhere the shadow, and like a dog, I followed the darkness through the darkness. Dugg's signal was weak, dissipated, maybe corrupted already. Kinsey was urging me on, screaming at me; sometimes just going quiet, frowning, letting me become entuned. There were the crowds on the streets, of course, with kids out late because of the occasion and that made it difficult; the noise, all that crazy joy getting in the way, like I was the only thing between them and nightfall, childfall, lovefall.

Following . . .

I directed the car into an open space, a parking lot behind a factory. I made to get out, but Kinsey kept me tight. There were other cars behind us, with armed cops, and they did the search. It took them fifteen minutes or so, but I already knew: the scent was lingering here but no longer around. The shadow of a shadow, which petered out, like twisted desire. To grow elsewhere.

'You know what this place is?' Kinsey asked. 'It's the place where he did the first one. Breakheart. This is where he started.'

I looked through the window, at the stark shape of the biscuit factory, while the cop woman hit the back of the seat in frustration:

'The guy's on a fucking tour.'

We spent the next hour searching the seven sites of murder. Every available police unit was on alert. No bodies were found, which was a comfort; and no sign of Breakheart, which was not. At four of the sites I picked up faint messages, thin tingles of mist almost gone, as though Dugg was distantly calling to me with a losing voice.

Somewhere . . .

As the last site was searched, Kinsey hauled me out of the car. She threw me against a wall and pulled a gun on me. 'This is your last chance, Carter,' she whispered close. 'Where the fuck is he?'

I could only shake my head, slowly.

The feeling was cold stone.

*   *   *

It was gone eleven when we got to the police station. On the way we'd called at Breakheart's dingy little flat. There were cops posted there, as though standing guard over the ramshackle stack of equipment perched on the desk. It was from here that the murderer had made his intrusion into the Monastery's dark, digital heart. I was this close to the carrier's nest, and yet I still couldn't feel anything, like Dugg had never been here, not at all. A sense of loss came over me like a heavy cloud; hopelessness, failure, anger at having failed, fear. Fear for the kids.

In the station, cops were hanging around, stalled, drinking thick black coffee as they waited for a call-out, hoped against being called. A call that would mean that the bad thing had happened. And the big clock on the wall crept towards midnight, victim of a thousand stares. There were some sad balloons strung up, and a drooping HAPPY NEW YEAR! banner. Nobody said anything to me, nobody would even look at me. If only the clock would reach for twelve early, maybe then the murderer wouldn't strike, following the established pattern.

'How do you know it was him?' I asked, to anyone.

Kinsey was working the drinks machine. 'What?'

'Breakheart. Could've been anyone breaking in.'

'Left his marker, didn't he.'

'What, a greetings card?'

'Yeah. Fixed on all the screens it was, animated, with the severed heart spinning around.'

'Could've been anyone, leaving the message. It was in all the papers—'

'The message . . . you wanna know what the message was?'

I nodded.

'Happy New Year, Douglas.' Kinsey laughed cold and I don't blame her.

'That's my middle name. John Douglas Carter. That's why he chose me? For the name? Stole me, I mean. Stole my . . .'

'He tried others. All prisoners called Douglas. Didn't work. They fought back.'

'Oh.'

Dugg always was a sucker slave. Any good master would do.

'Just find this Douglas,' I said. 'Find all the kids called Douglas, their parents, warn them . . .'

Kinsey was looking at me in disgust, shaking her head.

'But how will he do it?' I asked. 'Breakheart. I mean, murder somebody now. How can he? Perhaps he can't. Perhaps . . .'

'This is so comforting, Carter. It really is.'

'No, listen. It's not his sex, is it? His was killed, turned off. It's mine. I've never been into hurting people, never into kids. Not ever. He's just a body, a shell. The desire's not in him, it's in the shadow.'

'Shadow?'

'The sex, the gnome.' I had stood up now, excited. 'Dugg's a masochist, not a sadist. What's Breakheart going to use? Perhaps he can't. Perhaps he can't do anything!'

Kinsey crunched her coffee cup into a ball.

'Well, he's out there. He's searching for something.'

We fell back into silence then. One of the cops, Kinsey's partner, got up and ripped down the HAPPY NEW YEAR! banner. I went to the Gents, washed my face, stared at myself in the broken mirror, rubbed at the back of my neck. Somebody stood behind me, a dark shape in one of the open cubicles.

It took a few seconds to realize that both my hands were still resting on the faucets. My neck was still being touched.

Close.

I turned: the shadow turned with me.

*   *   *

Copcar, rollercoaster, streets laced with dancers, slick with vomit, kissing couples. Kinsey beside me, holding on. Me with the eyes shut, me with my hands clenched tight, sweating, cold. Hot inside, with the strongest feeling ever felt. This was him, this was Dugg, but stronger, more powerful, somehow darker, more in control. Doing the wanting. Turned inside out, not wanting the doing.

Doing the wanting.

Close. It was close to the station.

Street lamps flashing, music pounding, all the clocks of Manchester ticking, ticking. Eleven twenty-five. Honking the horn to part the crowd that knew nothing of the darkness that lay within them, waiting, hiding, prowling the moments, the laughter and the flashbulbs and the drunken sprees.

I had a map of the city in my head, following a black spot that crept along the streets, twisting and twisted. Hair bristle. With Kinsey broadcasting the constant changes of our whereabouts over the radio. It was strong, the black mirror in my head, like Dugg was broadcasting as well, calling me, fighting back. SOS. Distress signal. Find me, help me, retrieve me. Stop me.

Stop me.

Doing the wanting.

Somewhere the shadow and a crooked somewhere, almost lost, fading out, with me directing the driver until the shadow darkened again, the tingle like broken glass, coming into focus, sharp head-blinding focus.

'Here!'

Copcar, rollercoaster deadstop, engine panting, tyre screech. Breathe out, at last. Dust settle, slow rain, radio squawk. Out. Me, the cops, other cops. Not thinking any more, just following. Listening. Dugg, calling, calling . . . but so many people. Banks of the Irwell, the river. Pathway crowded, brass band music from the other side, clear.

Clock: 11.47.

Running, pushing people away. The cops behind me, some ahead already, making way, ordering people aside. Good. Clear run. Boats on the river, partying. Rave music, mixing in. But where, where now? A man and woman, distraught, shouting. 'Douglas! Little Douglas? Where?' The woman screaming and then crying to see the police, so many police. 'Please God . . .'

All this in a blur as . . .

Shadow, pitch black. Don't leave me! Find me! Crowd thinning out, gone. A fence, broken. Muddy ground behind some shops, half-built shops, can't remember. Kinsey beside me, gun out, breathing sharp. Climbing through, hair on barbed wire. Figures, ahead. Two. A man, a young boy. Boy on the ground, clothes torn, please God . . . the man scrabbling about near some waste bins, desperate, wailing he was.

Coming in close. Kinsey checking the boy. Alive, OK. She stood up, got the gun tight on the man in the shadows. 'Breakheart!'

He comes up from the darkness, turns, shocked. No, scared. No, empty. Empty sack. His face, his eyes, drawn wide, nothing behind them. Alone. He comes forward, slowly, midnight chimes from Albert Square and over the river and great cheers on the air, flash of fireworks, exploding. Breakheart's face ghosted, gaudy orange and yellow as he stumbles in the mud, the rain, 'Can't find him . . . lost him . . . can't find him . . . please . . .'

Cops all over him then, but I was moving to the wastebins. A movement there, rustle of paper, plastic sheeting. A flap of binbag. Crackle. Closer, shadow dark. Somewhere . . . two glints from beneath a pile of rubbish; two dark, purple eyes. Jewelled, they were, and bright with fear.

'Dugg?' Gently said, so as not to . . .

The shape moves, slowly first, and then rushes out of hiding, running towards me. I open out my arms, wide to receive. A voice behind, 'Don't! Don't shoot!' Kinsey's voice, but then the firing of a gun, heavy blast, burning. Burning inside me, the pain, as the shadow jerks back, pounded deep into the metal side of a bin.

'Nailed him!' A cop voice, male, edged with shock.

It slides to the ground, this lump of stuff that somebody threw out one sad day. I walk slowly towards it, hardly breathing. Kinsey at my side, 'Carter, I tried to stop him . . . Jesus!'

I kneel down, stroke the thing's head, his small, broken misshapen body. The eyes are open, but barely so. 'You did it, Dugg,' I say. 'You stopped him.'

The eyes, the beautiful twin-jewelled eyes, slowly close.

The shadow inside me lightens, lightens to a cloud of scent that drifts away, finally, to nothingness.

CALL OF THE WEIRD

Dog J-Loop need a good head clean. Hungry worms crawling around inside his skull, making his mind go itchy. Bad enough scratching mad on the streets of Manchester. Bad enough with his Mistress selling copies of the *Big Biscuit*, and her saying all the time, 'What's wrong with you these days, J-Loop? You're supposed to look boneless and homeless, not rabid and stupid!' Worse still that the good Whistle not working, because all them worms got to it. Whistle is one smart bone-ticket to the intersnout. Mistress feeds your jaws with Whistle. Then you can talk to her, through the intersnout. Bad enough to lose the sharing, but worst of all that J-Loop's music starting to come up wrong.

J-Loop a robodog DJ at Howling Club, slipping latest Dogga tunes into the collective head of the cross-bred pack down on the floor. That night the whole pack-net very nearly collapsing when J-Loop misses a beat in his brain due to the worm invasion. Money-sucker bossman of the Howling, shouting down the DJ for the mishap.

Trotting home to Mistress-comfort.

'Dear pet, what is it?' Soft hands of the Mistress stroking all along his fur. J-Loop managing just enough intersnout to sniff the gist.

'Me got the worms, Mistress.' Hoping these ragged growls make up sense.

'Oh my poor doggy!'

Nanoworms being the fear of every good mistress; a curly intruder that make a robodog want to go *off-string*, being the urge to run weird.

'Oh my *poorest* doggy!' Mistress tugging tight on the string that binds their love together. 'Please don't leave me!'

But J-Loop no longer understanding the words, only the stroking hands. Makes for one urgent need to get the laundry done. The trouble being that J-Loop never cleaned his head before. Idea of it scary, because his tune-spinning at the Howling Club is only bootleg money. According to the Authorities, J-Loop is purely a jobless dog, linked up direct to the Basic Bones Allowance. Well known the Authorities make real cheap head-cleaning jobs of basic boners. Which laundry involves losing your robo-brain to the wave-kennel, whilst the cleaners make up new edition. Pack-rumours telling of how some dogs die in the process, it being a moment of losing your way. Scary losing of the way to a street-honed robodog.

'Loopy, don't you go being no mudpuppy now,' Princess Lickety snarls at him. She's one sleek robobitch at the Howling Club. 'Us dogness stick together, you catch the ball?'

Catching the ball real good, because dog-to-dog being his only intersnout since the worms came calling, and two days later Dog J-Loop sauntering out of the Town Hall, quite merry on the end of Mistress string, freshly laundered brain in his head. No worms, no nothing. J-Loop feel dog-ambient! Pair of them set up street-camp, J-Loop adopting perfect begging mode: front paws crossed just so, plaintive look in dewy eyes, fur raised in bristles against Manchester rain. Mistress starting out her melancholic selling-chant: 'Please help the homeless! Buy the *Big Biscuit*. Only fifty-four pounds!' And it's exactly now that J-Loop gets the call: yearning voice inside his brain. This no worm-sickness, this no itching; voice being strong and passionate. Constant hungering.

J-Loop goes off-string. Tugging string loose from his Mistress fingers. Running free, desperate cry chasing but no contest. Like, going weird in greyhound style!

Rain-drenched and guided, stranger's voice pointing the nose-way, fifty minutes later J-Loop arrives in Southly Poshtown. Voice making the dog scratch his claws against the front door of a big manhouse. Young girl opens the door, takes one look at J-Loop, starts to scream: 'Noodles! You've come home!'

Noodles? thinks J-Loop: Who the fuck this Noodles?

'Mummy, Noodles has come back to us!' young girl shouts back into the house, and then she's dragging J-Loop inside behind her, tugging hard on loose string.

Seven weeks, J-Loop lives a canine-prince of a Poshtown life: warm blankets, juicy steaks, ultra-flea powder, his very own platform boot to chew on. Each day at play with the young girl, and swallowing lots of good Whistle-bone but making only sniffing visits to intersnout. Not knowing what to say. Each night sleeping by the embers of dying fire.

Each night to dream a doggy-dream.

To let the floating voice of Noodles give free howl to final moments; the shivering to stillness of canine brain inside the

Town Hall doggy-bath. Each and every night, the repeated death of the robo-poshdog inside him: J-Loop feeling possessed by story. How Noodles had died during his high-class head-clean; how a bone-whisper of his doggy-mind keeping alive inside the kennel-waves. Like embers of dying fire, yes? How Noodles had waiting and waiting to do before J-Loop came for his clean-up: another black robodog! Exact same Labrador model! Slightly downmarket but no time for choices. How Noodles's pedigree patterns had slithered through the waves, straight into J-Loop's brain.

Seven weeks passing by, this nightmare stupid dog inside of J-Loop, never leaving him no peace! Seven weeks, the stupid games of second-rate Mistress; cloying warmth, wet meat, platform boot leaving too many sequins in the mouth. Oh-so-tight leather collar around his chafing neck! Too much. Too chafing much! Seven weeks then J-Loop gets up one night, snuffles around twisting backdoor key in front paws, full robo-mode.

Door against superdog. No wailing contest!

Running the streets of Manchester, old-time memories: rain and piss and rancid cats to chase. Noodles howling upside his head, demanding his whereabouts. 'Catch this ball, Noodle-brain!' Dog-to-dog intersnout talking. 'J-Loop in charge of the two-pack.'

Noodles only a growling at the edges then. Belly up.

Back to the old ground, early morning: there's the old Mistress, newly issued robodog on the end of her latest string. J-Loop feeling down to dirt from the sniffing of this but still making a keening goodbye from across the way. *Got my own trip to make, Mistress. Sell some Biscuit!* Hoping this got through. Then trotting over to Howling Club to find the Princess Lickety, tied to a table leg. 'You want to go off-string, good robobitch?' snarls J-Loop.

Well weird and travelling. The three of them, J-Loop and the Princess and the Noodles inside, running away from Manchester's clutches. Paw to paw to paw they scamper, outlanding to where the smell of fresh meat plays above the city's gates. Sniffing at freedom's tang, making homeless home beneath the sparkle stars.

You catch this ball yet?

This little story being told by J-Loop himself, his ravenous dogself.

DUB WEIRD
(crawling kingdog remix)

hungry worm come a crawling
(I said)
slow hungry worm come a crawling
bad beat upside me brain
dogga tune! dogga tune!
those worms sure got me mauling
gonna bite me some chain
howl down the moon

devil worm sure got me itchin'
(I said)
bad devil worm sure got me itchin'
aphrodisiac in me feed
dogga tune! dogga tune!
gonna do me some serious bitchin'
chew me off some lead
howl down the moon

bad arse worm sure got me belly up
(I said)
that bad arse worm sure got me belly up
natty furlocks and ting
dogga tune! dogga tune!
gonna find me a bone to sup
chew me through some string
howl down the moon

crazy worm ain't got me afeard
(I said)
crazy mad worm ain't got me afeard
got me legs ten feet tall
dogga tune! dogga tune!
sniffing tang well fuckin' weird
gonna catch me some ball
howl down the moon
(you catch it?)
howl down that big old moon

THE CHARISMA ENGINE

■
■
■

Emerson and Scott's *Complete Tables of Charismatic Value: 1895 to 2105* records the personality ratings of all the many thousands of people who have scored over 1,575 jaggers, for the years stated in the title. The copy I possess has a natural tendency to fall open at the pages corresponding to the year 1999, this being the period of history I had studied for my final paper at university.

I had, for that paper, concentrated on the more well-known personalities, my work being a comparative analysis of the various examinations already done. For this, the first project of my leisure, I had a more ambitious notion: to undertake the study of a figure as yet untouched by the academic hand. Consequently, on the occasion I speak of, it was towards the lower end of the charismatic scale that I made my perusal. What governing, overarching mind guided my eye towards the name I eventually chanced upon, I cannot say;

but guided I was, of that I now have no doubt. I give here the exact entry:

LUCINDA TONGUEBRIGHT (1978–1999)
vocalist, composer, musician, actress
charisma rating (estimated): 1,576 jaggers

It seemed a dreadfully thin summation of a life, even for a person who died so young; twenty-one years old, when she left this world. And such a low score; why, only two less jagger points and she would have been unlisted. It goes without saying that I had never heard mention of Lucinda Tonguebright before this moment. One fact was immediately obvious: she had achieved her entry in the same year as her death – 1999. A quick study of the preceding years confirmed my suspicions: her very death had produced the interest in her life. This is often the case, especially if the death be a mysterious or notorious, or a cruel one.

Perhaps it was the name; the wonderful name – a singer bright of tongue. Perhaps it was the way she hovered so, barely on the edge of being remembered at all. Whatever the reason, I found myself strongly drawn to this young woman born over one-hundred-and-fifty years ago. I could only hope she was suitably, so to speak, unexplored. Moving quickly to my computing engine, I entered the candidate's name and her year of birth into my expert locator. You may imagine my dismay to find that an archaeology had already been performed. A researcher whose name was unfamiliar to me – Professor Alexander Bringhome – had already examined the archives for this very same singer. It seemed I would have to choose again from my Emerson and Scott.

However, something still drew me towards the woman. I quickly established from the data that Professor Bringhome had last consulted the archives in 2047, fully eighty-two years ago! On a whim I activated a search for any papers or theses dealing with the young woman. To my delight, none turned up. The professor had obviously decided she was too uninteresting for a published study. Excellent! I now had a subject worthy of my burgeoning talents.

The few days following my decision were spent in the most delightful manner, as I gathered together copies of all the known artefacts of the singer. They amounted to a surprising testimony, for one so young: four albums of recorded music; a leading role in a moving picture; a book of poetry; several appearances on television. Add to this the various newsprint items I collected – interviews, profiles, reviews and photographs – as well as the few personal items I managed to uncover – candid snapshots, fan letters, demonstration tapes and the like – and I soon had enough material to begin my examination.

The task was made substantially more interesting by the very appearance of Miss Tonguebright, which was most displeasing to the eye; in truth, she was a woman of uncommon drabness, a fact that leads one to believe some other, more tantalizing aspect must have led to her charismatic value. Of her life little need be said, containing as it did nothing that could not be found in all such media studies of the late twentieth century. As I originally suspected, only the study of the young woman's death – at the very height of her fame – seemed to offer a promising outlet for my talents.

Miss Tonguebright's transport was found abandoned near a notorious river, across which a high bridge offered dire temptation to the lost. She had been due to appear that weekend at a prestigious music festival; it was entirely another audience that greeted her body being dragged from the waters fully two weeks later. A public inquiry reached a verdict of 'death by misadventure'.

Using my collection of media traces I did my own measurement of the woman's charismatic rating; finding it to be worth 1,629 jagger points, a score somewhat higher than Emerson and Scott had estimated. Having posted this new rating off to the publishers of the book, including in the package all the relevant equations, I then spent another week or so attempting to uncover further traces, specifically relating to the death, thinking perhaps to reveal the psychological trauma that had led to it.

Coming across only some press reports referring to the singer's apparent nervousness about the upcoming festival, and a certain listlessness in her recent performances – 'thin and wasted', one reviewer called her – it seemed inevitable I would have to abandon the study. This I prepared to do with a heavy heart, for I had become quite enamoured of the young artist's work; listening to her recordings almost every night, and watching the film she had starred in over and over with increasing frequency. In truth, Lucinda's charismatic force, over myself alone, was far, far higher than the new public rating I had submitted.

This new-found passion would have been entirely in vain were it not for a remark made at a dinner party I attended a few weeks later, at the behest of my former personal tutor at the university. I had accepted the kind invitation with some gratitude, for I had hardly ventured outside my house in a good number of weeks. After a delightful repast, the professor and I settled down to discuss matters of mutual interest. When asked with what project I was occupying my skills, I had told, quite innocently, of my interest in the woman called Lucinda Tonguebright; a remark to which the professor had replied:

'Ah, the Bringhome Project!'

Somewhat taken aback at this, I immediately asked: 'What? You know of Professor Bringhome's work?'

'Know of it? A little; merely rumours.'

'I have seen mention of his name,' I said. 'He too consulted the archives regarding Lucinda . . . I mean, Miss Tonguebright. The only other consultation on record. What was his interest in the woman?'

'I'm not entirely sure. The older members of staff sometimes whisper his name.'

'You mean Bringhome was . . . ?'

'Yes, he was a professor at our university.'

Upon hearing this fact, I once again had the curious notion that my interest in Lucinda Tonguebright was no mere affair of chance. Barely able to contain myself, I at once enquired as to the nature of Bringhome's field of study.

'Ah, now . . . image retrieval systems, I believe,' replied my host. 'Apparently there was some kind of scandal. Bringhome was forced to leave his post because of it.'

'What kind of scandal?'

'Something to do with a sponsorship deal. But really, I know very little.'

Suffice it to say, not a day later I was paying a visit to my former place of learning, the University of Manchester. Seating myself at one of the ports of entry for the university's computing engine, I entered into it the words: BRINGHOME, ALEXANDER. As suspected, the engine refused my advances. Pausing only to establish my privacy, I then brought from my travelling case my recently purchased unlocking device, the Houdini Model Superior. Affixing this to the engine, I had only to wait a few seconds before a successful, if somewhat illegal, revealing was performed.

Unfortunately, the information so gathered seemed of little use; evidently the authorities of the time had deemed it wise to archive as little as possible regarding the professor. Nothing was said of the so-called scandal, except that the reason for his dismissal, in 2050, was listed as 'Unprofessional behaviour, regarding the Xikon sponsorship'.

Once back in my own study – with the exquisite voice and playing of Miss Tonguebright as my muse – I consulted my trusty locating engine, seeking out any publicly available information on both Professor Bringhome and the company calling itself Xikon. The professor yielded little more than a few mentions in papers on the history of image retrieval, and these were all in praise of his expertise. It was as though the scandal had been erased from all memory. I did manage to unearth a photograph of the man; it revealed a dark, hooded countenance etched by some inner pain. The Xikon location search produced a more fruitful bounty, including a history of the company, relevant parts of which I now summarize:

Xikon Ltd was founded in the last years of the twentieth century, with the stated intention of becoming a major provider of media-effects technology. Success with the pioneering Image Retrieval System – most famously in the year 2009 with the Marilyn Monroe vehicle, *Some Like It Hotter Than Ever*, where an entirely new performance by the actress was constructed out of all the films, photographs and voice-recordings she had produced during her tragically short lifetime – established the company as a world leader in its field. Miss Monroe was only the first of a long line of regenerated artistes.

The even greater success, four years later, of the

'enhanced reality' version of the software led to an unprecedented public hunger for the 'new and improved' actors. The extent to which the more gullible believed in these fake stars was shown by the increasing demand for 'personal' appearances. The invention of the holograph engine, in 2034, gave Xikon the power to satisfy these demands. From now on, all manifestations in public could be generated in three dimensions, powered by a simple laptop computer. Movie stars, television personalities, politicians, famous sportsmen, even members of the royal family: anybody who had left enough media traces behind could now be retrieved, enhanced, given a kind of pretend life – copyright permitting. Artificial Intelligence systems gave these 'simutainers' a projected voice, and a somewhat limited personality.

But still, something was missing from the equation; as one correspondent to the company wrote: 'Loved your Princess Di. But where's the twinkle in the eye?' Subsequently, in 2046, and in the face of increasing competition from rival companies, Xikon initiated Project Propagation. This visionary scheme, to be led by Professor Alexander Bringhome of the University of Manchester, was intended to offer the most lifelike regeneration the market had ever seen. According to their publicity material, the company would make 'a simulation so enhanced, even its own mother would greet it with a big sloppy kiss!'

I must admit to a feeling of disappointment at reading this; it seemed the professor had only been interested in Miss Tonguebright for the purposes of resurrecting her image, with purely commercial reasons behind the scheme. I knew a little of the fashion for retrieved images in the middle of the last century; indeed, I had studied the scientific basis for it as part of my course. However, the above-quoted history passed over Xikon's grandly titled Project Propagation in a few dismissive lines, calling it a failure of the first order, and the seed of the company's eventual demise.

One aspect of this history puzzled me dearly: surely Miss Tonguebright's charisma had been too low for a successful image resurrection? Usually, such operations were performed on the very famous, for only they could possibly supply the necessary range of source material. The explanation, when it hit me, caused me to feel a profound affinity with Professor Bringhome: for he too must have been enamoured of the mousy young woman's strangely appealing image. He too must have given her a personal rating far above any effect she may have had in her real life.

However, all my researches had brought me no closer to uncovering the reasons for Lucinda Tonguebright's suicide. Again, an unfathomable despair shadowed my every thought; a despair kept scarcely at bay by a continuous merging of my senses with the woman's collected works. Even when the music fell silent, still it seemed to echo through the empty rooms of my house, as if through the chambers of the heart. You may imagine my surprise therefore, when, a few days later, I received the following unsolicited message over my communicating engine:

Dear Mr Newne,

I pray you will forgive this stark invasion of your privacy. During the last few days, by means of an expert (and quite illicit) monitoring service, I have become aware of your interest in Professor Alexander Bringhome's life and work. I must pray forgiveness also (shall I run out of prayers before this letter is through?) for conducting a covert research into your background and social standing. Professor Bringhome was my father, and if your interest in his work is truly genuine, I entreat you to reply in the first instance. I have a proposal that may be of interest.

Yours,
Miss Hildegard Bringhome

The reader may safely be assured that I did reply to the communication, and in the very first instance, and that I made thereby an appointment to meet with Hildegard Bringhome at the earliest possible convenience.

Her house, conveniently enough, was located in the village of West Didsbury, a well-kempt leafy suburb some few miles outside of Manchester, and not very far from where I myself lived. I arrived there charged with a nervousness I had hardly felt since my early youth. It was the winter of the year by now, and a weighted bank of cloud gave a darkened aspect to the large, and very old house that stood before me. No shred of light escaped from its windows, despite the lateness of the hour.

The door was opened by a young man, a servant of some kind, who ushered me into a dismally lit drawing room; a number of candles, set here and there on the antique furniture, created a flickering dance of shadows rather than any significant illumination. One wall was entirely filled with books, and it was with these that I settled my nerves as I awaited Miss Bringhome's arrival. One volume was a handsomely bound copy of Emerson and Scott's *Tables of Charisma*, the rare 2077 edition. I had opened this at random, and was studying the entries for whatever year it had fallen to, when a voice at my back announced, 'We have similar tastes, I see.'

Startled, I turned around, the book still open in my hands. Seated before me, in a corner of the room not even the candle-light dared approach, was an old woman. She was dressed in a simple off-white shift, above which her lined, wizened face seemed to float in the gloom. 'Miss Bringhome,' I stuttered, 'You surprised me. I did not think—'

'Please, sit down,' the old woman answered. 'We have much to discuss.'

I took the seat proffered, some distance from where she herself was perched. The woman had a face that seemed to shift constantly between aspects – at one moment she would appear old beyond measure; at other times, a glimpse of the strikingly beautiful young woman she must once have been would shine through the furrowed mask. We talked a little of her father, and she revealed that he had died in 2053, at the age of thirty-nine; 'old', as she said, 'well before his time, and dragged down by that wretched Xikon business'.

Upon hearing the company spoken of thus, I immediately asked for details of the scandal. I might well have been more circumspect, had I anticipated her reaction.

'Scandal!' she said, fairly hissing the word. 'I will have no such word mentioned. *No* such word, do you hear? My father followed the company's orders to the letter. Later, they claimed he had failed them. That could not be further from the truth. If anything, my father was *too* successful with his workings. Too *damned* successful!'

The curse shocked me, coming from such an elderly personage. Hoping to conduct the conversation back to gentler ground, I enquired about the proposal mentioned in the letter.

'That is simply stated,' the old woman replied. 'I have prepared my father's various papers for your inspection.' She referred here to several bound notebooks set on a small table beside my chair. 'It would give me great comfort, sir, if you were to look over them.'

'Miss Bringhome . . . I feel hardly qualified for such—'

'I wish only that you would read my father's notebooks. That is all I ask. And that you write a short report, giving your honest opinion as to the work's commercial viability. I have a great desire, you see, that my father's reputation should be salvaged, and by an academic such as yourself.'

'If I may venture . . . is it not a little late, for . . .'

I could hardly finish the sentence.

'Sir! You speak of lateness, to one as old as I? I have waited many years for someone to take an interest in my father's work. I shall not be ungenerous, let me assure you.'

If only to calm the lady down, I quickly agreed to the sum mentioned. In truth, I was already eager to take the papers away with me, the better to study them. Even this was against her wishes, however: 'I cannot allow the papers out of my sight,' she said. 'I will ask you therefore to accept the hospitality of my home while you make your report.'

So began my sojourn in the old woman's house. I moved in the very next day, bringing with me a few simple provisions, clothes and suchlike, along with some of my textbooks. I was given a spacious bedroom of my own; the very same one, I was informed, that her father had slept in. Pausing only to ruminate upon the twisted pathway that had brought me to this most curious task, I opened the first notebook of Professor Bringhome and started to read:

'Some people', he began, 'burn themselves into the film-strip, the photographic plate, the painted portrait, the pixels, the vinyl disc, the video screen. Admitting of their magical presence, we call these people photogenic, audiogenic. Or more simply, and even if they are ugly, we call them beautiful.

We say they have "charisma", from the Greek *kharis*; a religious term, signifying a divinely bestowed power or talent. To say that these favoured few belong not only to their time, but to *all* times, is a long-held poetic truth. However, I now believe that such transcendence is a physical fact of the universe itself. The great and the good do not die; rather, their base matter transforms into pure, undiluted image, contained alive within the traces of all they have touched. There they await us, scattered in clouds of information, pending only the invention of a suitable gathering device.'

It was a standard text, in all honesty, and typical of the time; only the final statement – that charisma was a physical property of the universe – seemed out of the ordinary. Certainly, in all my readings I had not come across this idea before. I automatically presumed the professor was speaking allegorically. But as my days and nights at the house progressed, I came to see that he had a material, if somewhat delusional, ambition behind the philosophical ramblings. He evidently believed such a machine could be built; a machine that would gather charisma from the ether. He referred to this as the Charisma Engine.

The complex equations and tortuous mathematical diagrams (only some of which I could understand) gradually homed in on one recurring image: that of two spirals, winding around each other like acrobatic snakes. At first I thought these the representation of the DNA structure, led to this belief by the numerous references to the so-called genetic properties of an image; a process the professor termed the 'photogenetic continuum'. Only slowly did it dawn on me that these were actually diagrams of the machine itself; blueprints, if you will, of the Charisma Engine.

I will freely admit I found all these ideas more than a little hard to take. The professor was claiming that the current image-retrieval technology could be augmented and vastly improved by his own invention, to produce not a copied *image* of the chosen person, but an exact *replica*; 'A reverberation in the charismatic field,' in Bringhome's own words, 'entirely indistinguishable from its material source'. As if this were not madness enough, he further went on to claim that 'the successful Charisma Engine will be a *nurturing* environment; by this I mean that the products of the retrieval will be sentient. They will have a life of their own.'

Shortly after this passage came the first mention of Lucinda Tonguebright. Hers was but one name in a long list of possibilities. It had however been underlined in a different pen, as though at a later date. And from that point on the notebooks were filled with speculations about her life and works. Of course, I was reminded of my own growing obsession.

During all this time of study I saw very little of the professor's daughter. The lady of the house kept to her own quarters most of the time. As for the young, silent manservant; I saw him only when I requested meals. I could ask for nothing more. And so, the first week passed.

I had now reached the section of the papers dealing with the Xikon sponsorship. The company had shown great interest in the professor's stated ideas of a 'fully enhanced replication', although nowhere in the correspondence did he mention the idea of sentience, as though realizing that such notions were strictly for private thought. Project Propagation, as it became known, was a prestigious undertaking for the university, and it was clear from his writings that Bringhome felt an immense pressure to deliver results. This may have caused him to throw all accepted scientific caution to the wind. How else to explain his decision to present a first tentative retrieval using only an untried prototype of the Charisma Engine? Lucinda Tonguebright was his chosen subject. To this demonstration were invited the board of the university, along with the directors of Xikon.

In the circumstances, it is perhaps fortunate that the resurrected image flickered into life for little more than two minutes. Two minutes in which (according to the professor's highly charged account) the half-formed Miss Tonguebright spat and howled, and verbally abused her creator; two minutes of precious life, in which she vomited blood and attempted physically to attack one of the Xikon directors. Somewhat reluctantly, the professor turned off the Charisma Engine; the image dispersed into thin, screaming air.

Even taking into account the professor's fevered view of the occasion, it seems hard to credit such things. An image that could produce saliva, could scream, could physically – *physically!* – attack a human being? No, I could not allow myself to believe such monstrosities. More likely the professor had exaggerated; more likely Miss Tonguebright's image had been badly reproduced. Some fault in the mechanism had caused the image to appear more alive than it could possibly have been.

But still, *something* out of the ordinary had taken place that day, in the university's media laboratory. Within a week Xikon had withdrawn their sponsorship, and Bringhome was given a month's notice from his position. However, so angry was he at this treatment – and the notebooks fairly explode with bile at this point – that the professor left at the first opportunity, taking all his workings with him.

Obviously of independent means, he had already set up a laboratory of his own, in this very house where I now lived and slept. Here he continued his studies alone, attempting to construct an improved version of the Charisma Engine. Only after a year of intensive work did he feel able to call up another image from the past, again that of Miss Tonguebright. Again, the retrieval failed, this time living for five seconds only. The professor now shunned all human contact. One can only imagine the passion that fuelled him during the next two years. Finally, he believed he had made the necessary adjustments, determined this time to allow the image to emerge, 'only at her own desired speed'.

Now begins the strangest part of the recorded account. On 22 August 2053 Bringhome activated the machine for what he stated would be 'one last final attempt to reach longingly into the past'. Here, for the first time, the notebooks stand empty. The next entry is dated seven days later. It begins, 'I have dragged her out of the air. At first, only a wave shimmer, at the centre of the engine. A princess of doubt.' He then starts to refer to the image in the second person. 'Slowly, so very slowly, your form has gathered, taking molecules from the realm. A thing of dust, with the faintest memory of a shape. And written then, alive in masques of dark light. My princess of the codes, how dare they disparage your appearance. My jigsaw girl, my lady of dreams!' The next entry, in a more controlled hand, states: 'The precise amount of charisma in any particular field is always a fixed, constant amount. By this I mean, in order to bring about a successful resurrection, some other, lesser body will have to relinquish its image. The system remains in balance. So be it; surely, any sacrifice is worthy of such a vision. Lucinda shall be mine alone.' And then, and given a page of its own: 'Tomorrow, she lives!' Here, the final notebook comes to an end.

With a somewhat palpitating heart, I closed the volume. I was sitting in the library where Hildegard Bringhome had first greeted me; sitting at the very desk no doubt at which her father had written this account. I could not help but remember that the professor had died in 2053, the very year of his final experiment. Had the strange undertaking – or failure thereof – somehow brought about his demise?

The room was quite dark, except for the few guttering candles I had been reading by. I had no sense of the time, and when I examined my pocket watch I was surprised to find it past midnight. The library seemed to be alive with another presence, as though the professor's writings had animated the air. Slowly then, I became aware that this feeling was no illusion. I turned around to find Miss Bringhome perched on her usual seat. I had by this time become used to her sudden appearances, but still, how could I not be unnerved?

'You have finished, I see,' she said. 'And have you formed an opinion?'

'Yes, I have.' Steeling myself, I went on: 'Miss Bringhome . . . I believe your father, for all his undoubted expertise, was suffering from a most profound delusion.'

The old woman was silent for a moment. Then she rang a small bell at her side, which summoned the young servant into the room. I really thought I was to be shown out of the house. Instead, she said to the servant, 'William, the kind gentleman wishes to visit the workshop.' Before I could say anything in reply, Miss Bringhome turned back to me: 'My father's laboratory,' she said, by way of explanation. 'I will meet you there.'

From the very first moment my eye chanced upon Lucinda Tonguebright's name, I had felt myself caught in the grip of some superior force; now, following the servant down a short flight of steps, to the basement of the house, I knew that force had me completely in its thrall. The steps led to a short corridor, at the end of which the servant unlocked a heavy door. Inside, a dark cavernous room was dominated by a large cylindrical shape. Even in the darkness I had no doubt as to its nature. The apparatus was perhaps six feet tall by four feet in diameter, consisting of a broad base out of which a pair of entwined pipes rose upwards. The pipes were made of brass, or some similar metal, and were folded in such a way as to leave an opening through to the empty space at the very centre of the machine. I could not stop myself from gasping out loud:

'The Charisma Engine!'

'Do you still not believe?' answered a voice from behind me. Turning, I saw that Hildegard Bringhome was now approaching along the corridor. She glided past me to take up a position beside the machine. 'Surely, now, you will write a favourable report?'

'I . . . I . . .' Stuttering, I then said the words that would continue to haunt me for as long as I lived: 'I should have to see it in operation.'

The old woman looked at me deeply for a moment, and then nodded to the servant. This young man activated a few switches set into the base of the machine, causing the pipes to hum with some spectral energy, and the central space to glow with expectancy. A soft emission of light seeped into Miss Bringhome's skin, and she grew more vigorous than I had ever seen her, as though she were taking strength from the machine. She moved around the Charisma Engine with what seemed a youthful energy, directing the servant in his work and every so often looking at me with a crazed expression on her face.

But even with my limited knowledge of the Engine and its processes, I could see that the apparatus was in dire need of repair. The pipes now made a fearful noise, as of so many wailing, electrified souls, and the light within danced erratically in a ballet of sparks. The machine seemed to be dragging the air towards itself, so that I could hardly breathe; and any breath I could inhale was layered with a stench of what I could only imagine was burning flesh! I felt as though I might faint, so overpowering was the experience.

I saw then a shadow forming in the centre of the machine; a shadow that pulled substance for itself from the air around it, growing darker by the second, and veined with fire. I could hardly move. Was I finally to see Lucinda Tonguebright's image appearing before me?

But the image seemed too dark, too full. It was a man's shape forming there, within the cylinder of light. Perhaps some poor, random soul was being pulled through. But no; as the figure congealed, and the face gathered some small semblance of humanity – with a shock I recognized it. This pained, broken face, this half-formed mouth split in a hideous scream; they were the mutated features of Professor Alexander Bringhome himself!

And I thought back to what I had read earlier: the professor's theories about the exchange of charisma had proven correct. In order for the Charisma Engine to work it had fuelled itself on the image of its very own creator. Evidently, the machine was still not functioning properly, perhaps because of its age. Now that same creator was trapped within its force field, howling to be released.

With a shock, I came out of my frozen mood. Miss Bringhome was standing by my side, gazing rapturously at her father's caged image. Without even looking at me, she said, 'Now, do you believe?' Before I could say a word, I felt two strong arms grab me from behind. It was the manservant, William. Under Miss Bringhome's direction, he was forcing me ever closer to the Engine. They meant to exchange me! To feed my image to the machine, in order that the professor be released.

I struggled as best I could, but my body seemed almost hollow, as though the process had already begun. Only when my face was actually over the threshold, and I felt my spirit being sucked from me, did I find a last vestige of strength. With an almighty effort, I managed to swing around, taking the servant with me. This young man was now in the position I had just been in: pressed up against the opening of the Charisma Engine. I heard Miss Bringhome scream, and felt a cold shiver run through me. I then, and with no remorse, pushed the servant away from me.

The machine had him. For a moment the two figures within it – the shadow of the professor, the terrified, struggling form of the servant – seemed to perform a little dance, a perverted waltz. There was an explosion of light, which engulfed them both and from which only one of them finally emerged.

It was the professor. Or rather – his image. Floating above the prone body of the servant, this shimmering, transparent form raised its hands to its face, perhaps in disbelief. Only the eyes of the figure held any real semblance of life; filled with a burning desire, they fixed upon Miss Bringhome's smiling face. Descending now from the confines of the Engine, the professor floated closer to his daughter's waiting arms.

I was standing to one side, still in a profound state of shock from the events of the last few minutes. I may as well have not been in the room at all, for all the attention the two people paid me. Slowly now, as though nervous of the lost years, father and daughter came together in a tentative embrace.

It was only then that I realized that the professor had never had a daughter, and that his original experiment had been only too successful. For before my very eyes, Miss Bringhome discarded her old woman's image, and the image beneath that, of the beautiful young woman I had occasionally glimpsed. In their place stood the uncompromising appearance of Lucinda Tonguebright, albeit made from light, rather than flesh. I remembered then the words from the professor's final notebook: 'Lucinda will be mine alone.'

And the two gossamer contours wrapped around each other, in intimate reflection of the Charisma Engine that stood behind them.

Without saying a word, I left the room. I walked quickly up the stairs and out of the front door. I did not stop even to pick up my belongings. It was enough that I took this with me: *this* body; this trembling, thickset, awkward mess of flesh and blood.

SPACEACHE AND
HEARTSHIPS

.
.
.

This morning, the papers and the television were filled with pictures of the sky lit by fire. Now that the British lunar rocket has finally been launched, I feel duty bound to write of my own journey to the moon. Consider me mad or simply a liar; the decision is yours, whoever you are and whatever world you inhabit.

Five years ago I was asked to join the team of scientists in charge of preparing the flight path. As first assistant to the esteemed Professor Lucas Gull, the country's leading expert on gravitational science, my job would be to help him plot the optimum course for the mission, weighing all the sky's myriad factors.

What we actually found was an entirely new world to explore.

I would dare to claim the first sighting, being the witness to a slight blip on one of the instrument panels; a tiny kink in the gravitational field of the Earth, easy to ignore. Luckily I reported my finding to Gull the next day. Most senior astronomers instantly dismissed the anomaly, of course, calling it computational error. Or else, if real, too small to be of concern.

We worked for many lonely months, the professor and I, to track down the cause of the deviance. I will freely admit that I too disbelieved, when Gull came to his startling conclusion; namely, *that Planet Earth had a second moon in tandem with the first*. The slight fuzziness on the screen was in fact the shadow of another satellite, somewhere in orbit, invisible and strange. This extra moon would have to be extremely small and extremely close to the Earth, in order to satisfy the read-outs.

Professor Gull pleaded with the authorities to call off the launch, because the presence of the second moon could have an adverse effect on the flight path. Of course they thought him mistaken, misguided, mad even – because hadn't the Americans managed the journey years before, with no such problems? Gull's arguments caused him to be dismissed from the project.

So it was that the disgraced scientist and I set up our own mission to find out the exact size and orbit of Luna Two, as we called the new discovery. Working from Gull's own laboratory, we spent another year in constant search and frustration, surviving only on a pittance, until we could be certain of our calculations. The second moon was circling at exactly the same pace as the Earth, always floating above the same point on the planet, that point being somewhere in the city of Manchester, England. Twenty-four feet above the surface, the twin moon was, and only 11.0457 inches in diameter. Further work allowed us to pinpoint its exact co-ordinates: a street name, even a house number. Simple enquiries revealed that the house was owned by a Mrs Gladys Selene. According to the records, she lived there alone.

It was, I remember, early evening when we arrived, but already dark. The house seemed no different from any other in the street: a small two-up, two-down council property. A faint yellow light glowed from an upstairs window.

The door was opened a tiny crack by a middle-aged woman. Gull stormed into the place, pushing the woman aside. She began to scream and to argue, but then suddenly collapsed, as though the fight of years had gone out of her. Tearful, drunk on cheap vodka and resigned at our intrusion, she motioned us to go upstairs.

In the front bedroom we found her only child, a young boy, ten years of age. His name, she told us, was Joe; Joseph Selene. At first sight I could only wonder at just how very fat the boy was. Then I saw that his bloated, distended stomach actually glowed; glowed with wave-pulses of pure amber, the only source of light in the room. The boy had spent his whole life in that small space, with no schooling or contact. He could neither speak nor write, and lived his days in painful solitude. Only the various maps of the moon, images from the early flights, and models of the Apollo 11 spacecraft dotted around the room brought him peace. From our enquiries Gladys revealed that she had conceived Joe with the help of a travelling salesman, whose name she could not recall, nor his intentions, except that he was selling cheap atlases.

The instruments of measurement were prodded into Joe's veins, and a body-scan taken. A dark, poisonous smudge appeared on the printout, reminding me of nothing more than the original blip I had seen on the gravity read-outs.

I can hardly state the following without remembering my

horror at the revelation: the second moon was living inside the boy's stomach, desperate to be born.

'Beautiful . . .' whispered Gull. 'Quite beautiful . . .'

He decided it best that Joe not be moved, 'for fear of disturbing the gravitational field', so we carried all our equipment into the house, set up a field-lab there. I was to stay awake through the night, standing guard; nightwatchman to the Earth's second moon. Once alone, I rested myself in a chair next to the boy's bed. I very quickly fell into the slow, pulsating rhythm of the moonlight. I felt the moon was guiding me dreamwards . . .

Suddenly. Where am I?

An empty, grey landscape, pitted with holes. I imagine this to be the inside of Joe's skull, the convoluted surface of his brain, sluggish to think. Until a puffball-costumed figure comes slow-bouncing over the horizon. He's dressed in the antique NASA spacesuit, long studied from the old Apollo landings. Face hidden behind his visor, the astronaut speaks in a weary tone, words broken by radio static: 'It's been a long time,' he crackles.

'Who are you?' I ask, my own words floating through the loose gravity of this sleep-haunted world.

'Does no-one remember?'

I glance at the nametag on his suit. 'Commander Armstrong? Apollo 11?'

The figure nods slowly, reflections of the Earth pinballing around his helmet's darkness.

'But what do you want?' I ask. 'I mean . . . what are you doing here? I mean . . . I thought you . . .'

'Died? Yes. Many years ago, but there are journeys still to make. I have landed on satellite Selene to complete the mission.'

'Mission? What about the boy?'

I woke up in early morning darkness. It took me a few seconds to realize what was wrong. Darkness! The boy! I stood up from the chair in a panic, only to bang my head painfully against the wall. Someone must have moved me around in the night. Scared now, I tried to place myself—

Flash! Retinal burn. Light drenching me, like take-off.

Gull and the boy's mother burst through the door. One of them turned on the overhead light, to find me cowering in a corner, screaming. My chair was jammed up tight against a wall, far from where it had been. All the furniture had moved away from the boy's bed, blown by a stronger force. Plastic models of the lunar rockets lay in pieces all around. Joe Selene was lying on the bed, gently moving; alive at ground zero.

Gull was running to his beloved equipment, all of which was dead, night-dark; the woman to the beloved child, resting her hands disbelieving on the loose folds of empty skin where the stomach had once engulfed her world. The light had gone from there, to flow into the boy's eyes; to flow, smiling in the aftermath, at last and somewhere . . .

'What happened?' Gull was shaking me. 'What happened in here? Where's the light!'

I smiled. 'He took off, Gull.' Then I couldn't stop laughing. 'He took off! Neil Armstrong! He took off without us!'

DUBSHIPS
(blues for a lost astronaut)

sky lit by fire
consider me mad or simply a liar
world you inhabit
wherever whatever
sky lit by fire

it's been a long time
been a long long time

to let the sky swallow
orbital hollow
consider me moonmad
shadowdark shadowboy
belly of apollo

it's been a long time
been a long long time

we take poison's flight path
dreaming of spacecraft
gravity's clutches
descending unending
asleep in the math

it's been a long time
been a long long time

beloved equipment
journeying heavensent
retinal take-off
achespace tasting
illusion's ascent

it's been a long time
been a long long time

skull lit by fire
mother to the wire
he took off without us
somewhere and somewhen
skull lit by fire

it's been a long time
velocities climb
the heart's apogee
touchdown and touching
been a long long time

PART FOUR

REFLECTION'S EMBRACE

SPECIMENS

It was a small cage, roughly four inches square and two inches high. Somebody had placed it on the roadway. To call it a cage is perhaps an exaggeration, constructed as it was from a fine wire mesh. It had no door.

Inside the cage, a worm. A worm, a common earthworm (*Annelida lumbricus*), perhaps two inches long, quite thick, and with a slightly bulbous midsection.

It was the early morning, just after seven o'clock. A small group of people stared at the cage, curious, but no more than that. Nobody had seen it being placed there. A tram was forced to stop because of the gathering. The driver descended from his cab, to remonstrate with the people blocking his way. They pointed out the cage to him. The driver then tried to move it by hand. To his surprise, he found that the cage was firmly fixed to the tarmac, with some kind of bonding agent. Angry now, and fearing for his schedules, the driver warned the people aside, climbed back into his cab. He started the tram, and drove forward, slowly.

The cage was lying directly on the left-side track.

The tram hit it squarely, there was a crunching sound; the tram moved on. The driver did not stop to inspect the damage.

The cage was crushed, bent to one side, and the mesh was torn. The worm had been pushed through the gap, and lay wriggling in two pieces on the tarmac. The crowd drifted away, as though nothing had happened. Quite soon, somebody stood on one separated half of the worm, squashing it. In all likelihood, this person was not aware of what they had done.

Nobody knows what happened to the other half.

Two days later, and at approximately the same time, another cage was found. It was positioned in the same place – on the short section of Market Street that leads away from Piccadilly Gardens in Manchester. Constructed of the same materials as the first one, only this time of slightly larger size, being six inches square, and the same in height. The mesh was of a wider gauge. It had no door.

Inside the cage, a mouse. A mouse, a common field mouse (*Apodemus sylvaticus*), grey in colour, with clean fur and a long pink tail that swished, contentedly.

Again, a tram was stopped, and the driver tried to move the cage by hand, without success. He then decided to use his vehicle to move it. One or two of the crowd were horrified at this cruelty, and they protested vehemently with the driver. The driver would have no such discussion.

He did not stop to inspect the damage.

The incident was reported on page seven of the *Manchester Evening News*.

*   *   *

Five days later, a larger cage was found. This one was three feet square, two feet in height, with rigid steel bars down the sides and along the top. It was cemented to the tramlines. Nobody had seen it being placed there. It had no door.

Inside the cage, a dog. A dog, a mongrel dog (*Canis familiaris*), perhaps a mix of Collie and German Shepherd. It was a light fawn in colour, with patches of muted brown here and there. It was growling and obviously in some distress, the cage being slightly too small for it. The dog turned in a tight circle, again and again, and butted its head against the bars, trying to get its jaws around them.

A large crowd had gathered, and people were pushing to get a closer look. A woman was kneeling down beside the cage, trying to comfort the poor creature. The dog growled at her, in anger, in fear.

A tram was stalled in front of the cage. A long line of buses and other trams were piled up behind the stranded vehicle. Somebody called the police. A squad car arrived in ten minutes, and a puzzled officer radioed for help. Soon, the police had control of the square, diverting traffic, and trying to keep people back as workmen sawed through the bars.

The dog was released, and taken to the police station. The workmen then removed the cage, clearing the roadway.

The incident was reported on the local television news programme that evening, and was picked up by the national media. The story was connected to the first two episodes, with the worm and the mouse. The BBC featured it on the *Nine O'Clock News*, as the last item.

By now, most of the people of Manchester had heard of the strange happenings, and speculation was rife, in pubs and living rooms, in restaurants and launderettes. Some felt sure it was a political gesture, by an animal liberation organization. Others claimed it was merely a tasteless joke by a madman. Some even saw it as a brilliant piece of art, a trenchant protest at an unfeeling society.

The police, for their part, had made a forensic examination of the dog. Its fur was covered with grass seeds, bits of matted food, and the usual colony of fleas. The only item of real interest was a splash of silver paint found behind one ear. Chemical analysis of the paint revealed it to be of an unknown composition.

The police also examined footage taken from various security cameras in the Gardens. All five cameras had failed to operate during the early hours of the morning.

The next day, a small crowd gathered at the same location. The people were becoming intrigued; they wanted to see what would happen next. To witness the curiosity. Unfortunately, the road was quite clear, and after half an hour or so the crowd dispersed. The next day a smaller crowd waited there, but again, no cage. Each day the crowd got smaller, until people merely passed the spot, idly glancing to see but then continuing on their way.

Twelve days after the dog incident, when nobody cared any more, the fourth cage appeared. This one was the largest yet: twelve feet square, and ten feet high. The bars were spaced at two-inch intervals. It had no door. It must have been set into position during the deserted, early hours of the morning.

Inside the cage, a horse. A horse, a thoroughbred mare (*Equus caballus*), with a shiny black coat and a midnight-blue mane. It stood four square in the cage, quite still and at ease. Only the occasional *harrumph*! from its nostrils and the smoke of its breath disturbed the cold air.

The whole area was cordoned off, as the police decided what to do about the obstruction. A large crowd had gathered, increasing in numbers as the hours passed. A camera crew turned up to capture the event, and to add to the confusion. A team of workmen cut through the bars, releasing the horse into the trained hands of a veterinary surgeon. The poor creature was quickly examined, and then loaded into a horse-box. The workmen set about removing the cage. This operation took three hours to complete, and even then the road was ruined.

No traffic passed through Piccadilly Gardens that day.

The incident was reported on all the news programmes, and in every daily paper. A number of websites were set up on the Internet, dedicated to the cages and their various occupants. A round-the-clock police watch was started, and the camera crew and a large group of spectators camped out all night long, just to catch a glimpse of the next cage being erected. Everyone expected that somebody, some group, would surely come forward and claim responsibility. Nobody did.

So, the people waited. It seemed that all of the country was held in the same state of vibrant expectancy.

It took twenty-one days for the last, severely disappointed person to leave the site.

And fifty-seven lonely days after that disappointment . . .

Inside the cage, a jaguar. A jaguar (*Panthera onca*), native of Central America; a great snarling beast, breathing hot thoughts of its homeland. Spotted large, with deep black on orange, turning in its own tight circus, bound by the cage, but barely so.

Nobody dared come close; instead a circle of fear formed around the cage. Time and the city slowed to a halt, as though the beast controlled the clock's pace. It took two days to release the creature safely, and even stunned it provoked fear.

The incident was reported around the world, and discussed in Parliament. Crazed pamphlets were published, offering futile explanations; a desperate man came forward to be punished for the incidents. The police dismissed him after two days' questioning. Synopses for books and films were hastily prepared, many of them finding their price. A range of toy cages was put on the market, five in the series, containing exact models of the worm, the mouse, the dog, the horse and the jaguar. Each cage had a different secret mechanism that would unlock the bars and release the creature. They were the most popular gift that Christmas.

And then, nothing. No new cage appeared. Months passed by. People speculated that the process was complete. Talk drained away to memory, and then to dismissal. A few jokes remained, that was all.

Exactly one year on from the very first incident, finally, mysteriously, the next cage appeared. It was four feet square, six feet high. Bars at three-inch intervals. Fixed to the road so rigorously, it seemed to have deep foundations. In all respects similar to the previous five cages, except in this one particular: it had a door. A door that was open, slightly ajar, and a large, heavy, padlock that swung on a reinforced strut. The padlock was unclasped, and the tiny gap between the clasp and lock – it caught the eye, teasingly. There was no key in the lock. Once closed, it would remain so.

Inside the cage, nothing. Nothing, an emptiness. An aching sense of something not being there; and the people, the vast crowd of people who gazed in silence, they thought, at last, at last, something has escaped!

Until they realized.

The cage was waiting . . .

A man, a middle-aged man (*Homo sapiens*), dressed smartly as though for an insurance office, stepped forward from the crowd.

CREEPING ZERO

Tonight we caught five. We was pretty good. Mr Bone says we're nearly back on target. I'm thinking that was pretty good anyroads until Clingfilm says it don't mean fuck, we got yards to go before we gets us some bonus. We got some bad days see? We got us some bad days where we nearly didn't catch any at all. But now we're making up. Tonight we caught five.

Tonight we caught three. Pretty good. But not as pretty good as last night was pretty good.

Today we caught none. Some days you do that. You catch none. Sometimes you catch one, most times two. Sometimes three. Sometimes five. Once we caught six, and once we caught seven. That's the most we ever caught in one time, seven. That was a special day, we got prizes. We never caught four, not in one time. I thought this was just strange luck until Mr Bone tells us that you never see four together, they don't like that number. He don't know why they don't like it, and neither does Edie and not even Shiva who thinks she knows everything. But today we caught none, which is the same as saying today we caught four, because you never catch four, not in one time. But Mr Bone says it's cheating, to think like that.

Tonight we caught two. Not good, not bad, just the usual number to catch in any one night or day. I like the dark rides best. Everyone keeps telling me it's more dangerous at night because that's mainly when they come out and that's why we get more wages for the darkshift, but I don't care. I don't mind how much we get just as long as we catch as many as possible. Everyone laughs at me for this, because all they talk about is the wages and the bonus and the prizes, except for Edie who never talks much, and except for Shiva who's a little bit crazy but who cares because she catches more of them than anyone else. So that leaves just Mr Bone and Clingfilm talking about the wages. That's enough. I like it best of all around three or four in the morning when the whole city just belongs to us. So quiet the streets, so quiet and tender almost. It's not like we're driving, more like we're floating through Manchester. Tonight we caught two.

Today we caught another two. That's a lot of twos to be catching. Pretty soon we're gonna have to start catching the threes again, and the fives, and the sixes and who knows even the sevens. The best that any crew ever caught in one time was nine, but that was the Mambo Suicide Crew, they're famous for riding hard, and anyroads they clean the Gorton block. All you've gotta do in Gorton is walk out the door, you've caught five already, they're everywhere. Whereas we work the Levenshulme area, there's not nearly as many, and today we caught two.

Tonight we caught three. One time I would've called that doing pretty good. Now it's doing pretty bad. Mr Bone is cursing, and Clingfilm is saying that's it, no bonus, and Edie's getting quieter by the minute, and Shiva is going crazy in the van for some let-out. There's the five of us. We're the Creeping Zero Crew. There's always five in a crew. I think that's pretty neat, there being five of us, because that means that one can stick with the van, and the four others can go on patrol. So if you stick together out there, there's no chance of you being taken for a gang of them, is there? Because you never see them in fours. That's how Mr Bone explains it, anyroads. Mr Bone is the boss, and Clingfilm is the driver, and Edie's the tracker, and Shiva, well Shiva's just Shiva, ain't she? She's the gun. She's caught hundreds of them. Me? I'm the kid, the apprentice. This is my first ever crew. I've never caught any. I just drag them back to the van, and skin them.

Today we caught none. I don't even want to talk about it.

Today we caught one. What's to say? We just went out there, with Edie leading the way, and we found a loner, and we caught it, and we killed it, and I skinned it, and that was that. The rest of the day we just went around the streets, and I tried to do some talking to Edie, saying that I'd like to be a tracker one day, but she wouldn't talk back at me, just living in her own world, I guess. And Mr Bone says you don't get to be a tracker, kid, you have to be born a tracker, and Clingfilm said that was a pile of fuck. But what does he know? What does anybody know? Today we caught one.

*   *   *

Tonight we caught five. We did pretty good, and we were up for it, except we let one get away. That means we caught four. It's not the same as really catching four, because you never do, and that's that. It's just that one of them got away. That got Shiva mad, you bet. She hates it when they get away. And Clingfilm was cursing about the bonus again, when really it was all his fault that one got away. He was hiding behind the curses, even I can see that. But the strangest thing was when the one got away, and the four that were left went mad like, when they realized there was four of them, I suppose. Usually they come easy once they're caught, but these four went mad on us, and I was scared because I know that's how the Creeping Zero lost Wesley, catching five and letting one get away, and the four what's left going mad. But this time Shiva got them all. Got them good.

Today we caught none. I don't mind it. I was still shaken up from last night, and I can't stop thinking about Wesley now that I've started. I never met him, because I took his place. But all the crew, they go on about him, like he was brilliant or something, even though he got lost. I wish they wouldn't, because them going on like that means I'll have to be brilliant one day. I hope I am, one day, and that I get to be a top-notch tracker, but thinking about it just makes me shake even more. Today we caught none. Good.

Today we caught one. We did pretty good. Catching one ain't usually pretty good, but this time it was, because we had to keep it alive. Sometimes you have to do that, keep them alive. You get more money, so Clingfilm's happy. Mr Bone got word that the university wanted a live one, and so we had to be careful, because they would rather die than be kept alive. It's my first time at keeping one alive. It was a female. I wouldn't mind so much if it was a male, but it wasn't. It was a female. We had her tied up in the van, and all I could do was look at her struggling. I don't know, it's different. It's different close up. I thought it would be. I thought that close up it would be easy to tell, but it wasn't. Because she looked just like the rest of us. But, you know, beautiful. And that's why it was different. And Mr Bone says you have to be careful, thinking like that because them looking just like us is only the disguise. That's why Edie is so important, Mr Bone says, because without a tracker how would we ever know which to catch? And today we caught a live one.

Tonight we caught six. And everybody's going crazy good. But what is it, what's wrong? I can't stop thinking about yesterday and the one we kept alive, the female. Because why are we catching them? Nobody knows. I asked Mr Bone, he's the boss and he doesn't know. I asked Clingfilm and he said it's for the money, and I asked Shiva and she said it's just so we can kill them. And I asked Edie, and Edie didn't answer. And then Mr Bone says we shouldn't never ask that question, it's a stupid question, you might as well ask the moon why it keeps coming back every night. We just catch them, that's all. And tonight we caught six. And then I got to thinking about Wesley again, and why he went and got himself lost.

Tonight we caught two. Pretty good. Pretty bad. I don't know. Thinking about the girl, the female, I mean. And thinking about Wesley and the job and everything. There's only two ways to leave the job, so Shiva reckons. You can die, or you get lost. And you bet she said that dying is the best way, the only way, because getting lost is when you just walk out one night, away from the van, away from the crew, and you become one of them, one of the lost ones out there, wandering, wandering. Wandering until you get caught. But when I reminded her about Wesley, she just turned away and started messing with the gun. So I waited for the quiet time and I asked Mr Bone and he says you shouldn't be thinking about that. But Wesley got lost, I says. Yeah, Wesley got lost, and Mr Bone gets this look in him then. But he'll come back to us, he says. And I ask what that means. And he says, just like Edie came back to us.

Today we caught one, or was it two? I can't remember.

Tonight we caught some. I think we did. It's just that I can't stop looking at Edie now, knowing that she got lost, and then she came back, and now she's a tracker and can find the lost real easy. Maybe you have to get lost, to find the lost, to become a tracker. Maybe that's what Mr Bone meant when he said that you have to be born a tracker, because you certainly have to be born to get lost. And I'm scared, scared that I was born like that, with the losing inside me, and that one day I'll just walk clean away.

Tonight we caught something. What was it? The whole crew is damaged by the catching. Because ain't that the nightmare: to catch the ones who got lost and to have them turn around and not want to come back. Not like Edie, not like Edie came back with the tracking knowledge, but to just go crazy bad on us. It must be Wesley. It must be poor lost Wesley we caught, but Mr Bone won't mention it, and Edie's on the edge of something, and Shiva just sits there cleaning the gun like for ever, and Clingfilm won't even talk about the money any more, that bad. But we had a job to do. And we did it. We went out there and we caught it and we killed it and I dragged it back and I skinned it. We had a job to do.

Tonight we caught two and a half. We did pretty good and everybody's jumping because no-one's ever caught a half a one before. It's not really a half a one, that's just what we call them when they're in the changing state. Anyroads, it's very rare, so we're on for the bonus, most definitely. And everyone's saying I did brilliant, even Clingfilm, because I helped catch the half a one. It's the first one I ever caught, and it turned out real special. And then we just went floating through the night, and we was singing.

CRAWL TOWN

Old Tom Sharpsaw had this story that nobody ever left Crawl, that's why the cemetery was so crowded. That's why all the tombstones scratched up tight against each other. That's why the ground was so parched. That's why the housing estate was so rancid. That's why the food was so bad. That's why the buses always stopped at the edge of town. That's why we didn't have a football team. That's why the windows were always broken. That's why the roads curved around and kept meeting themselves halfway. That's why the sun worked like a fridge light, and the rain like a toilet flush. That's why all us girls wore sackcloth tracksuits. That's why the local library placed all the street-maps on the sex-education shelves. That's why the Town-Hall clock has only got one hand, and seven numbers. And it moves backwards. That's why, he'd say. That's why, that's why.

Old Tom lived on top of the Vanishing Palace. This was the

name of the amusement arcade, right next to the cemetery. To get there you had to step over the fallen stones, what was called the crazy paving of the dead. Us kids used to hang around the Vanishing Palace a whole lot, because what else was there, except for the Factory and that was too well protected. There were six machines to play. Five, really, because one of them was adults only. This was the famous Intravenus machine.

That's about as much excitement as you could find in Crawl, just thinking about what the beautiful Intravenus girl got up to. We just assumed the machine was female, it felt right somehow.

Crawl. Sounds like a strange name for a place, but believe me, you ever take several bad luck wrong turnings and end up here one day, you'll know where the name comes from. It's somewhere to the north of Manchester, so they tell us at school anyway. I won't say where exactly, just in case you're tempted. Anyway, I was born here, that's my excuse. I say born; nobody is strictly born in Crawl – you just wake up one day and find yourself here, alone in a stranger's bed, with nowhere else to go, and then you realize, oh shit, I've been here all my life already, what now? But like Tom said, escape isn't in the dictionary. Believe me, I've looked.

The machines in the Vanishing Palace only worked with old money. So when you went up to the change booth, and handed in your allowance, Tom would hand you back a little pile of antique coins. Most of them had a king's head on them, Charles III or somebody. And near all of them had teeth marks in the soft metal. Some of them had been bitten so hard, they didn't even work the machines. And anyway, the Intravenus machine would only work with one special coin that we never got to see. Tom kept it in a box behind the counter. And he'd sit there reading his paper while us youngsters played the kiddie games. Every so often he would mutter something about the state of the world, I mean the state of the town, of course.

The *Crawl Gazette* was four pages thin. It came out once a month. It was always four pages, even when there wasn't enough news or adverts to fill it; those times they just left some blank spaces in there. Sometimes they'd leave whole pages blank. One famous time the whole paper was blank, except for the title. When there was news, it was usually about the over-crowding of the cemetery, or the campaign to get rid of the Intravenus machine. Sometimes it reported on the latest product of the Factory. That was all I ever read it for, to see what the Factory had given this month. It always gave one thing a month.

Tom Sharpsaw had a robot that helped him run the Vanishing Palace. It was a crude spider of a thing, with two-and-a-half of its legs missing, and a single bulbous eye that was often clouded with a strange liquor. Out of its round body, a long needle sometimes protruded. This it would plug into the electric socket. The robot's name was Oris. Tom said that the name stood for Automated Retrieval of Information System, even though automated didn't begin with an O, it just sounded like it did. He'd stolen Oris from the library, so the machine wasn't up to much except maybe checking how many games had been played on which machine by whom. That kind of stuff. So Tom claimed anyway, but we reckoned it knew a whole lot more than that, including maybe the secret code to the Intravenus machine.

Tom had a thing about stealing things. He didn't see it as a crime, because everybody knew he'd done it. And mostly the stuff he stole was useless anyway, nobody wanted it back. Like I mentioned, the second hand of the clock was missing, and some of the numbers. Well who needed a clock in Crawl?

What was there to get to on time? So Tom had done his civic duty; the tall, spindly finger was planted in his garden round back of the Palace, with creepers growing all up it. The numbers, some he'd turned into furniture; the number two, for instance, he'd put legs on it to use as a dining table. But most of the things he stole went into the making of the game machines; the number four of the clock, that was the base of the Butterfly Circle machine. The machines were never finished, always something more would be added to them.

You can guess why Tom was just about the only grown-up I talked to much. He had some crazy stories, and the brilliant games, and all that. And sometimes he would take me on his stealing trips, and teach me some of the arcane secrets of breaking and entering. Other times I would help out adding new bits to the machines, that was the most fun. But mostly I liked him just because he was the only one who ever talked about getting away from the town's clutches.

It was all just talk, but what the hell.

Oris had come out of the Factory. Whenever anything comes out of the Factory, first of all we have to decide what it is, what it does. This is the Town Hall's job. Sometimes they can't ever find a reason for it. But with Oris, it was fairly obvious what was going on, what with those legs, and the eye, and the computing engine. That's why the library got to use it. Until Tom stole it off them, of course. I helped him do that. By then the robot was on its last five-and-a-half legs anyway. Nobody missed it.

If you've ever seen the Crawl library, you'll know why they really didn't need an Automated Retrieval of Information System. There just wasn't enough information to retrieve, that was it. The place was a shack, really. Small and grotty, made out of planks, and mostly falling down. And so small, they couldn't have more than a hundred books in there, surely. Tom claimed that one book was enough to last a lifetime anyway, especially if you read it in the special way.

'What do you mean?' I'd ask him. 'What special way?'

'One word a day,' he'd answer.

'One word a day, lasts a lifetime? I don't believe you.'

'Check it out, girl. Put up some money.'

Now Tom Sharpsaw had a whole bunch of books on the shelves at the Vanishing Palace. More than the library had, that was for sure. The thing about the books that Tom kept: they were all written by himself. So we made this bet. I said that reading a book one word a day wouldn't take a lifetime, and he claimed it would. And so certain was he of winning, he let me choose whichever book to test the theory on. So I looked over them all: unfinished novels, engineering manuals, dictionaries of illusions, a censored atlas of the world, collections of poetry. Of course I chose the atlas, after all wasn't it all maps?

'There's lots of words in there,' said Tom.

'Like where?'

'Place names. Here, in the back. Thousands of them.'

'OK. I'll choose a poetry book.'

The book I picked out was a tattered paperback affair, a slim self-published volume called *The Silvering*. The author's name was Zenith O'Clock, which was one of the names Tom sometimes used for his writing. I flicked through the book; there were only thirty pages, twenty-six of which contained poems. Actually, now I looked at it, it wasn't so much a bunch of poems, more a very short story, set out with only a few words on each page, and lots of empty space.

'Do we read all the book?' I asked. 'The bits at the front, the contents and all that? Or do we just read the poems themselves?'

'Just the poems,' Tom answered.

'What's wrong? Don't you want to win, or something?'

'Just read the words, one at a time.'

'OK, I'll read. You see how many days it takes me.'

'Begin.'

'OK . . . here goes.'

And then I read out the word 'Possibly . . .'

You can see the problem, can't you? I'm telling you this story about the poetry book, just so you'll get an inkling of how Tom Sharpsaw's brain worked. Because I couldn't read out the next word, which was 'you', until the next day. And then each day after that I had to go round to the Vanishing Palace, just to read the next word. I got as far as reading out loud the passage, 'Possibly, you could say that one evening, late in the future, all the mirrors in the world . . .', which took all of seventeen days, and then I just couldn't be bothered any more.

To this day I'm still not sure if I lost that bet, or if I won it. Certainly, no money changed hands.

So then, Tom Sharpsaw had a brain a bit like the roads around here; he kind of met you halfway through a thought, but from another direction, if you see what I mean. The best way to describe it is to tell about the machines he made. He built these strange contraptions out of anything he could get his hands on really, including some products from the Factory. Stuff that other people saw absolutely no use for, he would combine into these bewildering games. I call them games; there wasn't any obvious way of playing them. You just had to find your way around them, work out what they were for, try to unravel their mystery as you went along. I think the object of the game was to find out how to play it.

And I guess the Factory works in just the same way. Sometimes we would go and stand alongside the outer fence, just to watch if anything was being produced. It never was, of course. Nobody ever saw the Factory actually deliver anything; the products would just turn up, left on the special platform that was the only part of the whole compound we could ever touch. Every other part of the fence was electrified. Robot guards circled the spaces between the fences.

The Factory protected itself.

There it stood in the distance, nested within the three fences and the moat; the centre of attraction around which the town of Crawl slowly travelled. A giant of a place it was, made out of crumbling red brick, on which the words HERCULES MILL 1897 stood out in dirty white lettering. They told us in school that people had worked inside it once, a long, long time ago, before all the processes were automated. At the end, so they say, only one person was needed to operate the whole building. I was very excited when I learned that this last supervisor was a woman, I suppose because it's the kind of thing I could imagine myself doing, wandering alone around a cavernous factory, totally in charge of an army of robots. It was the kind of fantasy I had, when I was a young girl, and I would always see myself as wearing a long, flowing ballgown in these dreams, I don't know why. I would be dancing with a very handsome male robot.

Nobody knows what happened to that last supervisor. She must have died, years ago, centuries ago.

And now, at night, the Factory's lights come on, one by one, and the whole town listens to the constant purring of the secret engines. Tom reckons it just got caught in its own flow diagram one day, and had no more need of the human hand. But still, it produces, following the twisted instructions . . .

The best thing that ever happened was when I actually got to see the Factory make a delivery. No, that's not true. What it was, I was once the person who found a product on the delivery platform. I didn't see it being put there, nobody sees that, I just came down to the Factory early one morning and there it was, this . . . thing. It was a flat circular object, about thirty centimetres in diameter and made out of plastic. And this plastic was etched with a spiral groove on both sides of the disc. A paper label had been glued to the central area, and this was covered with writing. Reading this, I found out that the object was called Pixelkids Come Out Tonight, and had been made by somebody called Janus Fontaine. I didn't know what it was, but instead of taking it over to the Town Hall to be registered, I showed it to Tom at the Vanishing Palace. But he was just as puzzled as I was, and said that he would have to study it.

I kind of forgot all about the product for a while, because I never heard anything more about it from Tom. But then, about six months later, there it was, the thing I'd found, now a part of the Shark Magnet machine. Tom had set it up so the disc spun around, and the groove in it came into contact with a tiny shard of diamond he had prised out of a stolen necklace. And it made a noise! The spinning disc made a noise, a type of music I think, but nothing like I'd ever heard before.

So there you are; the Factory making these strange products that can hardly be used, until you break the code on them. And Old Tom Sharpsaw spending his lost days constructing perverse, uncontrollable machines. They were the mirror of each other.

Take the Snake Loop game he invented, for instance; all these metal pipes that twisted together, sometimes sending up clouds of green smoke. Here, the first thing was figuring out how to turn the machine on, because there was a different way of turning it on every time you put your money in the slot. And then, one day just when you think you've got the hang of turning it on, and you've successfully shot down all the fluffy green clouds with the attached perfume gun, what should you discover but that turning it on wasn't turning it on at all. Turning it on was just turning on the unlocking device which the clouds made. And killing the clouds in a certain order, that was the real way of turning on the Snake Loop machine. Only then could you really start playing the game, which had absolutely nothing at all to do with killing clouds, and a whole lot more to do with snakes and loops and the rhythm of the heart and the shadow of the eye . . .

Well, it's the Factory, isn't it? Tom's caught in the loop as well; we all are. And that's why nobody ever gets to leave Crawl, and why the goddamn graveyard is so crowded. And maybe one day we'll find out what the Factory is really making. The Big Product, Tom calls it. Because all these things it makes a gift of, they're just the side products, that's what the experts reckon anyway; things that have gone wrong, say, or failed experiments. Tom reckons it another way; he reckons the Factory is giving us these products just so we can help complete the process. And if we ever find out what the final product is, maybe then we all get to leave . . .

It scares me just thinking about it.

So there were five of these machines that Tom had made: the Snake Loop, the Butterfly Circle, the Plague Circus, the Shark Magnet and the Liquid Tiger machine. And like I said, all of them just kept on growing as the years passed by, and most of them included little things here and there that had come out of the Factory. But the Intravenus machine, that was different. Intravenus was a Factory product in itself. The whole thing had come out just as it was, complete in all its parts, ready for use. The only trouble being, nobody could work out the reason for it.

The shape of the thing didn't help any, being a perfect sphere made from a burnished metal of some kind. A hand knocked against it revealed a hollowness within, alive with echoes, and yet there appeared to be no way to open it up. Two small circular holes placed at right angles to each other allowed a glimpse of the contained darkness, which was smoky and smelled of ash. Certainly, at six feet in diameter, it was one of the largest products yet delivered, but that didn't mean anything; very often the smaller objects proved the most useful, like the bird shoes for instance, they were much sought after. But the Intravenus, what use was it? A large, hollow globe with two holes in it, that's it. So the thing was rolled on over to the Town Hall, which is where all products of the Factory were meant to be registered.

It wasn't called the Intravenus machine in those days, of course, it wasn't called anything. So that's when Tom Sharpsaw came calling. He paid a night-time visit to the Council Yard where all the useless objects were stored. And he found a home for the strange new machine in the Vanishing Palace. Of course he didn't know what the purpose of it was either, not at first anyway, not until he started to work on it, and I'm sure this is where Oris the Robot comes in handy. It was Oris that most probably discovered the secret code of the latest machine, because all the Factory's products are linked in some weird way.

We just don't know the weirdness of the way, that's all.

All Tom Sharpsaw had to do then was turn the secret code into a process that could be coin-operated, by the special coin naturally, and there it was, the star turn of the Vanishing Palace. He painted the sphere black, with the word *Intravenus* in swirling red letters. He only called it the Intravenus after he'd found out what the purpose of it was, so all us kids were real keen to have a go on it. And I was a bit mad at him anyway, because he hadn't let me help him work on the machine, that wasn't fair. The least I was expecting was first go on the new game. Except then he goes and paints ADULTS ONLY on it as well. It was the first time we'd ever seen such a phrase in Crawl. Tom was very strict about it being for adults only, and so it was only a few men of the town who got to play the Intravenus. And not only men, because some women started to play it as well. They would stare through one of the holes, while a beam of light that Tom had rigged up was shone through the second hole. What they saw inside, we just couldn't imagine. The arrival of the game didn't please everybody, however, because pretty soon some of the older and more conservative people of Crawl started a campaign to have the Intravenus machine closed down, even destroyed. This made us even more curious. We'd ask the players as they came out of the Palace what it was they'd seen in the game, what had happened, what was it like, what was the secret? Please, we'd demand, please tell us what the mystery is.

But nobody would. They'd just walk out of the Vanishing Palace with this glazed expression on their faces, as though they were drunk or something. Near everybody who'd played the game would start to gather around the Factory's outer fence, just staring at the place. Like it was a temple or something. We got so curious that some of us decided to hide in the back room of the Palace while Tom locked up for the night.

There was me, and Bobby, and Janet, and Flo.

Bobby dropped out because he was too scared, I think, so that left the three of us, three girls. I guess that's why we were so fascinated with the machine, not so much that it was adults only, but more because of the name; we all wanted to be in love one day. Because what else could you hope for in a town called Crawl? So there we were, all three of us cramped in the little store room, surrounded by all the bits of things that Tom Sharpsaw hadn't got round to using yet. And it was dark, and scary, and worse still I couldn't help feeling guilty at doing the dirty on Tom, after all he'd taught me. I was going to use the skills he'd passed on to me against him. So how could I not be feeling bad?

But the Intravenus Girl was calling, and that's all that mattered.

Tom lived in some little rooms above the Palace. We had to wait a few hours until all was silent from up there, and every flicker of light had been extinguished. Even then we still waited a while longer, just to make sure. Then we crept out.

It was easy enough to find the box he kept the special coin in. And easier enough with my stealing skills to pick the lock on it. There was the coin! How it gleamed, not like the usual coins at all. This one was shiny, with no marks of hunger. Freshly minted, but how could it be, with a queen's head upon it. Elizabeth II. How long ago was that? Nobody knew.

There was a plan to all this. Flo would keep watch, and Janet would help me with the machine, but I would be the first to look into the hole, that was decided because wasn't I the one who had stolen the key? Tom had suspended the sphere from wires, to bring the apertures up to eye level. Of course that was too high for us kids, so I had to stand on a stool to get to the right level. Janet held the stool while I climbed up, and then I told her to put the coin in the slot. Which she did, making the beam fire into the one hole while I put my eye, tenderly, nervously, against the other.

And I looked inside of Venus.

At first, all was a fog, a swirling of darkness that the light beam cut into fragments. And then the beam would bounce off the inside of the globe, and cross over itself, and where it crossed, a side beam would shoot out. In a few seconds the whole of the inside of the sphere was filled with these criss-crossing beams of light. So many of them now, they made a spectrum embrace; a meeting at the centre, where the lights fused into colour.

And inside the colours, an image started to form, giving shape to a woman's face. A woman's face I had seen before, in one of the picture books at school. The last supervisor! She was trying to speak to me . . .

Just then I heard Flo shouting from the doorway, and I thought Tom must've woken up or something, heard a noise perhaps, the woman's voice, or else he'd noticed the beam of light. And the next thing was Janet screaming, and pulling me off the stool.

I was on the floor, with Janet beside me, and Flo running over towards us. And there, rising up on what was left of his spindly legs, Oris the Robot was jabbing at my body with the electric needle and then I was screaming as well, especially when I saw Tom Sharpsaw standing over me, shaking his head in a fearsome rage . . .

All this has come back to me, because Tom Sharpsaw died recently. He never did make it out of the town, and now his body is just one more occupant of the graveyard. We drifted apart after the incident I've just described, and pretty soon after that he shut the doors of the Vanishing Palace once and for all. He more or less closed himself up in there, only coming out for food, or for the occasional stealing trip. Eventually even those stopped, and we never saw much of him at all.

And that was an end to playing the Intravenus.

I went to the funeral, I'm not sure why. I was the only person there. He meant a lot to me, I suppose, when I was a kid, and certainly my life without him became very boring. I work for the council now, processing the Factory's products. That was never a part of my youthful fantasies, was it? But still, we do know a lot more about the place these days, and about the mysterious fourth fence, the one within our minds. I think Tom was a kind of escape, just in his company, maybe that's it. But standing there amongst the rain-spattered tombstones, I couldn't help but look over to where the Vanishing Palace shadowed the thin, dying rays of the sun. The building was in a terrible state; the windows boarded up, holes in the roof where a few birds fluttered to and fro, the whole thing dusted with cobwebs.

What can I say? It was a simple job to work the mechanisms of the lock. Some skills you never lose. Opening the door, it was like going back twenty years, but the sight that greeted me was altogether a shock. The whole amusement arcade had been taken over by the machines. I couldn't say there was a definite number of them any more, because Tom had joined them all together, over time, into one giant apparatus. It was a game beyond all rules, and I could only wonder at the controlling loneliness that had produced this monster.

I turned on the overhead lights. Luckily, the electricity was still working. I stood then, in silent amazement at the sight. The room was filled, wall to wall, with the game. Pipes and wires sprouted here and there, in seemingly random display; wheels waited to turn; fanbelts were stretched over pulleys and cogs; levers were poised; gyroscopes were balanced on the horizon's edge. And there, at the very centre, was the suspended globe of the Intravenus.

I found myself remembering Tom's words about the Big

Product, and how we would all escape the town once we had helped the Factory build it.

Was this the Escaping Game?

A sudden noise startled me. Something scuttled from behind a part of the machine. It was Oris, the Robot. I saw that he had only three legs left. He stood somewhat awkwardly on this tripod, watching me, expectantly. So I walked over to the counter, found the coin box. For the second time in my life, I picked the lock on it. The special coin was there, waiting, with a note. It read, 'Here you go, girl.'

There was no clear path to the Intravenus machine, I had to clamber over various pieces of apparatus. Of course, I had no need of a stool this time, the viewing aperture was exactly level with my sight. I wasn't even sure if the game was finished yet. Knowing Tom, it never quite would be. Perhaps that was my job now?

The coin slid easily into the slot. The beam of light was fired, and all around me the vast engine of the Vanishing Palace stirred into noisy, clanking life.

I set my eye to ignition.

ORGMENTATIONS
(in the mix)

■
■
■
■

William Meta Meta III, artificial hair on hire, last night threw a sparkle party. *Strictly Robots Only* trumpeted the invite, but the Zoom Lens Maganauts managed an elegant gate-crash. Everybody, but *everybody* was there, and much sport was had by one and all. Machines both famous and flirtatious were seen in various states of undress and dismantlement. The Clan of Squeaky Clean made a frightful mess of table nine. Lady Swankish, she of the troubled Baby Metal Company, left various parts of herself in the trifle. (Dark gossip was told of DJ Pixel Juice.) Entertainment was provided, at table, by a newcomer to the scene, one Tony Tango, a magician of sorts. (Dark gossip so fast so deep.) He turned the wine into oil, which was drunk with glee. The Glee was supplied free of charge by RoboVaz International. (Let loose! Let loose!) Mucho sucking of the Vurt feathers, including a rather delightful pink, that caused an automated orgy to break out. (Hands of the DJ move around move around.) We can only guess at the cleaning bills! But quite the best part of the evening took place when Benji Spike showed off his latest 'cyborgmentation' collection. This self-styled Avant Primitive really has got the demi-mondo in thrall. (Landscapes of scratch.) Young models of stainless-steel beauty clanked up and down the catwalk, stripping off in tempo to the new Lab Test Residue album. (Hands of the DJ sonic bloom.) Oh the sight of so much naked burnished chrome fair dazzled the eyes! One shining boy of non-specific machinery had a human index finger pierced through his lower lip. (Such noise such crackle such slither!) Another, a female of the Paradroid species, had a human eye, still gazing! set dead centre in her polished brass tongue. Eyes and ears and nipples and navels, all carefully harvested from fully paid-for volunteers, were seen in gorgeous contrast against the sheen of metal skin. (Hands of the DJ wet to the traces.) We could go on, but the most impressive aspect of the collection was the advanced use of the new anti-decay fluids. (Rapid fire fingertronics.) These human parts were still alive, so well preserved were they. Benji Spike claims they will last for up to six weeks, before the stench becomes rather too unsociable. How marvellous! (Let loose! Let loose!) But we save the best for last. Imagine our delight to see mounted stylishly upon the platinum breasts of a young she-robot – yes! – a fully extended human penis! (Dark gossip so fast so deep.) Bravo, Monsieur Spike! (Hands of the DJ move around.) Oh, dear sweet reader, you really should have been there!

\\\\\\\\\\ FRACTAL SCRATCH \\\\\\\\\\\

\\\\\\\\\\V//////////

\\\\V/////

V

HANDS OF THE DJ

Dark gossip was told of DJ Pixel Juice, so fast, so deep, were the ranges of her landscape of scratch. They said her hands moved around at sonic bloom, making ghosts of themselves in the stage lights. She had to have more than two hands fully extended, surely, to let loose such noise, such crackle, such slither. Such expert play of the new anti-decay fluids. Vinyl went wet to the traces, held sway in time to rapid-fire fingertronics; etch-plate aesthetics, fractal scratches (really should've been there) out on the limits of the human edit. Echoes of beat that last for up to six weeks, revolving through clubland. Booked top slot at the Magnetic Field weekender, Pixel Juice drew a record crush. They say half the known universe got turned away (really, really should've been there) even the ones with tickets. Goon Guards Unlimited were on bonus alert to keep it tight on the invite, members only and strictly drug-free. Walls were high and fat around the field, and electrified. Blue sparks painted the sky as some loser got stung too good with an access-no-areas powder burn.

Deep in the night, when the music pulsed already from the warm-up; out where the walls went fizz, some kid was offering a baby goon something conducive from his shoulder bag. The babe turned him down, but the kid gave her the shot for free. Five minutes later the guard was seeing stripy penguins, and the kid was making foreplay to the wall with a spurt of hi-level Vaz. Bootleg police issue. Sure was slippy!

The kid, name of Marco, he was only sixteen. Skinny but tall, dressed to the tips in black silk, a touch of lace. He had a spark about him, something in the eyes, something in the way he moved. He found a space in the crowd to call his own. He didn't dance, not to look at anyway; but his mind was skipping to some home-made spectral beat. The night was smoked; lit with purple, hard at the edges, liquid in the middle where the music came into focus and the people moved. They moved! Pixel Juice had them down in the dazzle, up for the float. Over the field, cruising the giant relay screen, the gloved-up hands of the woman; a constant blur, magnified one thousand. Left hand cut deep bass rhythms, right hand worked the scattershot punctuation. She had all the old ones, the stuff you couldn't get any more, the voodoo grooves. Waves of colour came scudding from the decks with every hard slice of the stylus. The hands that makes the scratches that make the colours that makes the trance that make the crowd go wild in a dance that makes the colours that make the hands that dance to make the scratches. And deep within this feedback loop stands Marco; he ain't dancing, he ain't swooning. He's got some whole other kind of a thing going on. This was his time, he knew it was.

The after-gig party was a burn-out zone mainly, hogged by record company dandies, orbital candies, and the press gangers and depress gangers. The marquee was flooded with cheap lager and the sponsor's Braindeath Vodka concoction. Members of the Family Goon surrounded the tent and passed a joint around. They had dogs with them; plus some tasty concealed weapons, but no trouble was to be had; the liggers were out to business lunch on Planet Whiz. None of them cared that Pixel Juice had left the party hours ago. The thing about the DJ, she was never the one for hanging out. She didn't give interviews. Never turned up to accept awards. No known vices, which pissed the marketing boys off no end. OK, no drugs for the punters, fair enough she wants that, but stop hogging the nosebag will yer? OK, she's a lesbian, what's that supposed to mean? With the same partner for years now? Tell me about it. No fucking story! Sniff, sniff.

And this partner, her name was Molly, this partner was walking Pixel hand in hand back to the trailer. It was three in the morning, still dark. The way was lit by overhead lights. An Artists and Repertoire man was lying face down in the mud. A thin rain was falling. Molly unrolled a little umbrella. Behind them, a discreet somewhat drunken distance, a junior goon was keeping watch. Suddenly, Pixel stopped in her tracks. Music could be heard. The guard tensed, reached for the weapon. The music was coming from Pixel's personal bus. This was bad, this was strange. The vehicle was supposed to be high-security. It wasn't the damage to the bus, she didn't give a toss about that; it was the vinyl: she kept her priceless vinyl in there. So the party-guard was staggering forward, pointing his radio at the vehicle and calling up assistance on his gun, and Molly was hiding behind the umbrella. But Pixel Juice, she was just standing there, she was just staring. She was just listening. That music, wafting slow, slow, fast and funky from the open door of the bus . . .

The number-one call for all junkies of groove. Pixelkids Come Out Tonight. The prize catch. Angel dust, shook from the wings. Talked about, never seen. Neither touched nor played, and definitely never scratched, not in all the years since Pixel Juice had been making music, and then some. This sound was launched way back, 1970s style. Before the world was born even. A good tongue licking from an ancient god couldn't even come close.

Pixel told the goon to hang back with a hand gesture, a black-gloved gesture. Her left hand. With the right, the yellow-gloved, she opened the door to the bus. It came open easy, no damage, the catch still slippy from something warm. She knew that stuff. Hi-grade Vaz; she used it on the records for extra texture. But all she could hear now was the music. She followed it inside. The bus was dark, only the glitter of a record spinning on her personal decks. Catching fire. Time was, she would have killed to get that specimen. Now she looked beyond the music, into the dark. A figure was lounged on her couch. Stretched out, eating an apple, it looked like; looking cool and absolutely couldn't care less.

'Hi there, Pixel,' the figure drawled. 'How yer doing? Nice music, uh?'

'How much do you want for it?'

'Put the wallet away, Pixel. You know it's not like that.'

'Right.'

'And get rid of the goon, OK?'

Pixel called to Molly, who was waiting nervous outside the door. Somewhat miffed, Molly sauntered over to the guard. The two of them walked back towards the marquee. Pixel came back inside, closed and bolted the door behind her, turned on a soft lamp. It was just a kid, lying there, pretty good-looking with it. 'What's your name?' she asked him.

'You can call me Marco.'

'Do you mind . . .'

'Go right ahead.'

Pixel walked over to the deck. She turned up the volume a touch, and then, slowly, lingering, let her left hand rest exactly one millimetre above the spinning vinyl. She was waiting, poised like a cat for the beat. Now! She brought the hand down, added some black bass of her own.

'Oh!' sang the figure, in time to the scratching. 'Oh, I like that, I surely do.'

'OK.' Pixel mixed the music down to a soft but funky backbeat. 'What do you want?'

The figure took a bite of his apple. 'How do you do it? That's all.'

How do you do it? How do you get to scratch like that? What's behind those gloves? Is it true you've made a pact with the Devil? What's the secret? What's the deal? Why no interviews? What's behind the air of loneliness so cultivated? When do you smile? Why so distant? Who's the shadow that taught you? How do I get to be like that? Can you teach me? How much does it cost? The same questions again and again. And to throw all that hard-earned pop mystery away, all over a lousy 12-inch single from the last century? Come off it. No way. And even if this Marco kid says, 'There's more where that came from', which he does, well even then . . . to give in so easily, well, maybe, just a little, almost . . .

'Why do you want to know?' asked the DJ. 'To sell the story?'

'I want to be brilliant, of course.'

'You're a DJ?'

The kid nodded. 'I'd like to be.'

'There are easier ways. With access to records like this . . .'

'I can get records. No problem with the records. I just don't . . . I don't know what to do with them. I can't make the people move. They won't *move* for me.'

Pixel Juice nodded. Maybe, just maybe she was remembering herself at his age; remembering the fear of the empty floor. And the desire that made her go so far in finding the secret. The sacrifices she had made along the way.

'I'll do anything,' the kid said. 'Anything.'

So then, and slowly then, Pixel Juice peeled off the glove, the left-hand glove, the black covering. And her hand glinted hard and silver and tarnished in places. The noise it made, the soft whirr and click as the fingers unfolded one by one, hinged on tiny levers, and longer, far longer than any human fingers had ever reached. The sight and the sound of the revealed hand made Marco gasp; in wonder, not surprise. The wonder of the expert mechanism, not the surprise of the fact, because he had suspected as much.

'You're a robot.'

'No. Only my hand. The rest is real.'

'Can I . . . can I touch it?'

Pixel Juice nodded, and the kid reached out to stroke the warm, pliant metal. 'Nice job,' he said. 'Very nice job. Must've cost something.'

Pixel Juice nodded, but would not name a price.

'OK . . .' Marco drew back. 'That's the bass revealed. What about the right hand? The treble hand.'

But the DJ shook her head. 'No. That's all you're getting.' Already she was pulling the glove back on. 'Thank you for the vinyl. Now leave.'

'I've heard metal music, a thousand times. That's nothing compared to what you do. There's more. There must be more. The right hand—'

'I have tolerated you long enough, young man. This trailer is alarmed. I need only press a button.'

'Be my guest.'

Pixel tried it.

Silence, and the slow smile of the young man that said, what's it to be then? And then he produced a gun from somewhere, a blunt home-made affair.

'You wouldn't want to know,' answered Pixel. 'Believe me, you wouldn't.'

'Let me decide.'

'It's about evolution. And you're not ready.'

'Not ready? Evolution? I am. I am ready. I'm evolved.'

'With a gun in your hand?'

'Bitch.'

The whole night swung around that word, as though waiting for it to be said.

Pixel Juice went for the door, but Marco was easy on his feet. There was a struggle, and then she had him around the neck, so easy, her black-gloved, bass-driven hand around his thin white neck. And the mechanism tightened at her will, the long stretched fingers, following algorithms.

And the kid . . . the kid . . . ahh . . .

It was going further than he thought it should, especially when the loud report filled his head with fire, and her body relaxed against his.

Marco dropped the gun. Blood was on his suit, his best jacket. Apple juice and blood.

Pixel's left hand was still clamped around his neck.

With both his hands, his thin, human hands, Marco tried to

prise the metal fingers loose. But the DJ was still alive, barely alive, enough to keep the mechanism working. Marco's hands were sweaty as he struggled for air, release, a way out of a good night gone superbad. Finally, the woman's body went limp, the black-gloved hand opened slightly, but then locked into position. Final position.

Able to breathe now, at last, if only just, Marco considered his plight. He was searching for the old cool, the cool and the fire that had made him scheme for this. He should've been in, out; swap the record, find the secret, do the deal. Sure, maybe a little threat here and there, whatever it took, but not a killing.

Was she really dead? He couldn't tell. He looked down at the body that hung from his neck. Her other hand, the right hand with the yellow glove, was hanging limp, the fingers touching the floor.

Noises then, from outside: and a knocking on the trailer's door, a banging on it, and people outside, talking, shouting. The gun. He realized finally that he had fired the gun. He'd never meant to.

Fuck!

There was a face pressed against a window. What must they have seen?

Marco let his suddenly tired body slide to the floor. DJ Pixel Juice was now lying on top of him, on his lap. Marco reached over for her right hand. Almost distractedly, he noticed it was still moving, the last part of her still alive. With the black knowledge that he might as well finish this, he started to tug at the yellow glove. The hand inside it, he could feel, was warm, and very soft, and filled with a vibrant pulse. Finally, he got the glove off, finger by tight finger, and then the shank of it, finally.

Spectrum glow. Her hand was rainbowed in a thousand bright colours. Out of her sleeve, out of her *wrist*, throbbed a bundle of flutterings, a cascade of life upwards and along and stretched out, making only the *shape* of a hand. The shape of wrist, the shape of palm, the shape of fingers, five. The hand grew, lengthened, rose upwards, took flight, separated, became a cloud of colours following the music through the air.

All he could do, the boy, was gasp aloud.

The colours! The colours!

Her hand was made of butterflies.

He was screaming as the goon guards broke open the door.

BASSDUST

So they catch these beetles, right, they live in South America. And they pull the wing-cases off them, and they grind these down to a fine, fine powder. That's what the guy says, anyway. It's this crimson stuff, like blood-coloured. And what you do is, you sprinkle this dust on the record, old-style vinyl, you know, and then give it some scratch injection with the old bejewelled needle. And it's like – Hey, Mr DJ! Hit the club slippage! Groove eternal on the jelly-up moment, oh come on! collapse my dancing heart, I beg you. I mean, you ain't never heard bass like it. Like it's the reflection of the moon's bass in the ocean, that far down. The crowd were doing a floorgasm. It's true, I tell you, listen to me. And I wouldn't mind but just a sprinkle of this stuff near burned the place down, so I'm thinking what could I do with an ounce. So, yeah, I buys it off the man. Strange-looker he was and all, thin as a stiletto's heel, with these cheekbones that met in the middle like a pair of scissors. And it doesn't end there, because the next thing I know he's getting out the old ciggie papers. Making a Rizla Sizzla, isn't he? And I thought I'm up for that, except it's only this bassdust stuff that he's doing the rolling with. No, I swear, this happened. So he takes a backbrain drag, and then he's offering it to me. He says, here you go, mate, have a listen to this. I mean, what? Have a *listen*, he's saying? So, you know, I have a listen. I mean, I smoke that listen, you get me? All the way down, and the cloud of it fills me, the cloud of the bass fills my veins and all of a sudden I've got this fucking jazz funk living inside me. And I wouldn't mind but I don't even *like* jazz funk. Trouble is, I can't get the tune out of my head, it's like a beetle flying around in there, like the bassdust has turned back into wings. And he says, It's there for ever now, but that's OK, you can do the remix. How's that then? I ask. And he says, Oh, you need to buy some dub juice for that. Dub juice? I ask. And he says, Sure, I got some right here. So I have to buy this new stuff and swallow it and then I'm like, wow, you know, like a version, dubbed for the very first time . . .

EVENTS IN A ROCK
STAR'S LIMOUSINE

*N*ow, it begins. Let's rock! Let's crack this baby wide, wide
open. Tear it down, bring the slaughter on. Ain't nobody
here but us chickens. Drive the hellmobile!

Yes, he wanted to ride alone. We have his sworn statement,
and the ride itself is captured on video – including footage
from an in-vehicle camera – as well as being traced from
above by satellite. All evidence can be viewed. His spoken
testimony, recorded during the drive, certainly reveals a frag-
mented mind ill at ease with itself, but at no time does he
voice any doubts as to his volunteering for the task. Let it be
known also that we offered to have a robot drive the car. This
was refused. David Pool had been too greatly affected by the
original accident to allow its replication be handled by anyone
(or anything) but himself. Also, as the inventor of the controversial Roadmuse system, he claimed he was more in tune

with its complex algorithms than any machine could ever be.

Reluctantly, we had to agree with this.

It was imperative that this second drive should mirror the first one in all possible details. Accordingly it was at precisely the same time – 2.15 a.m. – and from the same place – the car park of the Burgess Shale Hotel in Manchester – that David Pool started the experiment. The car was the exact same type (with slight modifications for the purpose of the experiment) – a powder-blue Rolls-Royce Hesperus Limousine. And the night, as far as the forecasts could tell us, would be similar to the first in its weather patterns, traffic conditions (thankfully quiet due to the lateness of the hour) and other environmental attributes.

We did everything, perfectly.

Pool's first words on the commentary tapes are, 'Now, it begins.' Then he laughs, as though aware of the somewhat portentous nature of the utterance.

The only real difference between the two drives was the identity of the person in the car. We could have no control over this, other than fixing certain weights and governing devices to Pool's clothing; devices precisely calibrated to have exactly the same effect upon the vehicle's suspension and centre of gravity as the original driver did, this being the ageing and somewhat overweight rock singer, Lucas Novum.

We did everything. Everything, except tell the authorities of our intentions.

At 2.17 a.m., David Pool turned away from the hotel, left, into Peter Street. Our two monitoring vehicles followed behind the Rolls, keeping a judicious distance so as in no way to affect the outcome of the experiment.

Information recovered from the original vehicle's data banks has provided us with a partial model of the drive; it was this model that Pool followed as, at 2.21 a.m., he turned on the limousine's music system. He heard an exact copy of the music played during the first vehicle's drive. Pool then deactivated the manual drive of the limo, resting his fingers only lightly on the now self-turning steering wheel.

'Let's rock,' Pool murmurs; again, following the script.

From now on the music would be the engine.

Gonna make me some turmoil, slam some on it. Slice a hole in the night, climb on through, get my licks from the lunar kiss. Oh yeah, I'm la crème de la bass, baby.

The otherwise strait-laced Professor Pool seems to have whole-heartedly taken on Lucas Novum's speech patterns and vocabulary, indeed his whole personality, once in the vehicle. Pool gave us no indication that he was going to adopt this manner prior to the experiment. Obviously he had studied the recovered tapes from the crash at great length, in order to copy precisely the words spoken (or sung) during the original drive. Perhaps Pool felt this 'identification' was a vital part of success-fully replicating the journey.

Of course, we cannot completely rule out the fact that David Pool had shown evidence of substantial mental breakdown since the rock star's death, a death that the press had relent-lessly linked to the use of the Roadmuse system. It was these rumours that had determined Pool to test the system himself; by making the exact same journey, governed by the exact same musical passage, he hoped to vindicate the Roadmuse tech-nology.

As the journey progressed, however, this identification increased alarmingly, until the professor was fairly screaming the rock star's words. We did insist at this point that Pool abandon the experiment, only to be answered with a complete breakdown of communication between our monitoring vehicles and the limousine.

Pool had yanked loose the wires connecting his microphone with the roof aerial. He did not however deactivate the microphone itself, allowing his running commentary to be saved for later analysis. Some ill-advised reporters have posited this as evidence of a battle raging in Pool's mind, between the committed scientist and the wayward rock star.

A little background: On 15 October of last year, Lucas Novum had played a concert in Manchester, with his band, ElectroSpasm. The concert had been a resounding success, as befits his status as one of the world's most revered rock musicians. However, the after-gig party at the Burgess Shale Hotel disintegrated into a violent argument between the singer and the rest of the band. Lucas had then left the hotel to take an early morning drive around his home town, the city that had given him his stepping-off point to global pop dominance. He did not bother to wake his chauffeur. We know that this need to escape, like the argument that preceded it, was fuelled by a copious amount of recreational drugs on Novum's part. Indeed, the actual route taken by the limousine was a random, twisting pathway through the lonely city, governed only by the rock star's overcharged desires.

It was a journey that would take just slightly less than thirty-five minutes.

Almost one year later, David Pool now mirrored this route, with the in-car music recreating precisely every turn, every change of speed, every variation in the climate; the primitive, pounding rhythms making an expert soundtrack of the drive.

Novum had received an early demo copy of version 2.2 of the Roadmuse Drivetracking system. Developed by Professor

PIXEL JUICE

Pool at our sonic laboratory, Roadmuse was a real-time feedback engine, with every note of music, every rhythm, every choice of instrumentation created by the movement of the vehicle itself, and the state of the world outside. Our publicity campaign said it all: 'Roadmuse: Life's original soundtrack!'

For the purposes of this free demonstration model, Pool had programmed the Roadmuse system with samples taken from the collected works of Mr Novum himself, and his band, ElectroSpasm. The journey was therefore an improvisation derived from the most basic of musical elements: frenzied drumming, simplistic bass lines, screeching guitar solos, and the occasional high-pitched scream of vocals.

The technology enabling this interaction of life and music was fairly simple; Pool's genius being to invest the interface with a real, interpretative expertise. For instance, at 2.29 a.m. on the original drive, it had started to rain. Earlier systems would have matched this change of climate with a simple, synthesized drumbeat; version 2.2 responded with an altogether darker, more ambient refrain, each drop of rain becoming an echoed note in a brooding, yet elegant melody of the night.

Mr Novum may well have wished he could have produced such charming music from his somewhat limited source material.

Strangely, at 2.31 a.m. on the second drive, it also started to rain, as though this time the music was causing an effect in the real world, rather than the reverse. There is a gasp from David Pool as this happens, faithfully recorded on the commentary tapes.

All the way home, honey. Drive me hard. (Gasp) Oh yeah, I feel the rain falling, baby, all over the world. Lay that wetness on me!

*   *   *

The major improvement that Pool had introduced to this latest version of the Roadmuse system was an increased sensitivity to the feedback engine. Even the slightest change in the car's environment would now have a marked effect on the music produced. He claimed it would transform even the body temperature of the car's occupants into a melody. He also made further claims, for instance that the system would be sensitive even to the thought patterns of the occupants.

At the time we thought these claims preposterous. Now, after studying the results of the experiment, we believe they offer the only possible explanation of what took place during both of these night-ridden journeys. Indeed, it may be that David Pool didn't go far enough in his assessment of the interface's responsiveness.

After aimlessly circling the streets of Manchester for a while, the limousine, and its ghost, were now moving along Deansgate, away from the city centre.

The time was 2.37 a.m.

We believe that Lucas Novum was aiming to travel into Hulme, the village where he had spent his teenage years and first formed ElectroSpasm. The world knows he never made it that far, but only now can we reveal the precise circumstances leading up to the crash.

At 2.42 he turned onto the roundabout at the end of Deansgate. If he was heading for Hulme, he should now have left the roundabout at the Chorlton Road exit. However he continued to drive around the roundabout, and all the way around it, again and again. The music mirrored this circular motion precisely, itself caught in a complex rising and falling fugue of notes, awash with feedback squall.

Finally, at 2.47, he manages to break out of this strange

mental state, and to escape the roundabout's embrace, not onto Chorlton Road as perhaps originally intended, but onto the Mancunian Way. He shoots down this stretch of motorway, accelerating quickly, reaching a top speed of 110 m.p.h. He then veers to the left, onto the exit leading towards Princess Road.

Likewise, the music breaks free of its fugal matrix, to ascend into a sudden rush of squealing lead guitar. All the other instruments drop from the mix. At the very end of this musical run, harmonic feedback comes into play, creating an almost ethereal cascade of sound. The guitar's tone is bell-like at this point, and made of pure air.

At 2.49 a.m., Lucas Novum crashes his Rolls-Royce limousine into one of the supporting struts of the motorway's flyover.

The music breaks into fire.

The rock star's last words are, 'The glass! The glass!' A scream of pain we initially took to refer to the breaking of the windscreen.

David Pool was meant to abandon the experiment at this last moment. His intention to do so is plainly stated in his signed contract. We, as a company, feel we did all in our power to ensure his safety. Alas, we could not control the experiment fully.

Pool's last words are slightly different from the rock star's; for the professor screams instead, 'The glass! The looking-glass!' It is his only divergence from the script, and this tiny clue has enabled us to unravel the mystery of the crash. Any critical comments on Pool's mental state during this, his last musical journey, must be softened with regard to his scientific commitment. For he proved beyond measure that the Roadmuse did in fact turn human thought patterns into music.

What he could not have seen until those final moments was

how the sensitivity of the interface fed back into the user's mind. The Roadmuse system not only turned thoughts into music; it turned music back into thoughts.

The first crash, like the second, was caused by the rock star's drug-addled brain creating a melody of destruction. Caught in the feedback loop of this suicidal music, and programmed to reflect it endlessly, the vehicle took the only route left open.

In effect, both limousines crashed into mirrors.

SPECIAL PROMOTION —
HYPER-ALICE

Girls! Ever felt left out and lonely, simply because you're scared of showing your true self? Fear no more with Hyper-Alice, the best reflective image now on the market. No matter how bad you feel, no matter how tired or unresponsive, no matter how downright *bored* with the whole sad and busted merry-go-round; let Hyper-Alice do the looking good for you.

Simply activate the discreet control panel (fits in a handbag!), and within a second all will be bowing down to your radiance! It's like a fairground mirror, tuned to perfection beyond the norm. Your friends, your colleagues, your lovers, your family – they look at you anew, and see their own desires in the mirror. Psychologists have proven this to be the number-one technique for impressing people. Hyper-Alice! It's so simple: become the looking-glass. Works at parties and other social gatherings, simply by taking the aggregate of all the needs there present.

And, introducing this month: Men! Don't be left out of the face race, send off now for Hyper-Elvis. Specially formulated for the changing image bank of the modern male. Become the son your boss never quite managed to produce.

Both models work just as well in reverse mode (one click of a switch does it!). Be pestered no more; warp that mirror. Let them see their worst fears in your projection. Or, when life gets just too much, simply turn the device to neutral. Guaranteed zero personality! The ultimate escape.

Hyper-Alice and Hyper-Elvis: the future of personal appeal.*

* Important notice: please read the instructions carefully – your personal appeal may rise or fall according to the changing rates of the International Index of Beauty.

THE SILVERING

Possibly, you could say that one evening, late in the future, all the mirrors in the world decided to join together. Whilst most people would consider mirrors merely as reflective surfaces, some of the more mystical religions proposed them to be doors, into some other, deeper realm. Rather now, see them as veins; the veins of some vast hidden creature along which light can travel. A creature with blood photons.

For centuries this creature knotted its veins together, in such a way that each journey of light came back to its starting point. Thus, we saw ourselves. But now, with this joining at the silver, each mirror reflected not the astonished gaze of the owner, but the equally shocked expression of another, stranger face.

A stranger's face.

At which you could only grimace, or bellow, or stand dumb-founded in front of.

We have to imagine the mirror creature shrugging itself, perhaps, and coming out of the shrug with its tangle of veins rearranged into a new pattern. Perhaps it didn't mean this to happen. Perhaps it did.

Destroying the mirrors brought no respite, for each replacement mirror bought, or indeed created, would still reflect the same stranger's image. Also, it was quickly noted, no matter where in the world the viewer was, no matter through which foreign mirror he or she gazed, the same partner would always be waiting there.

This phenomenon became known as the Silvering. In time, the imagined monster through which the rays of light ran was called by the same name.

The exact mathematical shape that the Silvering's veins would have to follow, for the process to take place, was discovered to be a highly complex eleventh-dimensional curve. The abstract beauty of this curve may have pleased the scientists; but it was of little use to all the billions of people in the world who now found their mirrors completely useless for their given task. To take a most obvious example: how could some young woman with long tresses of flowing hair possibly groom herself in the reflected image of some old, decrepit bald man?

For yes, some men were reflected by women. The Silvering knew no prejudice. The old were mirrored by the young; gays by straights; blacks by whites; the rich by the poor. At first this dissolving of boundaries brought only anger on both sides of the glass. Fortunately, although light waves could travel through the Silvering's veins, sound waves could not. Curses were not heard, but, of course, easily imagined from the expressions on a face.

But then, and only after a very short time, the people of the world came to accept their new reflections, and to work with them. And thus it was that old, decrepit bald men learned how to mime the combing of long golden tresses. And the world was considered a better place for the joining at the silver.

The only distressing moments came about because of a simple mathematical property: each of the Silvering's veins had only two points of entry – a beginning and an end. Because of this, the process only worked when the number of people in the world was an even number. Given the eternal play of birth and death, every so often a person would go to their mirror, expecting their partner to greet them, only to find themselves staring at a blank space, an emptiness, a terrifying void.

This phenomenon was known as the Clouding, and brought about an avoidance of all mirrors, until such day as the global population turned back from odd, to even, and all the veins of light had both beginnings, and endings.

A new face would appear to embrace your reflection, and the smiles were perfectly copied. Making balance in the world.

Until the Silvering shrugged once more; not only through space, but through the past and the future as well. So that possibly one day, late in the evening, you could say that all the mirrors of all time . . .

BEFORE IT DISAPPEARS

I was dining out with Kid Signal the other day, when he happens to mention a new player in town, some girl making a nice little fish-pie out at the casino. 'Monkey Funk, they're calling her,' says the Kid, feeding his face, 'and quite obviously born to angle. Want to check her out? Maybe to get rid of the worm, and a little something extra for me and the mouse?'

'Just keep eating,' I told him. 'And leave the worm out of this.'

The Kid was a fine experiment; the mouse that lived inside his stomach was a friendly little creature, if kept well fed, and an expert on all the latest rumours.

Some of us weren't born so lucky.

I threw the Kid a fish, just a tiddler, mind, for the tip-off.

Then I lose it. Something gets eaten, and it's all just darkness until I'm riding on board this tramcat, crammed in tight and sweaty. I swear I was the only halfway-human on board.

The tram was a moving zoo, filled to overload with snakegirls, dogboys, pigpeople, birdbrains. All the specimens. Screechings and roars and a right old ruckus they made, about how this was gonna be their luckiest ever day.

Yeah, right. I'd heard it all before, a thousand times or so. But if this new girl in town really did have some monkey in her, that was way up the food-chain, maybe I could finally catch enough moneyfish to get my head laundered. Sure could do with one.

We all tumbled forth at the outskirts of town, into the catpark. The crazy herd rushed for the casino gates, with me following slow behind, feeling this sudden emptiness. The skullworm was nibbling at something vital, and another bit of my sorry life drifted away. Something about my mother, or was it my girlfriend, I can't remember. What the hell was it?

Darkness.

In the foyer I changed some fish into chips, and then sauntered into the Fractal Roulette room. The place was jammed, wall to wall sucker. Tony McHool was playing a wheel, nursing his cobra the same time. Tony was one of my sure-fire bets; a skinny kid and skinnier snake I'd found playing poker in some dogdive down town. The snake was wriggling out of his shirt, and I knew for a fact where it was joined to him, because he showed me in the Gents when we signed the deal. I won't go into the gruesome details, but after that I just had to loan him some fish to play with. McHool was now gambling a shark on all or nothing. Always a bad bet, even with a snake to help you.

'Do you know a Monkey Funk?' I asked him.

'What's that? A new disease they're testing us for?'

He looked nervous, the snake also. 'Are you sure?' I asked. 'Because she's been winning some lately.'

'Leave us alone, please. The wheel is spinning.'

Sure it was. This wheel of misfortune, containing all the numbers of the universe and then some. Stakes were high, with this tiny marble spinning around like a dying planet; coming up minus 7.01377, gravity-bound.

So close, but no shark, not even a salmon. McHool made a curse, strangled his snake a little, and then started to gather up what was left of his shoal. I stopped him at the door to the Hyperdice room. 'You're betting mighty high these days, Snakedick,' I said. 'You want to give me my share yet?'

'We're not with you any more, Tapeworm. We're working for Mr Pork these days.'

I shook my head, let the snake hiss at me for a while. There was nothing much I could do, except follow them through.

Hyperdice. Throw the numbers along the green baize; watch them tumble and fall, into and out of existence. Watch the croupier as she follows the dice with her alien eyes into the next untumbling. A four-dimensional crap shoot. Thirty-six numbers the hyperdice contains, only six of which exist in our world. Our paltry, little world . . .

There was nothing doing in there, no sign of anyone looking even faintly monkey-eyed, never mind the full fur-job that Kid Signal had promised. I tried a pike bet on twenty-seven. The dice came up with twenty-nine spots from another realm. So close, but no pike, not even a king prawn. Not even a fried cod, and absolutely no chips.

One time, I was sure of a good angle, because there ain't nothing like a worm to catch a big fish. Now, it was all I could do to even remember which planet the numbers came from.

I was about set to head for the Quantum Poker room, when who should come strolling up but Cleetus McPork, his very own self, with his twin piglets growing one on each hand. 'Tapeworm,' he grunts. 'Go grovel. This is my patch now.'

'Who says so?'

'Pinky and Perky, who else?' and he waves his piggy hands around till they're squealing.

Now then, hear me out, I could have taken out those two little squealers easy in a square fight, but Mr Pork had a mean litter of pigboys in tow. And in the centre of the meatpack, this beautiful girl of midnight fur. Monkey Funk no doubt, and Mr Pork had beaten me to the prize.

But something sure got to me even just looking at her, and her looking at me the same, with eyes of luminous human. Like she knew who I was, deep down where even the worm can't go. And as though he knows he's being beaten . . .

Dark time.

The next thing I remember, I'm being hauled into Mr Pork's personal tramcat, which was a beast of a thing and fitted out like a brothel *circa* 2017, all leopardskin and tortoiseshell. There was a framed picture on the wall of a little mouse with a human ear growing out of its back. According to legend, this was the First of All Living Patents, and Mr Pork genuflected to it. Then he sits Monkey Funk down all nice and soft and orders all his pigboys to wait in the next room.

'Make yourself at home, Tapeworm,' he says, pouring himself a shot of something, glass in one piglet's mouth, decanter in the other. Neat trick. 'Fancy a splash?'

'What is it?' I asked with a cheap smile. 'Pig Swill?'

'Actually, it is. Vintage Swill, mind. From my own cellar.'

'I'll skip.'

He settled his bulk down next to the monkeygirl, put one of his piglets around her shoulders. Pinky or Perky? I never could tell them apart. The girl didn't seem to mind, not that much. I guess a girl with fur can put up with much of anything.

'So, Tape,' starts the pigman, 'I hear you've been having a spot of bother.'

'Nothing I can't handle.'

'Not what I heard. What I heard, your brain's being eaten. What I heard, your tapeworm's set to erase. Can't be nice, losing all those lovely memories. You tried the Patent Office?'

'Sure. They claim it's my fault. Been feeding it the wrong stuff, they reckon.'

'Bunch of pures! They're happy enough to pay us for the experiments, but when it comes to back-up, eh? Nothing at all. Now one of my boys, his pig-part started playing up. Starting taking big chunks out of him. Wasn't pretty, not at all. Took ages to get the stains out.' Here, he lovingly smoothed his leopardskin sofa. The sofa purred deeply and arched its back to receive the strokes. 'I paid for the operation, of course. Bootleg doctor.'

'What happened?'

'Successful, if rather ugly. Of course, I had to lay the man off. I mean, what use is a man without some pig inside him? Isn't that right, baby?'

The girl let her furry tail rest teasingly on Mr Pork's giant thigh, although whether she was teasing him, or me, I couldn't say.

'The thing is,' the pig continued, 'I'd rather have you on my side, than fighting against me. After all, there's only so many patents with the fishing gift. What do you say? You want that operation?'

'It's a kind offer, Mr Pork, but . . . I'm happier alone, you know? Lone wolf.'

'I knew a lone wolf once, proper one. Strange guy, couldn't

stop howling at the moon. Had to have him put down in the end.' With that, he pressed a button on his tortoise table and the whole tramcat purred into life. The room rocked slightly as the vehicle unfolded its legs. Even the table was surprised: it made a dash for the door, maybe half a millimetre an hour. I wasn't quite that fast.

'Hey, what is this?' From the window I could see we were moving away from the casino.

'Please, Mr Worm, do sit down. You'll have an accident.'

I was already thinking about the accident I would be having, and maybe of trying for Pinky and Perky, maybe ripping both those squealers off at the root, when the pigboys come cruising through the door, sweaty and heavy, and the next bit the worm has already taken, taken into darkness.

That's why I have to write this down, to try and capture the story before it disappears.

Out of the darkness, I remember running through the streets with this Monkey Funk at my side and the grunts coming up close behind. We were set loose inside a vast genetic estate. From all sides came the pungent smell of sex, big vats of it where they brewed the primordial soup. I could hear the tramcat getting closer and the trotters of the littermen but I didn't dare look back, just kept on running. It was all I could do to keep up with the monkey, especially when she started to swing up a ladder attached to one of the vats.

Climbing wasn't something I'd gone in for lately, but I was dragged along by the fear. The vats were the size of churches and open at the top, with an observation platform around the outside edge. Looking down made me feel sick because a lump of something was swimming around in there. God knows what. So I turned to look back over the other side.

The pigboys were in deep-trough mode of course, because have you ever seen a pig climb a ladder? One of them pulled out a gun. The metal below me was punched through by the bullet, and a stream of the soup came spewing out of the vat. Somebody screamed down there as the stuff hit them. Then the tramcat starts to climb the vat, and would have done OK if Pork hadn't been so extravagant with the on-board accessories. One second the vehicle was creeping up towards me, the next overhanging itself as the patio and miniature golf course on its back slowly shifted the centre of gravity.

Like any cat through history it tried to land on its feet, doing that mid-air dance-craze twist that nearly always worked. Nearly always . . . but this time its dug-in claws took a side of the vat with them. Too much weight.

We didn't stay to hear the cries of the pigboys as the whole soup came down that night. Monkey Funk just took my hand and together we jumped from vat to vat, from species to species, from darkness to darkness to . . .

I've just read the above entry to Monkey. Every night we do this, me reading from the old diaries as the memories fade away, her trying to put the past together for me. She claims she was a childhood friend of mine, that we used to go stealing fish from the vats when we were young, and that's why she'd rescued me from the Pork, but I have to take her word for it.

I have to take everybody's word for it these days.

It's strange, but I'm quite ready for the day when the worm takes everything. I don't even think about the operation any more. I don't know, maybe the worm's doing me good. Just to live, forever now. Yeah, whatever. But reading the diaries is frustrating, and this may well be my last journey back. There's too many things I read about, they don't make sense any more.

I can't remember what Kid Signal looks like, for instance, and what the hell is a hyperdice? So far gone, I can't even remember what I look like myself, without the use of a mirror, or the look in Monkey's eyes as we kiss.

And all the stories disappear, one by one by one . . .

PIXEL DUB JUICE
(sublimerix remix)

Whilst shopping for magical stuff
Some children find purchasing tough;
And a very young pimp
Grows decidedly limp,
At the sight of his dad in the buff.

The whole book's rather hotchpotch;
A kid gets wound up by a watch;
Adverts improve,
A DJ goes 'groove',
And Godzilla gets kicked in the crotch.

There's a hobo robocanus;
A faded pop star called Janus –
Bit of a wet fish,
Gets killed by fetish;
A beetle lights fags with its anus.

The rain's always falling like tears,
On yobbos with pixelized sneers.
More DJs go 'groove',
What's Noon trying to prove?
He's not been to a club in ten years.

A robot in New York goes screwy,
With a tongue in his tummy – how gooey!
Mirrors receding;
Books kill by reading:
It's all nicked from Borges, Jorge Luis.

In style it's manic-frenetic,
With language mistreated genetic;
Brings K. Dick alive,
To join Famous Five
In acrobatic alphabetics.

Oh, there's weirdo perversions galore!
Guns, hookers and drugs by the score;
Critics should pan it,
They really should ban it,
Or at least put it front of the store.

NIGHT SHOPPING

And, years later, when Little Tommy was older, much older and not so very little, he was trying on a changing suit in the ninth shop, when he felt a slight pain in his forehead. Asking the assistant for a glass of shadow, he sat down for a moment to calm his nerves. The suit, noticing his mood, loosened itself around his neck and chest, and then turned from its show-off silver to a soothing pastel blue. The shadow juice covered the pain with its dark and gentle hand, and between them, the suit and the shadow did their best to relieve Thomas of his discomfort.

The assistant asked him if everything was all right, and Thomas said it was, thank you, and how much was the suit? So a deal was made, and the assistant asked if he would like it wrapped, and Thomas said no, he would wear it now, and please dispose of his old clothes.

Then Thomas stood up, and went to transfer his wallet to

his new jacket. The jacket made a pocket just where Thomas's hand was resting. But when he put his hand inside the pocket, something hard and warm knocked against his fingers. He pulled his hand back out, to see that it now held a key, a golden key. The assistant was surprised to see it there, and was puzzled, because the pocket had not existed until a second ago.

So Thomas started to walk back home, wondering whether a tramcat would be wiser, knowing his condition. Instead, he decided the walk would do him good, and the suit agreed, changing itself into a sturdy anorak, and the shoes into walking boots. Soon, however, Thomas found himself lost, something that had not happened in so many years, and he wondered if they had built a new shopping extension, because he had never seen such a precinct before.

He went into the first friendly kiosk, whose counters were filled with compass bugs of various directions. He bought one for his home-shop, swallowed it, and immediately felt better. Letting the beetle inside his stomach guide him, he set off confidently through the strange and twisted streets. But as he travelled farther, the places became less and less familiar. More and more of the stores were boarded up, and the streets almost deserted. Eventually he came to an area he thought he recognized: a small patch of lawn with a single tree, and a bench. And here, Thomas rested for a while, and slept. And his suit, slowly and gently, became a long, flowing nightshirt. He dreamed, for the first time in years, of his departed mother, and the brave shopping expeditions of his youth.

When he awoke, it was already artificial night, and the artificial moon hung from the precinct's sky. Strangely, his suit did not change from its long flowing shape. The square was quite deserted, and only one shop still whispered in faint light. The sign above the doorway was in a language he could not understand. He could no longer feel the directions in his stomach, and the headache was shadowless and almost like a long-lost thought.

So, he went into the shop.

It was filled with all the things he had ever bought, and all the things he had once dreamed of buying. The penny ghosts and the bird shoes, the word egg and song biscuit, the smoke-maps and dogseeds, and all the shadows in the world were on display like pieces of the night's calming sky. Reaching into a sudden pocket in his gown, Thomas found there a single penny of the old money. With it, he bought a lonely, whispering ghost.

Upon leaving the shop, he saw, or thought he saw, a group of people sitting beneath the tree on the patch of lawn. One of them, a woman, called to him by name. The children around her begged him to hurry.

And his suit changed to ashes.

WATCH

believed in the invisible watch so much that I went straight back to the classroom and hid it behind some books in my desk. I didn't want anybody else to see it; the watch was mine alone.

Every so often, during a boring lesson, I would open the desk, just to have a look at it. Never, not for one second, did it puzzle me that you couldn't tell the time by an invisible watch. The time wasn't important; it was the invisibility that got to me.

The magic of it.

I took it home with me that night, actually strapped it to my wrist. I slept with it under my pillow. And wore it to school the next day, but then, nervous that somebody would steal it off me, I hid it safely in the desk.

Just thinking about the watch was enough, but then at play-time I saw Colin Bradshaw with his mates. He asked me how the invisible watch was doing. They were all laughing at me.

'What time is it, Noony?' they shouted. 'What time is it?'

I went back to the classroom, lifted up the desk lid, slowly, moved the books aside.

The invisible watch had gone.

Needle in the Groove
Jeff Noon

'AS FRESH AND COMPULSIVE AS ANYTHING YOU'LL READ
THIS YEAR'
Maxim

if music was a drug, how would you take it? if drugs were music,
how would you listen?

after years of playing bass in lousy two-bit bands, elliot finally
gets his big chance/ he meets a singer, a dj and a drummer who
seem to have everything/ passion, talent, hypnotic songs, and a
whole new way of funky seduction/ but just as their first dance
record is climbing the charts, one of them disappears/ elliot's
search for the missing band member becomes a wild, fiercely
emotional trip into the dark soul of rhythm/ and in the grooves
he discovers a world where the scratches of the stylus cut the
body/ a dj's samples are melodies of blood/ love is a ghost lost in
the boom box/ and the only remix that really matters is the remix
of the heart.

'HIS BEST SO FAR . . . THIS IS THE MOST STYLISTICALLY
AMBITIOUS, PUSHING HIM BEYOND THE QUIRKY
ORIGINALITY OF HIS EARLIER NOVELS'
The Times

'JEFF NOON'S BOOKS ARE SO GOOD THEY SHOULD COME
WITH A GOVERNMENT WARNING'
Jockey Slut

'*NEEDLE IN THE GROOVE* IS WHERE THE MAINSTREAM OF
LITERATURE OUGHT TO BE IN THE 21st CENTURY . . .
SEETHING, SEXUALISED, CHEMICALLY ENHANCED'
The Wire

'BRILLIANT . . . LUSH, LOOSE RHYTHMIC PROSE WHICH
STUTTERS AND JUMPS, SCREECHES AND SPLINTERS ALL
OVER THE PAGE'
City Life

0 552 99919 9

BLACK SWAN